ONE

There was a smell of gas in the Queen's Old Castle. Although the Reverend Mother had not been there for over fifty years, the shop looked more or less the same, but the smell, she thought, was new. It caught in her chest and brought on the cough that had been troubling her for the last week.

Despite its royal name, the Queen's Old Castle was nothing but a fairly low grade of department store housed within the decrepit walls of what had been one of two castles, built at the entrance to the city of Cork, over seven hundred years ago in the time of King John. Its subsequent history had not kept up with its origins, the Reverend Mother had often reflected, as the name tripped off the lips of her pupils as a source of cheap stockings and other bargains.

The castle had become a court house, then a manor house and then an abandoned ruin. Sometime towards the end of the last century it had fallen to the heritage of an enterprising member of the Fitzwilliam family who had plastered the medieval stone walls, removed the dangerously unstable upper storeys, replaced sections of missing roof with sheets of glass, re-laid the ancient flagstone slabs on the ground floor, added an enormous boiler with a series of hot pipes leading from it, snaking up the walls, and had turned the whole into a shop selling cheap clothes and household linens.

Today the shop, though enormous, was full. Everyone looking for a bargain. Garish posters in the windows and on boards throughout the city had announced in large, bright red letters the magic word: SALE. In the background, a past pupil of hers, Eileen MacSweeney, who worked for the printers, was standing, holding a large bundle of similar posters. The Reverend Mother congratulated herself silently on her quick-wittedness. Having read the article in the *Cork Examiner*, entitled 'QUEEN'S OLD CASTLE CALAMITY', detailing the damage done by the recent floods, she had immediately written to Joseph Fitzwilliam, expressing her sympathy and reminding him of their acquaintanceship of over fifty years ago.

It had worked even better than she had expected. He had written back, thanking her and inviting her to come and take her pick of the river-damaged goods, had implied tactfully that no money would change hands and when she arrived on the Monday morning, punctually at nine o'clock, he had been on the look-out for her, had escorted her past the queue, allocated to her the use of a young apprentice, equipped the lad with an enormous basket, and told her to take whatever would be useful for her school and assured her that it would be his donation to her charitable work among the poor of Cork city.

An immense sacrifice for a man who, reputedly, was so fond of money that no one who worked in the shop was ever allowed to handle even a single penny of the intake.

Joseph Fitzwilliam was very proud of his shop. As the Reverend Mother looked around, she admired the way light came in from the huge sheets of glass that had replaced the remaining slates on the roofs and from the gas lamps on the bronze pillars set at intervals throughout the shop.

'Twenty-seven of them,' he said proudly, following her eyes as she looked up at the gas bracket over her head. 'Had to have the pillars to support the glass in the roof, so I made a feature of them. You wouldn't believe how much that bronze cost, but I don't grudge it. Lovely glow they make, don't they? Hollow they are. The gas pipe goes up through the middle. Makes a feature of them, you see, Reverend Mother,' he repeated. 'I'm a great one for making features, you know.'

'I can see that, Mr Fitzwilliam,' she said, wondering when the talking would end and the shopping begin. Mr Fitzwilliam was not to be stopped, though, and he continued with the guided tour.

'Look at those change carriers, Reverend Mother,' he said enthusiastically, pointing to the small, barrel-shaped canisters, strung on wire that went from each counter, right up to the top of the building, to where his office was perched, supported against the ancient walls on a wooden platform by a series of

MURDER AT THE QUEEN'S OLD CASTLE

Cora Harrison

This first world edition published 2018
in Great Britain and 2019 in the USA by
SEVERN HOUSE PUBLISHERS LTD of
Eardley House, 4 Uxbridge Street, London W8 7SY
Trade paperback edition first published
in Great Britain and the USA 2019 by
SEVERN HOUSE PUBLISHERS LTD

Copyright © 2018 by Cora Harrison.

British Library Cataloguing in Publication Data
A CIP catalogue record for this title is available from the British Library.

ISBN-13: 978-0-7278-8830-3 (cased)
ISBN-13: 978-1-84751-956-6 (trade paper)
ISBN-13: 978-1-4483-0165-2 (e-book)

Typeset by Palimpsest Book Production Ltd.,
Falkirk, Stirlingshire, Scotland.

iron bars. 'The change canister fits inside the barrel,' he explained and then went into a series of elaborate calculations designed to show how much time this saved the counter assistants as they would just post the sales document and the customers' money up to him and the change and receipt would come whizzing back. 'Have them all over the place in England, you know. You'll have read about them in Mr Wells' novel *Kipps*. Might be some places in Dublin have them, but I'm the only one in Cork.'

The Reverend Mother nodded silently, looking around at all the water-stained goods piled on the counters and wondering how quickly she could get her hands on some of those gymslips – a boon for poverty-stricken girls whose mothers could not afford to dress them decently. She had already expressed her thanks for his generosity and now could not wait to join the bargain hunters. Thankfully, at the sight of a couple of small barrels hurtling above their heads, he hurried off, climbing the steep stairs like a man of half his age, leaving her to the apprentice and the enormous basket.

'I'm Brian, Reverend Mother,' said the husky-voiced youngster. 'Brian Maloney,' he added.

'Goodness, Brian, I didn't know you. How is your mother?' This Brian had not been the first Brian, and would not be the last to spend his early years in the convent at St Mary's Isle where boys of tender age stayed until they had made, at the age of about seven, their first confession and their first holy communion and were then supposed to be equipped to face the rigours of the Christian Brothers. However, by some miracle she remembered him. A bright and enterprising boy, she thought, an only child. Fatherless, also. His mother had done well for him to get this apprenticeship. The shop, she thought, looking around at the huge number of counters, employed a lot of Cork people. It would have been a disaster if the floods had caused irreparable damage. Its owner would have got insurance, but the employees would be left with little option than to pick up a reference and to get the boat for England. Young Brian Maloney had been lucky and his mother clever to pick up this apprenticeship which might guarantee him a permanent job as a shop assistant.

'Hey, Maloney, don't you touch them wellington boots!' The tone was extremely harsh and the Reverend Mother turned around and looked at the middle-aged man behind the counter.

'Brian is fetching these for me,' she said clearly and distinctly, and the man muttered something.

'Don't you worry about Mr Dinan, Reverend Mother,' said Brian, returning to her side with the boots. 'He's had the sack yesterday and he's got the hump, stupid old *bolger*.' He spoke with the easy insouciance of youth, but the Reverend Mother looked back at the face of the man and at the dark shadows under his eyes. Not an old man, well under thirty, she thought, but there was a look of premature aging about the tight lines around the mouth and bent shoulders. She had a shock when Brian continued, 'Just finished his apprenticeship. He was an Improver, but he didn't improve enough for Mr Fitzwilliam and so he got the sack. They do that here in this place. As soon as they have to pay you a decent wage, you get the sack. He's married, of course; that's what is upsetting him. Shouldn't have done it, should he? I'm not going to get married and have kids, Reverend Mother. Never, ever, not in a thousand years! I've made up my mind about that. I'm off to England before that happens. I want to be a soldier but if I can't manage that, I'll try one of the big shops in London. I'll get a job there easy once I'm trained. I'd like to try haber-dashery while I'm here, get myself trained to do that. You get haberdashery everywhere.'

A cheerful lad whose spirit had not been broken. Still, optimism didn't always guarantee success. The unfortunate Mr Dinan was now taking out his feelings on another young apprentice who was staggering under the weight of a heavy roll of curtain material. Perhaps eight or nine years ago he, too, had been a fresh-faced youngster, but now he was embittered and prematurely aged.

'Look at them over there, want some of them, Reverend Mother?' The Reverend Mother's mind left the unfortunate Mr Dinan and returned to business. She nodded at Brian who shot off on one of his detours, this time to get her some damaged kitchen cloths.

The Reverend Mother went back to thinking about Joseph

Fitzwilliam, now ensconced in his little office on high, and, as far as she could see, rapidly unloading the contents of the change barrels, refilling them and sending them shooting back, each on its own wire, down to the correct counter in the cavernous shop. Not a great way of spending one's days for a wealthy man as old as herself. Still, perhaps he was silently making the same remark about her, she thought as she wandered down the aisle and picked out river-stained socks, a few pairs of child-sized trousers, some blouses and a pair of navy gymslips, some towels and sheets, too. Not of top quality, and marked with water stains, but serviceable and a boon to a Reverend Mother who never seemed to be able to make ends meet and balance her books to the satisfaction of the bishop's secretary. She took up a kitchen towel, felt it, popped it into the basket and somewhat shamefacedly, added another couple. There were water stains right down the middle of each one, but that was something that she was sure the efficient Sister Bernadette and her kitchen team would be able to get rid of. Did Joseph Fitzwilliam, looking down from on high, wonder about her, someone he had known in his youth and danced with at parties, or was he just too busy, unloading the contents of the barrels and sending them whizzing back down again? Perhaps both were satisfied with a demanding and active life, she thought, as she fingered the goods on display.

'Everything nice and dry,' she remarked to her young assistant.

'We've had all the stuff in the boiler room for the last few days,' said Brian with the same chatty confidence that he had displayed at the age of seven. 'Holy Mack! Didn't half smell after that flood! Worst stink that you could imagine, Reverend Mother. Oh, not now,' he added rapidly as she dubiously lifted a towel to her nose. Old age, she had discovered recently, to her horror, had diminished her sense of smell and was rapidly reducing the acuity of her hearing. 'Not now, Reverend Mother,' he assured her confidently. 'Mr Fitzwilliam's son, the major, he's got them gas things, had them in the war. You put everything into a room, shut the windows, throw in one of them little canisters, shut the door and the gas gets rid of the smell. They used to use them during the war to get the stink out of places, the major told me that. Told me all about it, "fumigate" that's what he called it. Got the idea from tree growers in California who used to shoot them into trees to get rid of the fungus that grows on them. The major told us all about it. And the army bought thousands of them so they could fumigate the uniforms and boots and everything. I'd like to be a soldier in England, Reverend Mother, but me mam won't let me.'

'Well, you've got a good job here, Brian,' said the Reverend Mother, feeling an obligation to support the mother of this fresh-faced youth who might well be lost to his parent for ever if he went off to join the English army. The shop was doing a great business, she thought. The change barrels from at least twenty of the numerous counters in the enormous shop were whizzing up towards the proprietor, seated in his little office, high above the shop, and a similar number were whizzing back down again. Six barrels were queued up, she counted, looking upwards. Perhaps the owner of the shop allowed six barrels to accumulate before he took out the contents and returned the receipt and the change, or had he just taken a quick break from the demands of his task. Did it really save such a lot of time for the counter assistants or was it, as rumour hinted, a way of keeping complete control over the cash that came into the store.

'Your mother must be pleased for you to have this apprenticeship,' she added. The mother, she recollected hearing, had gone back to her own family farm in Mallow, north of Cork. Brian's father, like a lot of men in the city, had disappeared. Gone to England, probably. Possibly to be a soldier. A lot of Cork men still seemed to join the British army despite the numbers that were killed or maimed during the war.

The boy made a face at the mention of his mother. 'She's gone off with my new dad. Not my dad, really,' he added after a minute. 'Left me here.'

'Well, if you work hard, you'll get a job when you are older,' said the Reverend Mother trying to sound cheerful and positive though she doubted the truth of her words. Brian, she thought, was not impressed.

'I don't like it here, Reverend Mother,' he said. 'We have to work for twelve hours a day, here. I hate it. Start at eight in the morning, end at eight in the evening, when the shop closes on time, and that's not often. If there's only one or two people left, Mr Fitzwilliam won't close the door. I'm here for more than twelve hours. They never let you sit down for a minute even if there's nothing to do. Makes your legs ache. Boring, too. And you should see the place where we have to sleep, Reverend Mother. Terrible place. Desperate damp. Water running down the walls. All right for those who live out. At least they can see their friends sometimes. Though I wouldn't want to work here even if I lived out. You don't see Major Fitzwilliam working here. Not usually anyway. He'll be off as soon as they can get another war going in Germany or Africa or something. He was telling me that he'll be off soon. Wish I could go too. Sixpence a week, that's all I get for working from morning to night. And it's so boring here! It's dead boring. Have to work all of Saturday, too. I just get Sunday afternoon to see my ole mates. And if it rains, I've nowhere to go except sit in that stinking dormitory.' Brian turned a hopeful face towards her, looking, she thought with dismay, as if he felt she might do something about his woes.

But just as the Reverend Mother sought the words to encourage him to make the best of the present, to believe that his mother knew best, she became aware that something was going wrong in the shop. The traffic of change barrels upwards had not ceased, but the traffic downwards had come to a complete halt. Looking up to the office forty feet above their heads she could see that there was an accumulation of change barrels waiting to be dealt with. The shop assistants, women and men, were looking upwards, dismayed, uneasy. A young man in an old-fashioned morning coat, with tails flying out behind him came running up from the back of the shop and then started to climb the stairs. All eyes followed him and then swung around to look towards the front door. The crowds had parted, had left a passageway. Another man, this one dressed in a uniform, had just come through the front door, pausing for a moment and then breaking into a run and following rapidly the young man in the morning coat.

'That's the major,' said the young apprentice. 'That's him, Reverend Mother.' He sounded quite excited.

'And who is that man, Brian?' queried the Reverend Mother.

'Ah that *fuster*, that's young Mr Fitzwilliam, Mr Robert. He's just the shop floor manager.' The boy sounded scornful and the Reverend Mother concealed a smile. That good old Cork word 'fuster' did seem to suit the harassed and worried air of the younger Mr Fitzwilliam, but now there were genuine grounds for concern, she thought, looking upwards at the motionless change barrels. The work of the shop seemed to have come to a full stop. The busy barrels on the wires over their head were jammed one behind the other. The twin daughters of the owner, Monica and Kitty, emerged from their counters and looked upwards at the static queue of small canisters.

The door in the tiny office above was flung open. A figure, an elderly, heavily-built, tail-coated figure staggered out, lurching his way to the safety rail of the landing outside the office and leaned over it. And then, while the noise and chatter of the huge crowd of people quite suddenly ceased, Mr Joseph Fitzwilliam toppled over the safety bar and fell heavily down on to the stone floor beneath, almost directly at the Reverend Mother's feet.

'Janey Mack!' exclaimed a blond-haired young apprentice from the Ladies' Shoes department in horrified and frightened tones. 'He's had a fit. Old Mr Fitzwilliam has gone and had a fit.'

The Reverend Mother moved forward. There was a strong smell of gas, and Major Fitzwilliam, his hurried ascent towards the office having been interrupted by the old man's fall, now descended the stairs rapidly as he pushed himself through the dense crowd of people, still with a lit cigar between his first two fingers. She glanced around hastily. All of the gas lamps on the bronze pillars seemed to be burning steadily with a clear, white light. The aroma of gas, she thought, came from the man lying stretched out on the ground at her feet.

The Reverend Mother knelt down. She touched the man's forehead, picked up the flaccid hand, her finger on the pulse. The major, extinguishing the glowing end of his cigar against the stone floor, knelt opposite to her. He took the other hand, his finger, like hers, on the pulse and their eyes met across the body. He got to his feet instantly.

'Robert,' he said authoritatively to his younger brother, 'take Mother and the girls home.' He nodded at the three black-garbed figures who had made their way through the crowd and now stood silently looking down at the dead man.

Mrs Agnes Fitzwilliam had changed greatly. She would be over seventy now, thought the Reverend Mother. A pretty girl in her youth, Agnes had turned, in middle age, into a smart, well-groomed, well-dressed woman, but was now an elderly figure with a bowed back and white hair. Did she really still work at the shop? The Reverend Mother wondered about that, but the black frock and the pair of scissors, attached by a piece of black tape to her waist, seemed to suggest this. Her two middle-aged daughters, Monica and Kitty – only a brother would call them 'girls', both dressed in black and both with a pair of scissors attached, stood silently on either side of their mother and looked down at the dead body of their father. None of the three wept, or made any gesture towards the corpse. A murmur rose from the crowd. News spreads fast, thought the Reverend Mother and wondered when the efficient Major Fitzwilliam would think of sending for a doctor.

And then, to the Reverend Mother's enormous relief, a rotund figure made his way towards them, tentatively moving his bulk around the shocked and now silent figures, with a touch on a sleeve, an apologetic whisper until he reached the cluster around the body. It was Dr Scher, with a pair of men's shoes in one hand and his purse in the other. His eyes went immediately to the dead man. He dumped the pair of shoes on top of Brian's basket, replaced the purse within his pocket and knelt down upon the flagstones, one competent finger on the pulse, the other lifting an eyelid. The Reverend Mother watched. Dr Scher was her own doctor, doctor to all of the nuns in the convent, a professor at the university and the man whom the police instantly called in the case of any suspicious death. He would handle the matter. She saw him bend over the corpse and inhale and knew that he, like she, had perceived the distinctive smell of gas.

Her eyes followed his and went to the bronze pillars. Twenty-seven gas lamps had said poor Mr Fitzwilliam, and it did look like that. Nine tall pillars in the row ahead of her, each with its metal glowing a warm bronze, illuminated by the bracketed gas lamp. Moving her head discreetly, she counted another couple of rows behind her and each bracket seemed to be lit up in a similar way – not a bracket without a light. But yet, there was that smell.

'Look at that!' Brian's half-broken voice cracked on the last note. Dumping the basket on the floor beside the Reverend Mother he plunged forward, scattering some of the crowd that pressed around. 'Look at that, Major! It's one of your canisters, one of your gas canisters. That's where the smell is coming from.' He bent to pick it up, but Dr Scher was too quick for him. He also had noted the canister.

'Just leave that alone, sonny,' he said. His hand went to his trouser pocket, pulled out a large, well-laundered and newly ironed handkerchief. He draped it over the canister and then picked up the small canister with great care. In a moment he had opened his attaché case and made a space where the canister could rest, still swathed in the handkerchief. A crescendo of sound swelled as half the crowd commented on the movement to the other half.

And then, quite suddenly, Mrs Fitzwilliam began to scream. 'I knew it, I knew it,' she shrieked. 'He's been murdered. The wrong person has been murdered. That stupid boy made a mistake. He murdered my husband and he was supposed to murder me.' She swung around and pointed a finger at Brian Maloney. 'He murdered him with that gas!' By now she was weeping hysterically, but her words in a high-pitched voice were clear to all. She would be heard all over the shop, thought the Reverend Mother, as she took a step forward and put an arm around the woman, watching Dr Scher open his medical attaché case and take out a syringe.

TWO

I t was when she heard that blood-curdling scream that Eileen changed from being a clerk and delivery girl in a printer's office to being a reporter, an author, a person who put feelings, atmosphere, sounds into words, and wove them into stories. Frequently she had short articles, news items, commentaries published in the *Cork Examiner*, but this, she decided instantly, was going to be aimed at the style of the English newspapers, the gutter press, according to the priests on the altar, who disliked the salacious tone of the stories that they uncovered in England and also in the cities of Ireland. But say what you like, these newspapers grabbed the attention and almost forced the money from people's pockets. She slipped rapidly behind the curtain of the kitchenware counter and began to write.

A good headline; she would need a good headline.

DEATH SOARS ALOFT IN THE QUEEN'S OLD CASTLE

She was not quite pleased with that, much too long, but would work on it. In the meantime, she had a dramatic story to tell:

> *An ordinary morning in an ordinary shop in the city of Cork, [she wrote, the rapid shorthand symbols filling up the page as fast as her thoughts were flooding through her mind]. The Queen's Old Castle was full of people taking advantage of the Flood Sale. Shoppers shopped; counter hands wrapped up parcels. As is the custom in this shop money was sent up in small barrels to Mr Fitzwilliam, owner of the shop, perched aloft in his office high above the ground. Change was sent back down again in those same barrels. As always was the practice in the Queen's Old Castle.*

But something went wrong on this morning. While shoppers watched, mesmerized with horror, Mr Fitzwilliam came out from his office, clutching a small barrel, staggered to the railing, and toppled over, crashing down to the floor.

There was no doubt that he was dead. No man could have survived that terrible fall. Or was he already dead when he fell? The shop was alive with rumours and information. 'It's gas,' went the whispers. 'You can smell it. The man has been gassed.'

And then his wife had screamed out hysterically, out of her mind with horror. And the terrible word: 'Murder'. The word first uttered by the wife of the dead man and then spreading outwards until it began to be whispered through the ranks of the shoppers in the Queen's Old Castle.

They had been married for over fifty years. Mrs Joseph Fitzwilliam, wife of the dead man was a hardworking wife, a devoted wife. She had stood this morning, as she always stood, behind the counter of the shop that they had built up together. And then came the terrible tragedy, the moment when, as her gaze wandered up towards the balcony where her husband sat, as always, counting out his money, she saw a terrible sight. Slowly, heavily, the body tumbled over the rail and fell to the floor. The man was dead!

And now his hysterical wife, distraught with anguish, her wits muddled by tragedy, screamed out that there had been a mistake; that she had been meant to be the victim, that she should have been the one who died.

That was a good way to put it, thought Eileen with satisfaction. No paper would publish an allegation that the husband had tried to kill the wife, but this implied something sacrificial, something like those Indian wives who threw themselves on to the fire where the body of their dead husband was being cremated.

'He made a mistake,' she screamed. 'I was the one that was supposed to be killed. It was a stupid mistake. That stupid boy killed the wrong person.'

Eileen leaned on the counter and wrote the words as Mrs Fitzwilliam succumbed to a fit of hysteria and began laughing and crying.

> *All listening knew that shock had momentarily robbed her of her wits and there was a murmur of sympathy from all over the shop. Her sons and daughters rushed to be by her side. No one could do anything for the dead man, but the live wife needed help. Soothing voices and gentle hands.*

Eileen stuck her pencil between her teeth and climbed onto a stool behind a counter. Now she could see over the heads of the people. There was a cluster around Mrs Fitzwilliam. Her two sons and her two daughters. Someone holding a cup to her lips. Keeping her quiet, thought Eileen. No one could scream and drink at the same moment. And now Dr Scher had arrived. She climbed back down from the stool and continued the bare bones of an article which she was sure she could sell to the *Cork Examiner*. She had to be quick, though. Soon the story would spread over the city and a reporter would be despatched. She could do better, though. She was an eyewitness. She would go straight to the *Cork Examiner* office as soon as she finished and she would read her notes to the editor, promise to have them typed up in time for the *Evening Echo* or if not for the *Cork Examiner*.

> *Doctor Scher, well known in the city of Cork, had come to their aid. Even as the elderly doctor bent over the body, the bereft wife still cried out, quite mad with grief, convinced that a mistake had been made. The doctor then took out his hypodermic needle. The poor woman still obviously distraught.*
>
> *But what was it that had killed her husband? Gas! The one word was muttered from person to person. The smell pervaded that end of the shop. The shoppers began to move towards the door. The family of the dead man, his two daughters, Miss Monica Fitzwilliam and Miss Kitty Fitzwilliam, Mr Robert Fitzwilliam, the floor manager and his older brother Major James Fitzwilliam,*

all huddled together and stared with horror at the
corpse.
*   And at the open, shrieking mouth of their mother who*
was saying the unthinkable. 'It's that boy. He sent the
gas up.' The woman's finger pointed at a young boy, faced
him with an accusation. 'I saw him!' she screamed and
then the merciful power of the drug took effect and she
slumped back into her daughter's arms.

Would the *Examiner* wear that one? Well, she could try,
anyway. Eileen took a quick look around the shop. She
wouldn't have long, but she had a dramatic story and
she needed to paint the scene. She noted the crowd – she
could do a little about them, hunting for bargains, but now
huddled together.

Whispers hissed! Bit by bit the words surged through the
air, became distinct. 'Gas!' 'He's been gassed!' 'Gas sent
up from one of the counters!' 'Someone had it in for the
old man!' 'Not hard to guess who could have done it!'

These mutters would fill the spaces between her descriptions.
    She began to plan the article, and how to set the scene.
    She noted the cavernous space, remembering the history of
this ancient building, writing a description of the strange slabs
of glass on the roof, the steep steps and the long passageway
that snaked its way high up on the ancient wall. She wrote a
headline at the top of her piece: 'MURDER IN THE QUEEN'S
OLD CASTLE'. She wondered whether she could get away
with that. Well, it would do for the moment. It would be such
a shame if it was just an ordinary accident. Her eyes wandered
over the staff, gathered in a cluster. Michael Dinan, she had
heard of him, knew the company that he kept; Séamus
O'Connor, the man who was running two love affairs behind
the counters – and one of them with the daughter of the owner.
And then there was the family. A mad mother, two sons, one
the floor manager, the other, very posh, a major in the British
army, and two daughters, each of them with a counter of
her own. She would have to find out some more details. No

accusations, no, the paper was not the kind to take risks. Just a whole lot of information without comment. It would be fun to do. She wondered how much she would earn from a series of articles. A description of that little office, forty feet up, almost touching the roof of the old castle. A description of the place where the dead man had spent his last minutes. That's what I need now! Quickly Eileen shoved her notebook and pencil back into her handbag, picked up the batch of posters and sedately slipped up the stairs, keeping close to the wall. There were heavy black clouds drifting across the sky and the light in the upper section of the shop had dimmed. Her black leather coat, leather breeches and black hair would not show up until someone switched on the gas lamps. And the Queen's Old Castle shop owners were notoriously mean and careful not to spend any unnecessary money.

In any case, Eileen told herself, I have a perfect right to be here. I was sent here by my employer to deliver the printed posters to Mr Fitzwilliam. Downstairs, the shop was being cleared of shoppers, commands to put back the goods being shouted. That was Mr Robert. Always made a great fuss about everything. She kept as close to the wall as she could and climbed the stairs as quickly and as silently as possible. There was a great commotion from downstairs. No one was happy to have to abandon goods that they had picked up. Eileen quickened her steps. Now she had reached the top of the stairs and was on the thin, long corridor that was supported on a structure of iron pillars. It felt a little shaky, but she told herself that the elderly owner of the shop went up and down this corridor and those stairs twenty times a day. Nevertheless, she avoided glancing down at the floor of the shop forty feet below where she walked. Why, on earth, had Mr Fitzwilliam wanted to have an office up here? She would add a little to her story about it, she decided, shaping the idea in her head. A man's obsession with supervision of his employees and his customers, and that obsession leads eventually to his death. She could manage to write something that delicately inferred, but did not spell out, the sheer oddness of the man and of his family, too. She felt less dizzy and less vulnerable as she planned her story.

Nevertheless, she was glad to reach the sanctum of the office. The door was closed, but she opened it and she slipped inside, closing it behind her. A gas fire burned in one corner and the place was stiflingly hot. She held the bundle of posters in her hand and went forward to look at the desk.

And at that moment she smelled the strong, suffocating smell of gas. She hesitated for a moment, and then self-preservation sent her flying for the door. It was opened before she got to it and she burst past the man standing there, gulping in great noisy gulps of the damp cold air outside the little airless office. It was Robert Fitzwilliam, she noticed, the younger son of the dead man and the shop floor manager.

He caught her by the free arm before she could go back down. 'What the hell are you doing up here?' His tone was low, but there was no mistaking the aggression. Eileen did not hesitate. Quickly she stamped on his foot with all of her strength and then thrust the heavy bundle of the printed posters up into his face. His hands came up automatically to shield himself as he grabbed the bundle.

'Sorry!' said Eileen and smiled to herself with satisfaction as she watched him try to regain his balance. She was a match for any shop man. She had spent a couple of years with the IRA when she had left school and had learned the elements of armed and unarmed combat. Surprise! That's what Tom Hurley always said. And automatically she had followed her training. Now Robert Fitzwilliam had been taken by surprise and stood awkwardly on one foot with both of his arms encumbered with the load of printed posters.

'Just delivering these from the printing works, Mr Robert,' said Eileen casually. Never explain, never apologize, that had been one of the rules of unarmed combat. Make your opponent's body work for you, had been another. Robert Fitzwilliam wasn't much good at this sort of thing. He was still slightly off balance and trying to cope with the pile of posters she had thrust into his arms. 'What's happened?' she asked, making her voice sound casual. She went to the railing and looked down at the cluster of people. The body was still stretched out on the ground. Shop assistants, apprentice boys, the Fitzwilliam family, Dr Scher and the Reverend Mother. What on earth had brought the Reverend Mother here? Eileen took a step backwards before she could be seen.

'You'd better get out of here,' he said harshly. He wasn't looking at her, but towards the front doors where Séamus O'Connor was standing, almost like a sentinel. 'It's the police,' he hissed. 'Now scarper! None of this is anything to do with you.'

He was right. Never a good idea to get mixed up with the police. She had had enough of that in her past life. Now she was nineteen years old and a law-abiding citizen. She said no more, just sidled along the passageway with her back to the wall and her eyes on the figures by the front door. When she reached the stairs, she put out her hand to hold the safety bar and trod lightly, doing her best not to attract any attention.

Robert Fitzwilliam, floor manager, son of the dead man, wasn't going down to greet them. Not straight away, anyway. He had gone back into the little office. Eileen heard the click of the door as he opened it and she paused, holding on to the inner railing and turning back to look. The office was made almost wholly of glass with windows on three sides, and she could see the shiny texture of Robert's frock coat. What was he doing? Bending over the desk? Rearranging the change barrels? She thought that she saw a wire flicker. And then she heard footsteps coming up the steep steps and hastily she turned around. She knew that head of hair. It was Joe, the sergeant from the police barracks.

He looked taken aback to see her when they met at the halfway point of the stairs.

'Just delivering some additional posters for the sale,' she said, instantly seizing the advantage. 'What's up, Joe? What's happened? Why have they shut the shop?'

He pulled out a notebook. She knew he would. Very predictable, these policemen. Went along the same lines all of the time. Name? Address? Business? As if he didn't know everything about her.

'There's a fellow up there in the office and I'd lay you a substantial bet that he's interfering with the evidence, Joe,' she said in a loud whisper.

He looked at her, unsure, torn between the two duties, but

then a twang from the wire overhead galvanized him into action.

'Stay here,' he ordered and set off with long footsteps that made the flimsy passageway rock.

She followed him. After all, she said to herself, I have an article to write. In any case, I'd like to know what Mr Robert is up to. Underhand individual if ever there was one. She stayed at the policeman's heels until they reached the office and then taking advantage of a momentary hesitation, she stepped in front of him and wrenched the door open.

'Sergeant Joe Duggan, Mr Robert Fitzwilliam,' she said with a flourish as though she were an official introducer.

Robert swung around instantly. There was a dark red flush on his face and a look of fury in his eye.

'Could I trouble you to come downstairs, sir?'

It was amazing how polite these policemen were. Didn't mean anything, of course. Everyone knew that. Robert had an ugly look of disappointment and frustration on his face. Nevertheless, he had to do what he was told and he went silently to the door, allowed the policeman to lock it with the keys that were stuck in the doors and then went down the stairs with his head bowed. What had he been looking for? Or was there something that had to be hidden before the police came and if so, had he managed to achieve that? Eileen wondered how she could work this frantic search of Robert's into her article – perhaps a series of mini snapshots of what everyone in the shop was doing? She did not look at him again and kept her head demurely lowered until she reached the floor of the shop.

'I'll be off now,' she said as soon as she was within sight of the front door. 'You know where to find me, Sergeant Duggan, but I'll be of no use to you. I'd only just come into the shop when it all happened. Just delivering another set of posters. Mr Robert will tell you all about it.'

She did not wait for an answer from either man, but went quickly towards the door and slipped through it. Once outside she began to run up Patrick Street. Get there before they managed to send a reporter, she told herself as her side ached.

No excitement in evidence in the *Cork Examiner* office

when she burst in through the door. Everyone calmly typing, or talking on the phone, or discussing last night's new film. Eileen paused dramatically inside the front door, holding up her notebook and only speaking once everyone's attention was on her.

'Hold everything! Stop the presses! I've got a scoop of a lifetime!' She waited for a moment and then walked across the floor towards the desk of the chief editor.

'How would you like an eyewitness account of the murder of a prominent citizen?' she enquired as she seated herself in the chair beside him.

THREE

The Reverend Mother looked across at Dr Scher. He was kneeling on the ground beside the hysterical woman. He still kept his finger on the pulse of the woman, but now in the sudden quiet that had ensued after his injection, the Reverend Mother knew that Dr Scher was now aware of the many curious glances that were sent in the woman's direction. This story and the account of her words would go all around the city of Cork. He looked deeply worried. The Reverend Mother wondered how strong a sedative he had administered and whether he could guarantee that there would not be another outbreak. Judging by his anxious expression she thought not. His eyes had gone to Major Fitzwilliam, the most authoritative figure around him.

'Close the shop, Major. What do you think?' His apologetic, tentative tone made a suggestion rather than an order out of the sentence but the major nodded. He immediately took his hand from his mother's arm, moved well away from her and then climbed upon a chair behind the nearest counter.

'Thank you all for your concern for my father,' he said. His voice, accustomed to the parade ground, rang from the rafters and seemed to be heard by all. 'I'm afraid that this shop will now have to close immediately.' He left a silence after this, but then went on, giving directions about which doors to exit. His voice was firm and without emotion. A man used to emergencies and well able to keep his feelings under control.

'And do please put any unpaid-for goods that you are carrying back onto the counters,' shouted his younger brother, Robert. His tone, in an effort to make his words understood by all, had a harsh, rather unpleasant sound and it was resented by the people standing around. A murmur, that had an indignant note in it, rose up as people turned their backs on the dead man and went towards the doors, dumping baskets as they went. Poor things, thought the Reverend Mother, giving a thoughtful glance at her own basket full of treasure. They had hoped to secure some bargains this morning. Prices, she had noted, were all extremely low.

After a few more harshly spoken words from Robert, the staff began to usher the customers out. The Reverend Mother wondered about the loss of witnesses, but decided that there were enough staff present to answer any questions that the police might pose. She thought about asking Brian to replace her own items, but he had wandered away from her and was standing near to Dr Scher, gazing at the corpse with an exaggerated air of ease, belied by the whiteness of his face. She decided to leave him there. He would have a wonderful story to tell all of his one-time school friends on Sunday afternoon, his one holiday of the week, and she could not grudge it to him, given the dullness of his life. Despite the pallor of his face, he had a thrilled and excited look about him. Death of an elderly man for a boy of that age meant little and something as bizarre as this death could make an action-packed recital and ensure his popularity among his friends. She doubted whether he had been particularly well treated by the dead man. Sixpence a week did seem to be a very poor reward for work which lasted from eight o'clock in the morning until eight o'clock in the evening; that must be over seventy hours a week, she calculated. She then failed miserably in an effort to divide up that sixpence into an hourly rate. How much of the hysterical woman's accusations had he taken in, she wondered. They had been almost incoherent and punctuated with gasps and sobs. Nevertheless, they had clearly accused Brian of being the person who sent up the barrel filled with gas.

The shop was now emptying rapidly. Robert Fitzwilliam was turning down the gas, moving rapidly from bronze pillar to bronze pillar. An odd idea, but perhaps a reflex action on his part to the departure of the customers. The wife of the dead man seemed to be coming back to herself, blinking her eyes, standing up and then, gently urged by Dr Scher, had sunk back down on a chair, holding hard to the hand of one of her daughters. She still shook her head to the major's suggestions that she might go home. Dr Scher patted her hand in a kindly way, but then left her in order to open his attaché case from which he gave the major a piece of paper with a scribbled telephone number. 'Ask for Inspector Cashman', she heard him say, and the major gave a nod and sped off towards the telephone, looking relieved at having something to do. The two plain-faced sisters wept silently, but their mother sat on her chair and stared stonily ahead.

Dr Scher had asked for the police. Did that mean this affair was a murder?

'A prayer or two, what do you think?' said Dr Scher in the Reverend Mother's ear and she nodded understandingly. There was a lot to be said for prayer, she thought. It punctuated tragedy and joy, gave the voice and the mind something to focus on when mental probing for answers to almost unanswerable questions would prove unbearable. The Latin words, *Profiscere, anima Christiani, de hoc mundo, in nomine Dei Patris omnipotentis*, came to her mind, but she rejected them for the vernacular. She sank to her knees, joined her hands and lowered her head.

'Eternal rest grant to him, O Lord,' she prayed, 'and let perpetual light shine upon him.'

Patrick, she thought, as the words flowed smoothly from her lips, would take at least five minutes to come speeding down from the police barracks, through the traffic of South Main Street and then to the back entrance of the Queen's Old Castle on North Main Street. Dr Scher would want that five minutes to be filled in a decorous and calm fashion and so when she had run out of prayers in English she embarked upon the *De Profundis*. She could only recollect it in Latin, but Latin was, she thought, a sound familiar to all Roman Catholics. She was, however, pleased and touched when young Brian, probably an altar boy at some stage of his time with the Christian Brothers, chimed in with the response: '*Et lux perpetua luceat eo.*'

The traffic must have been worse than she had anticipated, or else Patrick had been out when the call came for him. In any case, he was longer than she had expected. Still, she kept the prayers going and while they lasted no one moved or spoke. Robert, flourishing a bunch of keys, had ushered all of the customers out and now the shop seemed bare and empty, filled only with the staff and with the family of the dead man. Her voice echoed from the high ceiling and against the plastered walls and there was an odd uncomfortable atmosphere with no voices to support her prayers. She had finished the *De Profundis* and had launched into *Dies Irae* and then in desperation had begun on the rosary by the time Patrick arrived.

Patrick, she thought as she finished the last 'Glory Be to the Father', had like young Brian once been a pupil of the Reverend Mother's school. He had come from a much poorer background than Brian, but had been a far harder worker, both at the convent school and at the Christian Brothers from where he had managed to win a scholarship to the North Monastery Secondary School and subsequently pass the examinations which qualified him for a place in the newly formed unit of the *Garda Siochána*. Once there he had continued to work hard, gaining a reputation of being a careful, accurate and industrious young policeman who spent his evenings studying in order to pass further examinations. He had risen in the ranks to become first a sergeant and then an inspector. The Reverend Mother was proud of Patrick and admired how he had matured into a confident, though quietly spoken, young man.

He came in unobtrusively, followed by his sergeant, Joe, and brought with him a stretcher and some junior members of the force to carry it. He nodded at Dr Scher, well known, of course, as the police surgeon, gave a respectful half bow towards the Reverend Mother, and had a quick glance around at the assembled members of the dead man's family. Despite Major Fitzwilliam's efforts to remove her, and suggestions that she would be better off at home, the widow had stayed there, flanked by her two middle-aged daughters. Her eyes were empty and almost unfocussed and the Reverend Mother wondered how much she understood of what was going on. Her son, the floor manager, Robert, hovered uneasily, making an effort at lining up the numerous sales staff in a position, according to rank, where they could be questioned by the police. Brian, noticed the Reverend Mother with a twinge of amusement, had decided to attach himself to her shielding presence and had ignored the signals from the floor manager to take his place beside the other apprentices. In any case, his eyes were fixed eagerly upon the major, who, as the eldest of the dead man's family, had taken charge and was explaining the situation fluently to Patrick. The words, 'a fit', she noticed with interest, had appeared in the major's account with such frequency that even the dimmest police officer would be expected to take the hint. And yet the major had not been present during that crucial time before his father had fallen to his death. He had definitely come in through the Grand Parade entrance just at the very moment of him falling. In fact, she had seen his car pull up in front of the main doors just seconds before the tragedy. So far as she could hear, the major had not brought up the matter of the discarded change barrel. Nor of his mother's strange accusation. The Reverend Mother looked anxiously at young Brian Maloney. The boy must have heard and his face did still look rather white. A strange accusation.

FOUR

As soon as Inspector Patrick Cashman came through the door of the Queen's Old Castle, the first thing that he heard was the voice of an elderly nun reciting the rosary. It was a familiar sound to Patrick and instinctively he hesitated for a moment before proceeding. His first three years of schooling had been spent under the guidance of the Reverend Mother and he was still deeply grateful to her for encouraging his efforts, fostering his natural disposition to be accurate, conscientious and hard-working and always to pursue a line of enquiry to its utmost. He remembered how she had stood patiently beside him when he had taken it upon himself to count the number of ants going into a crack in the pavement wall. Sister Philomena had smacked him, but he had still refused to leave the playground until he had finished the task. Once the Reverend Mother had arrived she had shown a deep interest in his task and allowed him not only to finish, but also to bring his results into the rest of the class. Later that week she had accompanied his class to the library and had requested the librarian to find him a book about ants. It had been a good beginning for the careful meticulous work of a police inspector.

'Inspector Patrick Cashman and Sergeant Joe Duggan,' he said to Séamus O'Connor who was standing at the door and produced his badge for inspection. Unnecessary, of course, but that was the procedure and Patrick always followed procedure. It saved any awkward questions afterwards if no exceptions were ever made. The man, of course, didn't bother looking at it, but that was up to him. Séamus O'Connor, he thought as he walked into the shop, must have worked at the Queen's Old Castle for a good twenty years. He was already a counter hand when Patrick had been a boy.

'Who's that, O'Connor?' A harsh voice called out an unnecessary question. Always one to throw his weight around, Mr Robert Fitzwilliam. Patrick knew him and he knew Patrick.

He doesn't need any introduction to me, thought Patrick. The police had been sent for and so they would have been expected. Nevertheless, the man never missed any opportunity to pretend to everyone that he was the boss.

'Inspector Patrick Cashman and Sergeant Joe Duggan, sir,' called out Séamus O'Connor. Heads turned in his direction and the quiet voice of the Reverend Mother in the background held a note of finality as it enunciated, 'Glory Be to the Father, to the Son and the Holy Ghost'. Patrick made his way towards that voice. The body would be there, he thought as he listened to the voices gabbling a response. 'As it was in the beginning, is now and ever shall be, world without end. Amen.'

By the time he reached them, the Reverend Mother was on her feet and Dr Scher was standing beside her.

'Took your time, didn't you, inspector!'

Always found something to grumble about, that was Mr Robert. Always something to complain about. Patrick had had a few dealings with this man. Regarded any shoplifting as a failure on the part of the *Gardaí* rather than of the shop procedures where the goods were laid out on tables in a fashion that was very tempting to the poor of the city. Now Patrick ignored him. It wasn't a real question. A question had to be answered. A comment could be ignored or greeted by a polite nod. He had made that rule for himself a long time ago and had always managed to retain a composed face and calm manner. He looked across at the group around the body of the old man, saluting the Reverend Mother and exchanging a quick glance with Dr Scher, but not rushing forward, deliberately taking his time and waiting to see who was now in charge here. Séamus O'Connor also hesitated, looking from one to the other, but when he broke the silence, it was to the major, not to the floor manager, that he spoke.

'Inspector Cashman from the barracks, Major,' Séamus said, deliberately turning his back on Robert. He didn't introduce Patrick's assistant, Joe, but that was not intended as a snub, thought Patrick. The man was tense and worried. He wore a half belligerent, half frightened look on his face as he glanced from one of his master's sons to the other. There was a conflict there. Who was in charge? Major James Fitzwilliam was the eldest son, but his younger brother, Robert, had worked in the shop since leaving school. James had gone to university, qualified as a barrister and then joined the English army. As far as Patrick knew, James had never shown any interest in the department store. Seeing him in the shop this morning he initially assumed that he was merely spending a holiday in his parents' home. Joe, also, glanced from one to the other of the Fitzwilliam sons, as though he, too, wondered which one was in charge. But now, after Séamus O'Connor's selection of the older brother, Patrick watched with interest to see how Robert Fitzwilliam would react. Take it easy, he told himself. Feel your way. First things first. Deal with the body and then start the questions. Robert, he thought, looked angry, but neither surprised nor affronted by Séamus O'Connor's choice.

Patrick gave a quick glance around at the assembled members of the dead man's family. By now the shop had been cleared of all except the employees and the family members of the dead man. The widow was there, flanked by her two middle-aged daughters. Her son, the floor manager, Robert, hovered uneasily, making an effort at lining up the numerous sales staff in a position, according to rank, where they could be questioned by the police. A young lad in a shop apron was standing beside the Reverend Mother, looking as though he had decided to lock himself to her shielding presence and ignored an angry signal from the floor manager to take his place beside the other three apprentices. In any case, the boy's eyes were fixed eagerly upon the other brother, upon the major, who, as the eldest of the dead man's family, had taken charge. Patrick turned an attentive ear to the major, while eyeing the corpse and then looking up at the small office forty feet high above the shop floor. Eventually Patrick gave a nod of such finality that the major dried up quite suddenly and Patrick turned his back on him.

'Good morning, Mrs Fitzwilliam. I'm Inspector Cashman and this is Sergeant Joe Duggan,' he said now, looking neither at the major nor at Robert, but bending solicitously over the widow. She looked dazed and unwell, he thought, and he was very sorry for her. She did not reply, nor did she even look at him but stared bleakly straight ahead of her. 'I'm very sorry for your trouble, Mrs Fitzwilliam,' he continued. 'We will have to take your husband's body away now so that Dr Scher can find out what happened to him. I'll let you know as soon as I know myself.' His tone was as gentle and soothing as he could make it, but there was no response from the widow. She neither looked nor spoke to him but stayed sitting on the chair staring intently ahead. Monica and Kitty looked down at her uneasily and Monica murmured something indistinguishable. Dr Scher bent down and patted the woman's hand once more. He was very solicitous towards her. Patrick saw the Reverend Mother look from one to the other and he wondered whether Mrs Fitzwilliam had been a patient of Dr Scher. As far as he knew Dr Scher had given up all private practice when he reached the age of sixty-five, retaining only his position at the university and his work for the police. And, of course, he continued to visit the convent. In fact, when Patrick thought of it, this much vaunted retirement of his, this change in life-style which was going to herald a new leisurely time of getting up late in the morning and indulging in his hobbies, had not amounted to any great reduction in the doctor's work load. The poor of the south parish still blessed his name whenever he was spoken of and it was possible that he still attended some of his more vulnerable patients. Perhaps someone like that poor tragic woman slumped upon a hard shop chair. The sooner she was taken away, the better. He would keep questioning to a minimum. She wouldn't have anything to add over and above the account given by her son. His eyes went to Dr Scher. They knew each other very well. The sheer number of dead bodies found in the city of Cork, victims of violence, of sectarian killings, of suicide and of murder, were, he remembered reading, higher than any other city in Europe. Dr Scher had examined and pinpointed the cause of death of the majority of them and although he still had not clinically examined the body in the morgue, he probably, thought Patrick, had a fair notion of the cause of death of this body. Enough suspicion, anyway, to have phoned for the police. With his eyes, Patrick signalled and the doctor left Mrs Fitzwilliam's side, picking up his briefcase and following Patrick over to a dark corner beside the shoe counter. Once ensconced behind the high counter, he rested his attaché case upon a stool and clicked it open.

Patrick looked inside, but did not attempt to touch anything. There was the usual untidy clutter of pieces of paper, but lying on top of everything else was a handkerchief, loosely wrapped around a small brown canister.

'Lying on the floor beside the body,' said Dr Scher quietly. 'That bright young lad standing beside the Reverend Mother spotted it. He was going to pick it up, but I stopped him. Thought you might do something clever about fingerprints from it.'

'Fingerprints?' Patrick looked interrogatively at the doctor.

'Smell,' said Dr Scher.

Patrick bent over the attaché case and inhaled.

'Gas, is that it?'

'That's what I smelled too.'

'And the corpse? Did he die from the gas?'

'I think so. There's a blueish tinge about the skin. Tell you more when I've had a chance to have a proper look at him. Just as well to leave this where it is for the moment. I'll put it in an envelope once I have my rubber gloves on and I'll drop it into your office. You might be able to get some finger-prints from it.'

'But how . . .' Patrick broke off and looked where the doctor was looking. Dr Scher had raised his eyes to the wire that ran from the counter up to the small office high on the wall. He remembered how as a small child, he and another boy had sneaked into the Queen's Old Castle and had watched with fascinated interest as the sales staff moved the iron rods and sent the change carriers zooming through the air and waited to receive the change and the receipt. At the time, he thought that Mr Fitzwilliam, old even then, had the best job in the world. He would have loved to be the master of all those whiz-zing barrels, receiving and despatching them with the greatest of ease.

'It's just the right size,' he said, looking at the small canister. 'We can do a few experiments once I have tested it for finger-prints, but by eye, it would definitely fit into one of the change barrels.'

'He'd take it out – he wasn't a patient of mine, but very few men of his age would have perfect eyesight, so I doubt that he'd notice any difference. That's probably what happened. He'd take it out, unscrew the lid. Airless little place up there, probably. And the gas on, of course.' Dr Scher raised his eyes to the small, seemingly sky-high office. 'I've heard of these things used during the war,' he went on. 'A friend of mine, someone that I knew at medical school; he told me all about them. They used to throw them into a trench to get rid of the rats.'

'So he'd breathe it in. He'd know, of course. He'd have smelled the gas.'

Dr Scher nodded soberly. 'He'd get out of that tiny office. It would have been his first instinct to get out. But, of course, by then he would be sick and giddy. And so he pitched over the rail of the passageway. By the look of him, I'd say that he was dead by the time that he hit the stone floor. No bleeding or anything. Could have been a heart attack, but I won't know until I get him on the table.'

FIVE

Eileen hammered away at the keys of the typewriter. It had been good instinct that had prompted her to follow Patrick and Dr Scher into that dark corner. 'Gas', she had heard the word and now she knew how it had been done. The man had been gassed with something that looked just like the canisters for the customers' receipts and change. The storeroom had a shelf load of them. She had heard that said.

But if he had been gassed, who had sent up that deadly capsule?

And was he the person for whom it had been intended?

The shrieked words of his wife, the half-mad utterances, there was nothing secret about them. Anyone who had been in the crowded shop had overheard them. The trick was to make a story out of it. Rouse the readers' interest, get them debating what had happened, get them reading and rereading her article.

She revelled in the feeling of the words flooding out from her brain and oozing through her fingertips. She had read through her notes once, but that was enough and now she firmly put them back into her bag and concentrated instead on painting the scene. The enormous shop, the panic-stricken screams, the terrible sound of the body falling, the accusations – she would have to be very careful here, but she knew how to hint. By now most of Cork would have heard of the tragedy and if her article could appear in the *Evening Echo* and also the next morning's edition of the *Cork Examiner*, well then the papers would be a sell-out.

Did Mrs Fitzwilliam really think that her husband had tried to kill her? And that it was by accident that the deadly capsule had reached him, rather than her. Was the woman sane? Well, that isn't my business, Eileen told herself. But her mind went to the other members of the family and their reaction. *Stunned, shocked, dumbfounded, stricken*, all the words went through her brain and down to her fingertips as she typed away rapidly.

'That's not for me, is it? Don't tell me . . . No, thank goodness, something for the *Cork Examiner*, is it?' Jack, the compositor, had come back from his job of loading lines of type ready to print out some leaflets. He didn't wait for an answer but turned over the pile and began reading. Eileen wasn't worried. The owner of the printing works was quite happy for her to do articles for the *Cork Examiner* if there was no other job waiting to be done. She was a fast and efficient worker and so she had plenty of spare time to write about anything that took her fancy. But was this going to be printable? The editor had been alarmed. Fascinated, nevertheless, he had been alarmed and a little non-committal about publishing. Now she watched Jack's face with a degree of apprehension.

'Christ, Eileen! Are you hoping that the *Examiner* will print this!'

'Why not? It's the truth. It's what happened. I was there. I saw everything.'

Jack read it through again, a slight smile on his lips. 'And to think what a nice little girl you were when you first came here. Butter wouldn't melt in your mouth. A bit of a history of jail breaking and revolver firing, but apart from that . . . And now you're trying to ape the gutter press of England.'

'Oh, come on, Jack,' said Eileen. 'It's time that the *Examiner* woke up and made things a bit interesting. All this printing of columns of names attending a funeral and those tedious sports results. Wait until my article is printed. Can't you just imagine? The whole of Cork will be asking each other whether they've heard about the Queen's Old Castle. The paper will be a sell-out.'

'Doesn't bother you about the family, does it?' asked Jack. 'They're not going to like this, are they? You've skirted around it, but anyone reading this will be asking themselves what was going on in that family. They'll be wondering if this is really an accident.'

'Don't care,' said Eileen. 'The Fitzwilliam family don't do

much for anyone except themselves. It's one of the worst shops in the city to work in. What do I care about them? I just care about money in the bank and having enough to be able to go to university.' She could hear a note of defiance in her voice and knew that he could hear it as well.

'Don't get too hard, Eileen,' he said. 'Money isn't everything. University isn't everything. Lots of happy people around who never passed through the doors of U.C.C. Clever people too. People who read and think about what they read. Still, you have your heart set on it and if God wills it; well, you'll get there in the end.'

Eileen said no more. She had no belief in a benevolent God, but Jack had been very kind to her and had helped her to make a success of this job. She wasn't going to quarrel with him, but she knew what was important to her. And God, she thought, wasn't too good at responding to the most fervent of prayers or else the poor of the city might live in better conditions. Still, for people like Jack, God was important. He must be nearly sixty and he had gone on believing all of his life and wasn't going to change now. He was reading through the typewritten pages again now and a slight smile puckered his lips.

'Well, you certainly won't be popular with the Fitzwilliam family if anyone finds out who wrote it,' he said and added, 'as they will. You know what Cork is like.'

Eileen shrugged. She knew, as well as he did, what Cork was like. Her items always went under the by-line of 'From Our Own Correspondent', but that didn't guarantee privacy. Some other reporter would tell a friend who would tell a friend and then the news would be alive down the length and breadth of 'Pana' as the main street in the city was always known.

'And you won't be popular with the police either,' went on Jack. 'Still, what's new? Between ourselves, do you think one of them had something to do with it? Not a happy family from what I've heard.'

'What have you heard?' Eileen asked. Jack could never resist a good story, so she took her fingers from the typewriter keys and prepared to listen to him.

'Well, a neighbour of mine was telling me that Mr Robert, if you please, has been seen going into the cinema with that nice little girl from the Ladies' Shoes department.'

'Shock, horror,' said Eileen disdainfully. 'What's exciting about that? Are you talking about Maria Mulcahy? And she's no girl, either. She's twice my age if she's a day.'

'Ah, but listen to the rest of it. The woman who cleans the place in the morning overheard the father having a big row with Robert. Telling him that he wasn't to see the girl again. And threatening that if he did, he would fire him.'

'Fire him!'

'That's right. "For going out with a shop girl." That was the words. And, according to Mrs Murphy, he threatened that "he would tell the world about that other business".'

'What other business?'

Jack shrugged his shoulders. He had the air of one who had, perhaps, told too much. 'Haven't a notion,' he said. 'But anyway, it's a nicer story if it's about a son killing him than your one that seems to hint at the wife. Wives shouldn't kill husbands. There was the woman in Limerick who was hanged for that recently. Jury of twelve men. Didn't like that thought at all, not one of them, so they brought in a unanimous verdict. Judge put on his black cap and they hanged the woman. Going out with his own nephew, apparently. They hanged the nephew too, of course.'

'It's up to the police to get evidence,' said Eileen stubbornly. 'I'm just describing the scene, just in the same way as I would if Inspector Patrick Cashman bothered to ask me what I had seen. Fifty people will tell him the story. And do you know what, Jack, it will be buried because we're talking about a rich and respectable family, not a poor peasant. And that's Cork for you, Jack.'

She put her fingers to her typewriter and began to type. 'It is commonly rumoured that the inheritor of this prosperous shop will shortly be getting married himself. And that his choice, to the satisfaction of those who are romantic at heart, has fallen on one of the counter hands. A little bird tells me that Mr R. has been seen going into the cinema with Miss M.M. Perhaps this is what the Queen's Old Castle store needs.

Some young blood, an experienced couple, but young enough to take an interest in the fashions and tastes of the young people in Cork city . . .' She hammered on the keys and watched the words, line by line, appear on the page wound around the typewriter cylinder.

SIX

There is something very odd going on here, thought Patrick. The smell of gas from the small capsule was still in his nostrils. His eye went to the wires that snaked around the upper reaches of the tall building. No accident, anyway. He was sure of that. Dr Scher had done the right thing to call him. He looked appraisingly around at the staff and family who clustered around, standing stiffly to attention as though ready to serve him with some goods.

'I think I'd like to have a word with the members of staff who sent these change barrels up to the office. But perhaps, first of all, sir, you could show me the counters which sent them.' Patrick looked up at the wires that snaked across the ceiling and led down to the counters. He addressed himself to Robert, ignoring the major, who, up to now, had done most of the talking. Robert was the one who knew everything about the running of this shop. Major James Fitzwilliam was only seen in the city once or twice a year.

Patrick knew the Queen's Old Castle shop well. Once he had saved enough of his salary after his appointment to the *Garda Siochána*, he had bought a small house for his mother and furnished and stocked it for her. He had been in and out of the Queen's Old Castle, buying sheets, blankets and other such household goods on many occasions during that time and Robert had always seemed to be in charge of the shop floor. Robert would be the one who was most familiar with the working of the shop. Robert gave a rapid glance upwards, tracing each of the opened barrels back down its wire to its counter and naming it aloud. 'Ladies' Millinery, Ladies' Shoes, Gents' Shoes, Household Linens, Haberdashery, Curtains.' And then he frowned. Patrick took them down in rapid short-hand and when he looked up he saw that Mr Robert, as he was known in the shop, was still frowning heavily.

'There shouldn't have been anyone on the Gents' Shoes

counter. Don't know why money was sent up from there.' The words were uttered loudly and aggressively. He looked around at the staff and the apprentices, standing huddled together in silence watching the family, looking from the spot where their employer fell to his death and then back at the dead man's family. Robert's face had gone an angry shade of purple. 'Séamus O'Connor,' he called authoritatively, 'I thought I told you to leave the Men's Shoes counter closed this morning and to carry on with sorting the stock.'

'I did, sir. The counter was closed for the morning. I told one of the lads on the Ladies' Shoes department to come for me if I were needed.' Séamus O'Connor's eyes moved from the office up on high and turned back to look behind where they stood. A high wide counter, four chairs, arranged neatly, legs aligned with the counter and placed with an almost mathematically correct distance between each of them. Behind the counter, on the long narrow shelves were box after box of shoes and boots, each neatly arranged on a shelf bearing the appropriate size number. At the end of the counter was a large, high, wire basket filled with river-stained shoes, each knotted to its partner, but otherwise thrown in higgledy-piggledy. Then his eyes went to a pair of men's shoes which lay on top of the basket in front of the Reverend Mother.

Dr Scher looked uncomfortable. 'These are mine, inspector,' he said hastily. He went across and picked up the large pair of shoes. 'Quite right, Mr O'Connor. There was no one at your counter when I went there; I was looking for someone to pay for these,' he said to Séamus O'Connor and produced his purse, giving an embarrassed glance around.

Patrick glanced at him with surprise. He would not have thought that the Queen's Old Castle was the kind of shop where Dr Scher would go looking for a pair of shoes.

'They're a size 12, they'd be massive on you with your size of feet,' pointed out the young lad who stood beside the Reverend Mother.

Young Maloney, thought Patrick. He seemed to remember the mother. Had a job scrubbing out the barracks, but then she had gone back to her own people in Mallow. Some talk of another man, he seemed to remember. The lad must be an apprentice here in the shop. Brian Maloney, that's who he was. Brian had crimsoned and looked apprehensive as he got a withering glance from Séamus O'Connor.

'Smart lad,' said Dr Scher quickly intervening to save the boy from the wrath of the counter manager. 'No, I'm just a size seven. I just want them for the old chap that sells newspapers on Cornmarket. He has only one leg, lost it at the Battle of the Somme, a soldier like yourself,' he said to the major, 'but his one shoe is falling to bits and he tripped and fell over this morning on the mud by the river. Didn't do the remaining leg much good, poor fellow.' Guiltily, he produced his purse and looked from one member of the family to another.

'Take them and be welcome and anything else that would be useful to him. Tell him it's from one soldier to another,' said the major heartily.

Interesting, thought Patrick. He looked from the older brother to the younger brother and saw an expression of fury on Robert Fitzwilliam's face. The major had spoken as though he were now the owner of the shop and had authority to give away goods.

'The ambulance is here, ready to go now, inspector.' Joe spoke quietly, but everyone seemed to hear the words, everyone except Mrs Fitzwilliam.

Patrick watched as Robert began to make fussy arrangements about moving counter-front chairs from their position in the alleyway so that the men with the stretcher had plenty of room. Kitty Fitzwilliam wiped a tear and her sister, Monica, looked from one brother to another. And then Monica moved and joined the major. After another minute, Kitty, also, moved, but she went over to where Robert stood. The pair of them almost huddled together, standing under the gas lamp of one of the bronze pillars. It was, thought the Reverend Mother, as if the family were splitting in two.

Mrs Fitzwilliam stared drearily ahead and Dr Scher made no movement to assist her to rise, just continued to pat her hand. Again only the major stepped forward when the father's body was lifted onto the stretcher. He even helped with the lifting and then signed the dead man's forehead with the sign of the cross. It was a certain sign of affection, restrained, but it looked genuine. He watched the body go through the shop and then out of the door before he walked across and took his mother's hand.

'Could I ask you, inspector,' he said, 'is there any reason why my mother should stay here on these premises? There is really no reason why this terrible accident should delay her. My brother, Mr Robert Fitzwilliam, will give you all of the details while I take my mother and my two sisters home. I'm sure that you agree with me as to that being the best thing to do at this moment, inspector,' he said.

Patrick felt a surge of anger rise within him. There had been something very patronizing, very condescending in the major's voice.

'It appears that there may be grounds for investigating this matter of your father's death, sir,' he said carefully. 'I'm afraid that I will need to question everyone who was present when the unfortunate man breathed his last.' Not for the major to assign this strange death to a terrible accident or to any natural causes. This was police business. Looking around he could see very little shock on the faces around him. They had all known, he guessed. 'Perhaps I could just take a statement from you all and allow you to take your mother home, then.' He said the words in clear and determined tones and told himself not to budge.

'Well, I haven't anything to tell you, really,' said the major impatiently. Patrick had moved to inside one of the counters but the major had not followed him but spoke out in clear and very carrying tones. A parade ground voice, thought Patrick, but he did not turn around until he reached his destination. Even then, he did not look at the major, but it was of no consequence as the man continued fluently and confidently, seemingly careless of whether the whole shop could hear him or not. 'I was not here, inspector, at the time that my father came out from his office. I had just entered the shop when he fell to the ground. I'm sure that there are plenty of people here who can bear witness to this.' He looked around confidently and there was a murmur of agreement from most of the counter staff.

Patrick wrote this down, leaning on the counter and then

carrying it across to be signed by the major. There was no other question that he thought he could put out here in the open. Best to give way for the moment and question the man afterwards.

Then, without another glance at the major, he went over and took a statement from Monica Fitzwilliam, who said she had seen nothing as she was talking with a customer. Her apprentice, Tom Donovan, had sent up a change barrel about three minutes earlier, she thought, but couldn't be quite sure of the time. It could have been five. She had not thought that it was a long time in returning. Her father, as everyone in the shop knew, liked to do six barrels at a time when the shop was busy so she was used to waiting.

Kitty Fitzwilliam willingly followed him behind the counter and gave her statement. She seemed happy to speak in a low voice and to keep their interview private. She said she had looked up, wondering what had delayed her change barrel and she had seen her father stagger out of his office, clutching something in his hand and then seen him fall over the railing. Very clear-minded, intelligent woman, thought Patrick.

'And you thought that that there had been an unusual delay in returning your change barrel, Miss Fitzwilliam?' he said.

She considered his question carefully. 'I couldn't swear to it, inspector,' she said eventually. 'You must know that I always felt that whole system was inefficient and caused unnecessary delays to the customer and to the counter staff and so I was always impatient while I was waiting.'

'Not something that you would put in place if you were in charge of the shop,' said Patrick. She had, he thought, a very determined face. Perhaps the father's business ability had been inherited by his daughter rather than by his two sons. The major had no interest in the business and Mr Robert, as he was known in the shop, was generally considered to be a bit of a muddler. Kitty looked a different type and to his surprise she answered his throwaway comment with a serious air.

'The faster people are served, the better for business, inspector,' she said. 'If you delay a customer, then they will rush out of the shop, but if you serve them quickly, wrap their parcel, give them their change more quickly than they expected, then the chance is that they will delay on the way out and buy something else that catches their eye.'

'I see.' Patrick nodded his head while reading through her statement. He would say no more, he thought as he handed it to her to read and to sign, but she had given him food for thought. He had assumed that the daughters had been forced into working in the shop, but perhaps this daughter had enjoyed it, had accumulated ideas of how to run a business. 'Thank you, Miss Fitzwilliam, that will be all,' he said, but his eyes followed her meditatively as she went back to where her mother sat with Dr Scher beside her.

'Ask Dr Scher if I can have a word,' he said quietly to Joe and waited until the doctor came towards him before moving into the back room behind the counter.

'Is she capable of being cross-questioned?' he asked. No need to say a name. Dr Scher would know what he meant.

'No.' The syllable was uncompromising and Patrick bit his lip with annoyance.

'This may be a case of a murder,' he said quietly.

'That's your business,' said Dr Scher. 'You are asking me if my patient is capable of being questioned and the answer to that is no! Mrs Fitzwilliam is not well enough to be questioned by the police and I would like her to taken home as soon as possible. I have given her a strong sedative which will enable her to weather the immediate stress of her husband's death, but it may muddle her, or cause her to utter odd remarks. I think that her son and daughters should take her home now.' Dr Scher looked blandly at Patrick and then turned on his heel and went back to his patient.

He was right, of course. A statement should not be taken from Mrs Fitzwilliam after she had been sedated. Patrick had studied enough of the police regulations, sitting up past midnight and going over and over the rules for taking evidence. The whole shop was abuzz, whispering about the strange things that Mrs Fitzwilliam had said about her husband. But a policeman was bound by the rules and so he went straight over to the major.

'Thank you, sir, you are free to take your mother and your sisters home now. But I will be glad to have the assistance of

Mr Robert Fitzwilliam.' He looked across at Robert and received a sulky nod. *You haven't a doctor to protect you and you were here on the scene so you will damn well stay until I'm finished with you.* Patrick found a certain satisfaction in addressing these words silently to the man.

Dr Scher, with a half-guilty glance, picked up the enormous pair of shoes, indicated a badly stained tartan car rug from a nearby counter, and the major nodded, picking up the rug and adding it and a pair of socks to the doctor's basket before he stood back. The eyes of all present followed Dr Scher's rotund figure as he went out of the shop leaving the two brothers to escort their mother to the major's car.

'Is Dr Scher going off to cut him up to find what killed him?' whispered Brian in the Reverend Mother's ear and Patrick bit back a smile as she frowned reprovingly at the boy. The thought, of course, had probably gone through the heads of all adults present and Patrick saw how Séamus O'Connor gave a half-amused, half-guilty look at Maria Mulcahy from the corner of his eye. Something between those two? It was possible. He seemed to have heard something about that. Though if true, they had been a long time at it. They had both been there working in the shop since the time he was a child. Something else to find out about, he thought, as he made his way towards the room that Robert Fitzwilliam had indicated to him. He was just about to go through the door when a sudden silence alerted him and he swung around. Mrs Fitzwilliam had stopped dead in the centre of the aisle between the counters and was resisting any effort to pull her along. She had remained silent for some time, her chin resting on her chest as she stood there staring forlornly at one of the bronze pillars as though mesmerized by its gleaming illumination. But now she raised her head, turned back and pointed at the young apprentice beside the Reverend Mother.

'He didn't do it for himself,' she said in an almost conversational tone. 'Who told him to do it? Or he made a mistake. Brian Maloney was always a stupid boy.' She nodded her head and then turned back, almost wrenching her arm away from her daughter, going back to where she had been sitting and took several gulps from the cup of tea that had been brought to her earlier. 'He made a mistake,' she repeated. She pointed a skinny finger towards Brian. 'He did the wrong thing. He's a stupid boy. He was meant to kill me.' She said the words in clear and distinct terms.

'I never!' The boy's forehead was wet with sweat.

Patrick felt sorry for the boy, and the major, he was glad to see, turned a harassed face towards him and said reassuringly, 'Don't worry, lad. My mother is just a bit upset. Come on, Mother, let's get you into the car.'

With Robert taking the other arm and Kitty and Monica following they forced the dazed woman down the aisle and towards the front door. Patrick followed and waited at the entrance until he saw the woman safely into the car. Dr Scher was right, he thought, as he watched the efforts made to get her into the back seat. There was no way that he could have taken a statement from a woman like that. Once the car moved off, he waited to allow Robert to go back through the large glass door and allowed him a few minutes to disappear within before he followed him.

SEVEN

'**S**ilence!' Robert was shouting the words in an unsteady tone as Patrick came back into the shop. 'If I hear another word, everyone here will be docked a day's pay.'

Could he do that? Probably, thought Patrick. Those who were lucky enough to have a job didn't often complain, but just put up with injustice.

While Robert shouted out a few orders and doled out jobs to keep everyone busy, Patrick busied himself by putting the names of the counters into alphabetical order, writing them into his notebook and leaving a space beneath each for the name of the counter manager and the apprentice.

Joe took a step forward, showed his own notebook and said quietly into Patrick's ear, 'You might have a word with Mr Robert about what he was doing in his father's office,' he said. 'I went up there and found him rifling through things on the desk.'

'The change barrels?' Patrick also spoke in an undertone.

'Could be,' said Joe. 'They were on the desk, anyway. All I know is that he had his hands on the desk and he seemed to stop what he was doing and look up suddenly when I came in. He definitely seemed as though he were hunting for something. The drawer was wide open. I've taken a note of everything that was in the office.' Joe showed the page and Patrick nodded quietly. There was, he thought, something odd going on here.

'Mrs Fitzwilliam manages Millinery, inspector. And her daughters manage Haberdashery and Household Linens; Miss Kitty for Haberdashery and Miss Monica for Household Linens.' Joe whispered the names into his ear and Patrick, beneath an impassive face, cursed. This was going to be a complication. 'And Mr Michael Dinan for Curtains, Mr Séamus O'Connor for Gents' Shoes and Miss Maria Mulcahy for Ladies' Shoes,' continued Joe and Patrick gave another nod.

Really, Joe was invaluable. If he ever managed to solve this case he must make sure that Joe got his share of praise.

Maria Mulcahy, Michael Dinan and Séamus O'Connor exchanged glances and then they stepped forward. No one mentioned the daughters and wife of the dead man.

Patrick gave himself a moment to think. One thing at a time, he thought. First a meticulous interviewing of everyone on the staff. He would interview those whose change barrels had been opened by the dead man; Joe could do the rest of the counter staff and their apprentice boys. Aloud, he said, 'I wonder if there are a couple of rooms that we could borrow, one for me and one for the sergeant. I would like to get this over and done with quickly and cause the minimum of distress to your family, Mr Fitzwilliam.'

He did his best to sound calm and relaxed, but inwardly the case was worrying him deeply. It was obvious, he thought, that there was trouble between the two brothers. And the sisters, as well. Twins, they were, he was sure that he had heard someone say that. They, too, did not seem too friendly with each other. In any case, he would have to proceed very carefully with this case. It wasn't like a drunken stabbing at a North Main Street pub. This murder was going to have huge repercussions and he reminded himself to be very careful, to walk quietly and to say little, as the superintendent had reminded him when he was first appointed. He looked all around him. There was a small office at the back of the cavernous shop. 'Mr Robert' was written above it.

'Could I use your office, Mr Fitzwilliam?' he asked respectfully, indicating the place. Not for him to call a middle-aged man 'Mr Robert' as though this sad-faced man, a good fifteen years older than himself, was just a teenaged lad in an affluent household.

The tactful approach worked. Robert Fitzwilliam nodded. A fairly ungracious nod, but still a token of acquiescence. Patrick exchanged quick glances with his lieutenant Joe and received a nod in return. And he knew that Joe would find his own space in order to interview the remainder of the counter staff and, of course, their numerous apprentices. More apprentices than decently employed staff in this shop, thought Patrick, but knew these thoughts had to stay safely locked within his head for the duration of this enquiry. He took a look at the first page of this section of his notebook and said aloud, very calmly, without emphasis or stress, 'Mr Michael Dinan, could you come with me, please.'

There was a certain movement among those who remained within the cavernous depths of the Queen's Old Castle. Nothing could really have been discerned, but an atmosphere swept through the depths of the shop; it seemed that many people there thought that this name, the name of Michael Dinan, had a weighty resonance in the matter of the death of their master, Joseph Fitzgerald.

Michael Dinan himself stood up with forced assurance. He even swaggered a little as he came towards Patrick. Suddenly he was put violently aside. 'Just a moment, inspector,' said Mr Robert Fitzwilliam. 'I want to have a few words with you before you interview my staff.'

'Certainly, Mr Fitzwilliam, come in, won't you. Just wait for a moment, Mr Dinan,' said Patrick with a polite nod of his head. He held the door widely open for the other man and then shut it respectfully behind the two of them. 'Take a seat, won't you, Mr Fitzwilliam,' he continued in moderate tones.

The man was disconcerted by his politeness; Patrick could see that. Mr Robert didn't sit down but waited until Patrick had closed the door before he spoke. Patrick also remained standing and waited to hear what the man had to say. What had prompted that frantic search of his father's office, even before the dead body had been removed from the shop? What had he hoped to find? Let him do the talking for the moment. Patrick waited politely.

Robert faltered, hesitated, and cleared his throat a few times before he spoke. 'You see, inspector,' he said after a moment, and it did almost seem that he had spent the time racking his brains about what to say. 'I feel that perhaps I should be present when you interview the staff. After all, I have been in charge of them for the last ten, no, eleven years. My father looked after the money side of the shop and I was in charge of the staff.'

Patrick pretended to give the matter his most earnest

consideration. 'I can see what you mean, sir, but, of course, I am bound by police protocol.' He spread his hands apologetically. 'There's a manual that they give to us. It lays down all the rules, all the procedure, tells us exactly what we need to do when we question witnesses.'

'Oh, I see.' Robert Fitzwilliam sounded relieved to be given a way out of it. 'Well, of course, if that's the way of it. I wouldn't like to make you break any rules. I'll send Dinan in to you.' He began to back awkwardly out of the room leaving Patrick to raise his eyebrows in silent astonishment. What on earth had been behind that outburst? Was the man on the brink of a nervous breakdown? Or was he, perhaps, apprehensive about what might be said behind his back?

'Just a moment, Mr Fitzwilliam,' he said as soon as the man had his hand on the doorknob. Robert whirled around as though he had expected this summons, had been on edge waiting for it. 'I see that the sergeant reports you as being in your father's office just after we arrived in the shop. I wonder could you tell me what you were doing.'

'Just turning off the gas fire,' said Robert promptly. 'My father was an elderly man and he felt the cold, but that little office could get very over-heated.' The answer came out so readily it sounded as though it had been prepared.

'But apparently you were looking through the drawers. So the sergeant reports.'

'There's a lot of private stuff there . . .' Robert adopted a blustering tone. 'Confidential matters which should not be exposed to the eyes of strangers.'

'You have no need to worry, sir,' said Patrick. 'All that is found in the course of an investigation remains confidential, unless of course, it is found to have a connection with a crime.'

That word 'crime' bothered Robert. He turned very red and then just as suddenly the colour ebbed away leaving his face a pasty white.

'So, may I ask what you were looking for, sir?' Patrick put the question in a mild, unprovocative manner and Robert seemed taken aback.

'I just wanted to make sure that all the end of the month accounts had been paid. Just in case I forgot about them afterwards with all the stress of my father's death.' He eyed Patrick uneasily, as though he were conscious that this was rather a weak explanation.

It was, thought Patrick, one of the most extraordinary excuses that he had ever received. What on earth did the man mean by it? And did he really expect that to be believed. Even Robert himself seemed conscious of the oddness of his description and after a moment he stumbled into an account of what a terrible shock his father's death had been.

'I'm sure that you will understand my compulsion to do the right thing and to have all of my father's affairs sorted out before the police looked through them, inspector.'

'Yes, indeed,' said Patrick. It was a phrase that he had practised, and it meant nothing but soothed the atmosphere. He allowed the man to stand there for a moment in silence, alert for any further confidences. Nothing came, though. Robert cleared his throat, looked out of the window on the small back yard outside and shifted from one foot to the other in the manner of a man who would like to be dismissed, but who did not quite know how to end the interview of his own accord. *Compulsion. What did he mean by that? An odd word.* Patrick made a quick note in shorthand at the back of his notebook, headed with the word 'check'.

'Yes, please do use my office, inspector, and now, if you'll excuse me, I have some things that I must do.' Robert edged his way out of the office and a moment later Patrick overheard him shouting at an apprentice called Burke. He suddenly sounded in a very bad humour.

Patrick went on thinking about a possible connection between the death of the father and the obvious anxiety of the son. It would be worth running a check on the man's bank account. Money, he had found, was often at the root of crime and, even if old Mr Fitzwilliam was in theory keeping money matters in his own hands, in practice his son who was there in the shop for twelve hours a day and six days a week, might well have had the opportunity to put his hand into the till on a few occasions.

Except that all money matters went through that sky-high office, so no counter on the shop floor even possessed a till.

Patrick mused on the matter for a couple of minutes in order to give Robert a chance to move off to another part of the shop and then he went to the door.

'Mr Dinan, sir, would you come in here for a moment, please?' He made sure that his voice conveyed a request rather than an order. No point in putting anyone's back up at this stage in the enquiry. It was no good, though. The man was already worked up into a state as he strode through the doorway and slammed the door after him.

'I suppose that you think that I done it,' said Michael Dinan. His tone was very aggressive, but his legs shook and the pupils of his eyes were dilated with fear.

Patrick sat back onto the chair behind the desk and pulled the inkpot towards him.

'Take a seat, Mr Dinan, won't you? Now, which counter do you work on?' What was the matter with this man? He was in a state of terror, a terror that was working its way into aggression.

'Curtains,' he said and then added, 'until the end of the week. And then I get kicked out of the door, after all my years of working here for sixpence a week.'

This was interesting news. Never easy to get a job in Cork. Dismissal from a job meant that the door to any other job was slammed shut too. The only possible choice then was to take the boat to England. 'May I ask why you have been dismissed?' Patrick did not look at the man, but kept his eyes on his notebook, carefully noting the details and checking through the address.

'You may ask why, but I can't tell you. Not *won't* tell you, inspector. *Can't*! I don't know what I have done to be dismissed. Except for one thing, of course. Now that I am twenty-one years of age, then I need to be paid the minimum wage for an adult and they don't get me for half-nothing any longer.'

'Was that the reason given for your dismissal?' Patrick kept his eyes on the page in front of him but every sense was alert.

Michael Dinan gave an unpleasant laugh. 'You're joking, of course. These things are never said, are they? Oh, they found reasons, of course. They are expert at that. "Not polite to customers" – something that cannot be proved one way or the other. "Slow with your work" – same thing. "Not satisfactory" – well, that's all in the eye of the beholder, isn't it, inspector?' The man's voice trembled with anger.

'So you would admit that you bear a deep grudge towards the owner of this shop.' Patrick made the suggestion and then sat back to see the effect.

'Why do you say that?' Dinan's voice was harsh.

Patrick kept his own voice low and quiet. 'You have given me reasons why any man would be bound to feel resentment towards his employer.'

There was a sudden silence. Patrick looked up after a few moments. Michael Dinan wore the air of someone who was thinking hard.

'If you are looking for motive for this murder, inspector, then you won't have to look too far. In fact, you need not stir beyond his own family. He treated us like dirt, but he treated them like dirt, as well. What a life they led. These daughters of his are like slaves, and his wife, too, poor woman. All of them terrified of him. And what about that poor spineless Robert, scared to marry the girl that he was in love with. Oh, no, that wouldn't do for the high and mighty Fitzwilliam family. Marry a shop girl! But what was he but a shop boy, himself? A shop boy with the power to kick those under him, but a shop boy for all of that. Kept her dangling on, nice girl that she is. Too frightened of his father to act the man and take her to church. Lead a normal life. I tell you, inspector, there's none of them normal. They are not allowed to be. And I'll tell you another thing, inspector. If you want to make a list in that little notebook of yours, a list of those who might have wanted to kill Mr Fitzwilliam, well, I can tell you now that you haven't enough paper to write on. And that's all I am saying to you, inspector.' And with that Michael Dinan got to his feet and marched out of the room.

Well, well, well, thought Patrick. Have I got a suspect there? Perhaps? But would the man be so bold if he had anything to hide? A double bluff, perhaps. Whatever it was, there was a definite air of threat in his voice. Patrick made a note, added

a few question marks and then went to the door to summon
Séamus O'Connor.

Séamus O'Connor was almost a direct opposite to the man
who had gone before him. A relaxed, humorous man. A
bachelor in a city where the Catholic Church forbade all
contraception and marriage was usually followed by yearly
births and huge families.

'I understand that you are interested in the change barrels,
inspector, but I had nothing to do with one of these. I was
not serving that morning. I was down in the basement sorting
through the flood-damaged goods and putting them into
baskets.' His tone was perfectly relaxed. He pulled out a
chair from under the desk and seated himself upon it. 'You
don't mind, do you, inspector? In this job we are all on our
feet from morning to evening so we take the opportunity
of sitting down whenever possible. I've got flat feet and
varicose veins, like all the rest of the shop workers, so I
take the opportunity to sit down whenever I can.' He did
not wait for any affirmation from Patrick but stretched his
legs and continued in the same relaxed and unconcerned
tone of voice.

'To the best of my knowledge and memory, inspector, I
think that I only went up to the main shop twice during the
morning. The first time, soon after nine o'clock in the morning,
was to see what had become of my apprentice, and then when
I found that Mr Fitzwilliam had assigned him to Reverend
Mother Aquinas in order to carry her basket for her, well, then
I went back downstairs again.'

'Were you annoyed about that?' asked Patrick. It was, he
thought, a fairly stupid question. This matter of the apprentice
was hardly going to prove a reason for murder, but then he
had often found that an easily answered first question was
often enough to set the interviewee at ease before asking more
difficult questions.

'Not for me to be annoyed, inspector.' Séamus O'Connor
had a slight smile on his face. 'To be honest, I was just as
glad to be without him. The boy is a terrible chatterbox and
really there wasn't much fetching and carrying to be done.
The main business was in marking down the prices according

to how damaged the shoes and boots were and young Maloney was not going to be much help with that.'

'I see.' Patrick made a note. He had placed Séamus O'Connor now. The eldest boy in a family of twelve. Patrick had been in school with the youngest member of the large family. His father had a job on the docks when Séamus had been placed as an apprentice. Patrick remembered his mother exclaiming at how much money the apprenticeship had cost the O'Connor family and he also remembered her wishing that she could do the same for him when he was fourteen years old. Well, I've done better for myself without taking a single penny from my mother, he thought with an edge of satisfaction as he looked at the tired man with his flat feet and varicose veins.

'And the second occasion for going upstairs, when was that, Mr O'Connor?'

'Just when everything was happening, inspector.' The man's voice was still quite relaxed. 'I could be said to have arrived at the dramatic moment. I went across to the Ladies' Shoes counter to ask Miss Mulcahy whether there had been any enquiries for men's shoes and I found her looking up. She was waiting for change, of course. I don't believe that I even said anything to her and it's possible that she didn't even notice me. Because, of course, it was at that moment that old Mr Fitzwilliam came out from his office and tumbled down over the railing.'

'I see.' Patrick wrote all of this down. It had come out very fluently. But what if this plausible-sounding man had come upstairs earlier, slipped behind his own counter, not attracting any interest or any queries, and had sent aloft the change barrel with its deadly contents.

But what had been the motive for him to murder Mr Joseph Fitzwilliam?

Not a pleasant old man to work for; Patrick was sure about that. But would the younger Mr Fitzwilliam, Mr Robert Fitzwilliam, have been any better? Patrick rose to his feet and accompanied the man to the door. While he was murmuring a few words of thanks, his keen eyes were searching the shop. He spotted Miss Maria Mulcahy and made a beeline towards her. No point in letting the two of them exchange notes before he had a chance to interview the girlfriend.

That's if she were a girlfriend.

Judging by the look of her, they were leaving it very late if they proposed to start a family, but perhaps that was Séamus O'Connor's plan. The arrival of eleven more children as he was growing up on Barrack Street might have disillusioned him with the idea of rearing a family of his own.

Miss Maria Mulcahy was chatting with the Reverend Mother. Late thirties, thought Patrick as he made his way across the room. She had looked up at O'Connor's approach and had smiled at him, but there was no secret interchange of glances with the man who was supposed to have been courting her for the last fifteen years or so. In fact, Séamus O'Connor, after a cheerful farewell to the inspector, had turned and gone back downstairs to resume sorting out the water-stained stock that remained.

Robert Fitzwilliam, however, moved across the room and stood beside the two women in an almost protective fashion. The Reverend Mother, noticed Patrick, looked from him to Maria Mulcahy with one quick glance before she spoke.

'Would it be all right if I were to leave now, inspector? I know you wish to speak with Miss Mulcahy now and you have so many other people to see. Perhaps you might be able to take my statement on your way to see your mother this evening?' The Reverend Mother was on her feet now. 'I wouldn't ask,' she continued, 'but I have the bishop's secretary coming this morning.' Her tone implied the semi-sacred status of the bishop's secretary and those around looked impressed.

'And Brian should go with you to carry the basket,' said Maria Mulcahy. 'That would be all right, wouldn't it, Mr Robert?'

'Yes, yes.' Robert Fitzwilliam seemed almost embarrassed as he gave permission and covered it by several harsh admonitions to Brian to come straight back to the shop and not to dawdle around the quays.

Interesting, thought Patrick. Miss Maria Mulcahy definitely had influence over the floor manager. Perhaps Michael Dinan's story about them going to the cinema together was a true one.

The Reverend Mother, who had probably planned to go back by taxi, thought Patrick, immediately and cheerfully jettisoned the idea. By now her sharp brain was probably working on this mysterious death of the shop owner and Brian's chatty companionship down the north and the south main streets and across the bridge to St Mary's Isle would be quite enlightening.

'So if I could have a quick word with you, Miss Mulcahy?' Patrick uttered his request in very tentative tones, after saying goodbye to the Reverend Mother. But he was not surprised when Robert accompanied the two of them back into the room and personally pulled out a chair for Miss Mulcahy. She thanked him with a smile. Not a bad-looking girl in her youth, probably, thought Patrick, but definitely dropping into middle age now. There were a few grey hairs mixed in with the light brown, her skin had begun to line beside the mouth and by the eyes and her neck and hands showed definite signs of aging, he decided.

Thank you, sir,' he said to Robert and waited until the floor manager had backed his way out of the room, before continuing. She didn't look at all nervous, so Patrick plunged into the interview. 'Just tell me as well as you can recollect what actually happened this morning, Miss Mulcahy,' he said.

'Well, it was quite a dark morning,' she said immediately. 'Some of the gas lamps had been switched off and the shop was absolutely crowded with people, more than I've ever seen. The aisles were jammed. It was a really good sale, you know, inspector. I had pairs of shoes at half price that were really no worse than if you had been out in rain for a couple of hours.'

'A typical Cork day, in fact,' said Patrick and was rather flattered when she laughed so appreciatively at his little joke. A pleasant woman, he thought. The sort of woman that a lonely man would have liked to come home to. And then he thought of Mr Robert and wondered whether she had laughed at his jokes and whether that was the secret of her attraction for him. An intelligent woman, also. She had painted a scene that showed how someone with ill intentions towards the shop owner could have moved secretly to substitute the gas canister for the change canister. It would have been an easy matter, once that had been done, to have twanged the wire and sent the little barrel flying up to roof height, there to await being unloaded. Any one of them could have done it, he thought. Any one of the five: Maria Mulcahy, herself; Miss Monica Fitzwilliam; Miss Kitty Fitzwilliam; Mrs Agnes Fitzwilliam; Mr Michael Dinan; and then, of course, came the joker in the pack. The sixth barrel, the change barrel that went up from the Men's Shoes department could have been sent from anyone in the shop.

'And who would be normally in charge of switching on or off the gas lamps, Miss Mulcahy?'

'Oh, that is always Mr Robert,' she said readily. 'If anyone finds that it is too dark in their part of the shop they have to go and see Mr Robert, or else send him a message by one of the boys.'

'I see,' said Patrick. That, he thought, was a very interesting thought. Robert Fitzwilliam could have arranged for the murder of his father by choosing a dark moment – and Cork was a city where some rain fell in two out of every three days and where fog was almost permanent.

But did he have a motive?

He finished up with Miss Mulcahy as quickly as he could and began to plan his visit to the Reverend Mother that afternoon. By then Dr Scher may have concluded his autopsy and several pieces of the jigsaw would begin to fall into place.

EIGHT

'But he made a packet out of it! A great businessman, you know. He'd buy cheap and sell just that bit dearer, goods flooding out of the shop and all the time his bank account was building up.' The Reverend Mother's cousin, Lucy, could be relied upon to know the ins-and-outs of every wealthy Cork family.

'Odd the way that he had his wife and his daughters working there, wasn't it? Not the behaviour of a wealthy man,' said the Reverend Mother. She felt slightly ashamed of herself for indulging in gossip, and sometimes wondered whether it was a sin that should be confessed. Nevertheless, it was enjoyable and did no one any harm, so she encouraged Lucy with a glance of enquiry. In any case, she told herself, Patrick, Inspector Patrick Cashman, her one-time pupil, would need a little help. Patrick was doing very well since he had become an inspector. He had extinguished child prostitution from some of the seediest public houses on the quays by having a uniformed *Garda* conspicuously in attendance at closing hour, he had instituted police patrols on the back streets and prevented fights exploding into neighbourhood battles, but when it came to dealing with the merchant families of Cork, he could be at a loss unless she were available to give him a few hints. Now she looked at her cousin enquiringly. If anyone knew the ins and outs of the Fitzwilliam family, it would be Lucy.

'A miser, that's what he was,' said Lucy in her usual downright manner. 'Mind you, I blame the wife. Why did she do it? Why did she allow those two girls to spend their time in a terrible shop like that? No wonder neither of them married. And herself! Standing there all day. Terrible varicose veins, so my housekeeper tells me. Poor woman. A martyr to them. No wonder! But why did she do it?'

'I suppose that her husband wanted her help,' said the Reverend Mother mildly and Lucy snorted.

'Wanted! Well, that's men for you! I'd have allowed him to go on wanting. Imagine if Rupert asked me to come into his office and pound on the typewriter. Well, I'd soon get that notion out of his head, I can tell you.'

'Rupert is a rich man,' said the Reverend Mother, smiling to herself at the thought of her elegantly-groomed cousin placing her painted and well-manicured fingernails on the keys of a typewriter. And at the impossibility of Rupert, one of the wealthiest solicitors in the city of Cork, making any such demand upon his wife.

Lucy looked at her pityingly. 'You don't know the least thing about it, Dottie,' she said. 'Just because he sold goods to the poor, you think that he was poor himself. Not a bit of it! I'm telling you. You can believe me. He was as wealthy as any of them. Rupert was lifting his eyebrows and puffing out a few whistles when I asked him what the man was worth. Wouldn't tell me, of course; men are so ridiculous about confidentiality, but I got the idea. When Rupert puts his eyebrows that high, you can bet that a really good sum was left, but . . .' Lucy paused dramatically, leaned across the tea trolley and hissed the next words in a theatrical whisper, 'You'll never guess, Dottie, who gets it all. You won't believe it, but the whole business is left to the major – "my eldest son", that's how it went.'

'What!' The Reverend Mother put her cup back onto the trolley with immense care in case she should drop it with astonishment. 'But his wife, his daughters, the other son, Robert. And Robert was the one that worked in the shop, worked there all of his life, I think, and seemed to be working very hard,' she added, mentally suppressing the word 'fuster' uttered by the astute young apprentice, Brian Maloney.

'Didn't want to divide the ownership.' Lucy gave a shrug. 'Thought he was a member of the aristocracy where everything descends to the eldest son. Oh, there's the house, some shares and some money left to the wife, enough to keep her, though not in luxury. Same for the two daughters. Left them a thousand each. I suppose she might sell the house in Glenville Place and buy a small place for the three of them, somewhere in St Luke's Cross or something like that.'

'And Robert?' queried the Reverend Mother.

'Nothing. Nothing at all! Not a penny!' said Lucy, spacing out the last three words so as to give them maximum drama. 'Not that I know anything about it, not officially, you know.'

'What! Nothing to Robert! I don't believe it!' exclaimed the Reverend Mother, too horrified to be amused at Lucy's sudden withdrawal from the role of purveyor of information. She tried to recall the bustling figure in the shabby tailcoat. Aged somewhere between thirty and forty, she reckoned. Probably fit for nothing except the job of floor manager. What a dreadful thing for a father to do to the son who had probably served him faithfully and to the best of his ability.

'I suppose that his brother might keep him on at the same job,' she said dubiously. It would not be, she felt, a happy working relationship. Surely the business could have been divided between the brothers, or more fairly, bequeathed to the younger brother, since the major no doubt had cost his father plenty of money to equip him as an officer in the British army.

'Don't you believe it,' said Lucy, reverting happily to the person who knew everything that was going on in the small city of Cork. 'Not a chance!' she said dramatically. 'I know what James will do. He'll sell the place as soon as he gets probate. What would a major in the British army want with a shabby shop selling cheap goods? It wouldn't suit his style at all. He may have been doing a bit of hanging about the place for a few weeks on and off during the last few months, but that's only while he is waiting for something to turn up. The word on the town is that he's planning to go out to Palestine. He'll be able to cut a fine figure out there with plenty of money in his pocket. They'll make him an army judge, you mark my words. You knew he qualified as a barrister, didn't you? They say that it's a great life out there for the army officers, like a club. That's what I've heard. A friend of mine, Mrs Hayes, was telling me about Palestine. She said that she wished they could stay for ever, but the children were very unhappy at boarding school in England. And so they came back.'

The Reverend Mother thought about this information. There

was a question on her lips, but she didn't think that it was a good idea to ask a direct question of the discreet wife of a solicitor, a wife who would always, when asked a straight question, disclaim any knowledge of her husband's legal affairs.

And so she hospitably pressed fresh tea and more cake upon her guest, explained her cough as something that she got every spring and left a suitable interval before declaring casually, 'I suppose that the will was made some time ago.'

Lucy chewed her cake thoughtfully and then swallowed some tea before saying with huge enjoyment, 'Last week! Would you believe it?'

'Last week!' Thoughts whirled around the Reverend Mother's head and a question popped out before she had time to swallow it back. 'Did they know?' And then she was sorry that she had not phrased it more tactfully.

Lucy, however, had weighed discretion and the love of a good story in the balance and the latter had won. She leaned forward, her blue eyes sparkling. 'Oh, they knew all right, I'd say. The night before the major came home. Mr Fitzwilliam told them all about what he was going to do. Stopped them when they were going into the drawing room. Asked them all to stay after the dinner table was cleared. There they were all sitting around the table, all of them wondering what it was all about. An almighty row there was. Shouting at him, shouting at each other. Told them everything. So I've heard. Said he had asked the major to come home because he needed his help. Said that he would be the future owner of the business. The coffee was stone cold by the time that they came out of the dining room.'

'How on earth do you know all that, Lucy?' This was going too far. Her cousin's husband might have disclosed the contents of the will under a vow of secrecy to his wife. After all, it would all be soon in the public domain, but she couldn't see the discreet and reticent Rupert spewing out details of a huge family row, even if he were present.

'Their housekeeper is my housekeeper's sister,' said Lucy briefly, brushing this aside as an irrelevant detail. 'But can you just imagine, Dottie, what it would have meant to him, if they believed that he would do it. Why, every one of them,

Monica, Kitty and, of course, Agnes, herself . . . all of them are just left with a pittance. And Robert, not a penny. Turned out like a shop assistant who has had his hand in the till. Well, they must all have wanted to murder him.'

Lucy left a slight silence after her last statement and her cheeks went slightly pink. 'I don't mean that, of course,' she said hastily. 'Just a manner of speaking.'

'But if this happened before the major came home, and the day before the will was made, well . . .'

'He probably told them that he was going to do it. But they wouldn't have known when. Especially if he said no more about it. Popped out in his dinner hour, apparently. He'd just have five minutes' walk to Rupert's office in the South Mall. All signed and sealed. All done hours before James came home, though no one knew about it, I'd say. And, of course, there had been that terrible flood. And then the major produces those very handy little gas cylinders. Well, I don't know about you, but I'd say if I wanted to murder someone, these would certainly have given me something to think about,' said Lucy triumphantly.

'Yes, it does make one think, of course,' said the Reverend Mother thoughtfully. 'After all, the man is dead. We can't get away from that. And it does look, does it not, as if someone killed him. I saw the faces when Dr Scher handed over that gas cylinder. Everyone in the shop – all of the staff, even the apprentices – knew all about these gas cylinders. Certainly young Brian Maloney told me all about it and he's not yet fourteen years old, I'd say. They'd been using them to get the damp smell from the clothes that had been in the flood.'

Lucy brushed aside the question of the shop staff. Her eyes sparkled with excitement. 'And, of course, Robert and the girls, well they would have a motive,' she hissed, leaning across the tea trolley so that her face was very near to her cousin. 'But, of course, there's James, Major James Fitzwilliam. Think of that, Dottie! He gets the whole business, lock, stock and barrel. He's going to be a rich man if he sells that huge place now. Between ourselves we have to say that this death of his father has turned out very well for him. Gives him a nice little nest egg! Don't you think that gives him a motive too? Come on, Dottie, admit. I know that he would get it in the long run, that's if Mr Fitzwilliam didn't change his will once more – and I can tell you, in confidence, it would not have been at all surprising, if I can read Rupert's expression properly. I'd say that Mr Fitzwilliam was one of those people who made a habit of changing his will. Lawyers love clients like that!'

'Not after one week, surely,' observed the Reverend Mother. She felt keenly interested in the whole matter and sat for a moment, turning matters over in her mind. What a toxic brew was simmering in that household, she thought. A disappointed middle-aged son, now doomed to an existence with no money and no prospects. Two middle-aged daughters, with no hope now of a suitable marriage, and about to be denied even of such comforts as they had previously enjoyed. And a wife who had worked so hard in her husband's business, now to be left with nothing to show for it. 'So, Major James Fitzwilliam just had to sit and wait for his inheritance,' she said aloud.

Lucy shook her head. 'But remember he must be forty-five if he is a day. And his father was very spry. Just the type to live to the age of ninety. The money wouldn't have been much good to James by then. Quite a ladies' man, too, so I've heard. A few stories about him drifted over from London. Might have his eye on someone, but if it's the lady I heard mentioned, well, he could feel that he might not have enough money to set her up in the style she was accustomed to. But the way that it has worked out, it's been good for him. See for yourself, Dottie. His father is dead. He has the money in his pocket now. He's young enough to enjoy it. He could make a good match or else stay a wealthy and eligible bachelor.'

'And he was the one who, according to my young friend, Brian, was the source of those little cylinders filled with gas, a left-over from the Great War, apparently. Would know everything about their effect.' The Reverend Mother thought about the matter. War, she had often considered, was a form of licenced killing. And once licenced to kill, well, human life becomes of less importance. Somehow it seemed easier to think of Major James Fitzwilliam, a man who had probably shot many other human beings, being the murderer than any of the rest of his family, or even than any of his employees. All of them under suspicion, she thought and wondered how Patrick was getting on with questioning them. That unmanned counter made it possible for any employee to have sent up the deadly canister.

'That's right,' said Lucy enthusiastically. 'He was the one that supplied the gas cylinders. Rupert said that everyone was talking about it at the club last night. The major brought them back with him. May have brought them on purpose to give them to his father. My housekeeper tells me that the goods at the Queen's Old Castle often smell of damp. Says she wouldn't dream of shopping there for anything, no matter what the bargain. They're near to the river there. You get a flood going up North Main Street and it's bound to seep into the shop. And these old stone floors always hold moisture. I don't like them at all. Anyway, when that flood came into the shop itself, well, these gas cylinders were great for taking the smell out of the clothes and the linens.'

'I wonder how many of them he had?' said the Reverend Mother, half to herself and half to her cousin.

'What size are they?' asked Lucy.

The Reverend Mother picked up the sugar bowl, its silver polished carefully by Sister Bernadette who reserved its use for important guests. 'I suppose they are not much bigger, in bulk, than this sugar bowl, longer but slightly slimmer,' she said. 'The one found on the floor certainly fitted inside the change barrel, would have been about the same size as the little canisters that counter assistants put into them.' But one person at one of the counters put a different and a lethal canister into a change barrel. Which one of them? The Reverend Mother's mind wandered over the faces from that morning.

'Could put fifty of them in a suitcase, if you thought that they might be of use back home in civvy street,' said Lucy thoughtfully and the Reverend Mother nodded.

'He made no secret of it, though. He said immediately that they were his and Brian, the boy I told you about, said that the major had been using them to fumigate some of the flood-damaged goods.'

'Well, he would have been stupid, though, wouldn't he, not to admit to owning them. Probably most of the staff knew that he had brought them in, probably shown some of them how to use them safely. And, of course,' said Lucy slowly, 'his family would have known all about them. These people who were in the war, well, they are forever telling stories about it. In fact, I seem to remember Colonel Taylor ruining a dinner party of mine, lovely piece of venison the cook had dished up and this wretched man would go on telling stories about the men cooking rats in the trenches. I'd say that Major Fitzwilliam would have shown those handy little cylinders to all of his family.'

'His brother would certainly have known,' said the Reverend Mother. She was conscious that her comment sounded slightly distracted and was not surprised when Lucy pounced.

'Not just the brother. Those two daughters, the twins, Kitty and Monica, they worked in the place and then there is Agnes, herself.' She paused, took another sip of her tea and then said in a voice that she strove to make casual, 'Dottie, what did you make of Agnes?'

'Why do you ask?' The Reverend Mother knew that Lucy was bursting to tell her something, but she wasn't sure whether she wanted to know or not. Still, she thought to herself, better that I should know. Her mind went back to the woman's face, to the stiff pose, the eyes empty of expression. Was Mrs Fitzwilliam a patient of Dr Scher? And if so, why, when he had, by his account, given up his private practice, had he continued to feel responsible for her? Dr Scher had a very concerned look when he had stood beside her, not taking her pulse nor taking his stethoscope from his case, but stroking her hand and murmuring reassurances into her ear. Nervous problems, diagnosed the Reverend Mother. There was a lot of it about. Struck down the rich as well as the poor. There was that look about her, dull eyes, compressed mouth, trembling hands. Worse, and more distressing than any physical problems.

'For a moment Lucy looked annoyed at the curt question, but then she leaned forward and hissed into her cousin's ear. 'Agnes Fitzwilliam tried to commit suicide a few months ago. They sent for Dr Scher and he pulled her around. Poor thing.'

'Really,' said the Reverend Mother calmly. The housekeeper, again, she thought. She could just see the two women, the Fitzwilliam housekeeper and Lucy's housekeeper, heads together whispering pieces of gossip. So that's why Dr Scher was so protective of the woman. Cork was a terrible place for suicides; Dr Scher had reminded her once and had made her feel ashamed of her impatience. Now she thought with concern of the blank face of the woman who had just lost her husband of almost fifty years. Poor woman, not an easy life working in a shop in order to increase her husband's income, when there was really no need for her to do something like that. The Reverend Mother recalled to her mind the feel of one of the cold hands between the two of hers. The skin was very rough, rough, as though the woman, the wife of a rich man, had been scrubbing floors for a living. Not that, of course, but the continual handling of material, measuring it, cutting off a length, refolding the bundle. Half a century of work like that would roughen any skin. Not an easy life. Not the life for the elderly wife of a wealthy man. There had been something very odd about Agnes Fitzwilliam and her reaction to her husband's sudden and violent death. If she had loved him, would she not weep? If she had hated him, would she not show some brisk-ness of bearing, some consciousness that the business could be now hers to run, rather than a place where she, a woman in her seventies, had to work like a slave? Yes, something strange about Agnes Fitzwilliam's aspect.

Not sad. Not jubilant, nor even quietly satisfied.

Almost as though she were stricken by horror.

Aloud, she said calmly, 'If I am any judge, Lucy, I think that Agnes Fitzwilliam was horrified by the death of her husband.'

'Horrified at what she had done? It is possible, you know!'

'I don't think so,' said the Reverend Mother. 'Just horri-fied. Perhaps she wondered about the possibility that it was a member of her family. One of her sons, or one of her daughters. I don't see her able to carry out a murder like that. She seemed to think it was all a mistake. I really don't believe that she murdered him. Unless she is a better actress than I think she is.'

'You're probably right,' said Lucy. 'It did take a bit of nerve, didn't it? To put one of those canisters into the change barrel. I suppose the real barrel would be put under the counter, but one would have to be very quick and slick with movements, wouldn't one? How many of the barrels had been sent up when he tumbled over the rail?'

The Reverend Mother thought about it. 'I've forgotten the names of the counters,' she said, 'but I seem to remember that two of them came from people who worked in the shop, one came from an unmanned counter and the other three were from Agnes and her two daughters.'

'Unmanned!' Lucy seized on the word. 'That means that anyone could have sent that one whizzing up. Could have been Robert, or it could have been James. Whoever killed him, it seems likely that it was one of his family, doesn't it?'

'I don't know, Lucy,' said the Reverend Mother. Her mind had gone to the angry face of Michael Dinan, the man who had been sacked, according to the chatterbox apprentice, Brian Maloney. 'He's mad, furious about getting the sack. Didn't do nothing. They just do that here when people get too old to be apprentices or learners,' Brian had said and remembering the man's face, she could see what the boy had meant. Michael Dinan, she reckoned, facing facts, soberly and realistically, had looked as though he could kill.

'Tell me about the daughters,' she said. 'It's odd, isn't it? Their brother referred to them as "the girls" and I, too, think of them as a pair, almost as though they had been Siamese twins, joined at the hip as a life sentence, and having no difference, no individuality, no separate hopes and ambitions. Did they go to school?'

'I've no idea,' said Lucy cheerfully. 'But I don't suppose that school is important, one way or other. The fact is that both are plain-faced; Kitty very sharp and Monica with an odd and uneasy manner; and that neither had enough of a dowry, I should imagine, to make it worth any man's attention. And now they are too old. They would be about forty to forty-five, I'd say. What would you think?'

'About that, I suppose,' said the Reverend Mother sombrely. Too old to be considered for matrimony; too young to be reconciled to a life of drudgery, making money for a father who was too busy to spend it and for a mother who was lost in a sea of depression. 'But, according to you, they got nothing much from the will. Neither of them,' she said aloud.

'All the more reason for them to kill him,' said Lucy in a practical tone which belied the ghoulishness of what she was saying. 'He had robbed them of their youth, had denied them of marriage and of motherhood. I was reading something about Freud, the other day,' she went on. 'He would have had plenty to say about these two. The more I think of it, the more I think that one, or both of them, murdered the old man. I must say that if any man treated me like that, well, I'd feel like murdering him,' pronounced Lucy. She then added placidly, 'I say, what really excellent cake this is. That Sister Bernadette of yours is a treasure. I can never get my cook to make a nice moist fruit cake like that.'

The Reverend Mother ignored this. She was not personally too fond of cake and did not consider herself a judge. Nor did she find the subject to be of any interest. Her mind was on the murder, the deliberate cutting off of a human life. Could one do that out of anger, out of rage about lost youth, lost opportunities? After all, it wasn't wholly the fault of their father that Kitty and Monica had never married, that they had acquiesced dully and without any overt rebellion to spending their days in the shop. Was working in a shop any worse than hanging around the house with nothing to do? In her youth there had been many 'old maids' as she and Lucy had desig-nated them and they would sit for hours on end in chilly drawing rooms, putting a few stitches in needlework, doing a little knitting, playing patience and yawning over stale stories about their youth. At least when Kitty and Monica went home, although they would be tired, they would have spoken to many people, seen a good cross-section of the Cork population, would have had the satisfaction of knowing that their work had contributed to the comfortable circumstances of their lives.

But had they seen matters in that light?

'The more that I think of it, the more I feel that it was one of them,' said Lucy suddenly. 'After all, you said yourself that the mother looked horrified. What if she had suspected, had known that one of the twins felt murderous towards her father? What if she had overheard them talking about it? Perhaps they had drawn lots for it. One to kill and the other to lie about it.'

The Reverend Mother ignored this. Her mind was on the youth of those two unhappy-looking women. 'Surely they must be about the age of your Anne,' she said. 'Did she know them at all?'

'I wouldn't have thought so,' said Lucy. 'They wouldn't have been our type,' she said firmly.

The Reverend Mother thought about that. 'Strange, isn't it, how much money matters? You and I, Lucy, are descended from quite a modest ancestor; our grandfather was a man who had a good nose for tea and later on for fine wines. He made a lot of money importing it and selling it to his betters, the descendants of the Anglo-Norman families. People like the Fitzwilliams,' she added, 'well, they go back to the White Knight, don't they? The Gilbert line, wasn't it? I suppose that's how he inherited the Queen's Old Castle.'

'That terrible old ruin!' Lucy dismissed the pretensions of the Queen's Old Castle. She would be thinking of the modern elegance of her own large house in the salubrious and wealthy suburb of Montenotte, well out of reach of the slums and smells of the ancient city. The Reverend Mother thought it was time to get back to the present-day descendants of the ancient family.

'I was just wondering,' she said mildly, 'whether Anne might not have known them, seen them at dances, at parties. Anything like that.'

'Didn't know them at all,' said Lucy emphatically. 'I'm sure of that. I was talking to her last night and she asked me whether I was going to the funeral and I said that I thought not. Rupert will, of course, but I don't see any reason for me to go, as well. I don't think I've ever exchanged two words with the woman, or with him. And Anne said that she wasn't going either. I got the impression that she didn't know any of them. I believe that one of the twins, Kitty, I think, used to go in for amateur dramatics at one stage, according to Anne, but that was that. No, I won't go to the funeral.'

The Reverend Mother sighed. A lot of time in Cork was spent in attending funerals and grave offence could be given if there were any unwarranted absences. 'I suppose that I will have to. After all, the man dropped dead at my feet, literally. And I was very sorry for the wife at the time. She looked so stunned. And now, after what you have told me, I feel sorry for the whole family. There will be a lot of unhappiness.'

'I wouldn't waste your time feeling sorry for Major James Fitzwilliam,' said Lucy tartly. 'And don't put on any "holier than thou" airs with me, Dottie. I know you. You're as curious as the cat. You can't wait to have another look at them and make up your mind. I suppose I should go with you. I would, but I know that you would insist on going to that dreary funeral meats' meal afterwards. Would you believe it: they're having it in the shop! Very, very strange. Is she ashamed of her house, do you think? Did she refuse to have it? Anyway this is Major Fitzwilliam's idea. My housekeeper tells me that he is getting food and staff in from the Metropole Hotel, if you please. Going to put it on the counters, I suppose. Can you imagine anything drearier? Still, if you want me, I suppose I'll have to go.'

'It's very kind of you, Lucy,' said the Reverend Mother decisively, 'but I know how busy you are. I'll manage on my own. Dr Scher will probably be going and I'll ask whether I can go with him.'

The custom of giving food to those who went to a funeral was a very deeply ingrained one. It had originated in the country where relatives and friends might have walked long miles to pay a last tribute and would need to be fortified for the return journey. It had spread to the city and even the poorest tried to put on some sort of meal for those who attended a funeral. The wealthy made a big show of it; the not-so-wealthy did their best, and neighbours and even nearby shops came to the rescue of the slum dwellers. The idea of having the funeral repast in the family shop was, indeed, a remarkably odd idea.

Dr Scher, thought the Reverend Mother, as she made her way to the phone after saying goodbye to her cousin, would undoubtedly accompany her to the burial service at Brunswick Street and afterwards to the meal at the Queen's Old Castle. But it would be interesting to see how many others of Cork's professional and merchant class accepted this form of strange hospitality.

NINE

'Going to the Fitzwilliam funeral, are you? Holding it in that church in Brunswick Street, aren't they? And the meal afterwards in the shop. Did you ever!' Patrick, on his way out from the barracks, was met by the superintendent. The old man didn't wait for an answer. He was full of a piece of gossip.

'Heard something interesting at the club last evening,' he said. 'You'd never guess, but there's a rumour going around that the old man left the entire business to the eldest son, to the major. Not a penny to the younger son, to the fellow that has been working in that shop since the day that he left school. Robert, that's the name, isn't it? Makes you think, doesn't it? Amazing how these things get around,' he added.

'I heard that, too,' said Tommy.

'All sorts of rumours going around,' went on the superintendent. 'You'd want to keep your ear to the ground, Patrick.'

'Yes, that's true. I've been hearing lots of rumours, too,' said Tommy.

That might or might not be true, thought Patrick as, with a nod to both, he left the barracks. Tommy always did like to be in the know. And as he and the superintendent were the only Protestants in the barracks now, both of them leftovers from the time of the RIC, the British Royal Irish Constabulary, Tommy always echoed everything that the superintendent said.

But they were probably right about the inheritance, thought Patrick later in the morning, as he came out of the church after the funeral service. It was very noticeable that there was a small crowd of businessmen clustering around the major, while Mr Robert Fitzwilliam stood alone and awkwardly to one side, neither supporting his mother and sisters, nor joining his older brother. Funny how news travelled fast around Cork! He could have sworn that all of these men knew the contents of old Mr Fitzwilliam's will. Even the reporter from the *Cork Examiner* went to the major first, and completely ignored Robert. Reporters always liked to keep on the best side of the man with power and money, he reflected as he joined the queue to pay his respects to Mrs Fitzwilliam, before moving on to say a few words to Robert.

'You'll be welcome to come back to the shop, for a cup of tea and something to eat, inspector? Are you coming? You might as well. See us all at close quarters.' Robert Fitzwilliam gave a hoarse laugh. A man with a perpetual cold. There were a lot of them around Cork where the permanent damp and the constant fogs affected its unfortunate population with chronic bronchitis and catarrh. There was an awkward note in Robert's voice and because of that Patrick agreed immediately. Hard on a man, he thought. Almost everyone there, under a polite appearance of condolence, was avidly wondering why on earth the son, who had devoted so many years to his father's business, had been cut out of an inheritance.

'Yes, of course; very good of you to ask me.' The words now tripped off his tongue, though there had been a time when he had practised these forms of acceptance in front of his bedroom mirror. *I'm not ashamed of my upbringing. Poor but honest.* He tried to tell himself these things, but knew, that in a class-conscious society like the city of Cork, that he was always struggling under a disadvantage. He gave Robert a nod and moved on to say his piece to the major and then stood back, trying to look unobtrusive.

'Good morning, inspector.' A very upper-class accent and he knew instantly who it was. Mr Rupert Murphy, one of the foremost solicitors in the city. Married to a cousin of the Reverend Mother. Very posh, very suave, the type that always knew the right word to say. Discreet, too. Patrick admired the way in which the man had turned his back on the crowd and slightly urged him into a triangular space where the chancel widened out into the nave of the church. Out in the open but with their backs to two walls. No chance of being overheard.

'I've been having a word with Major Fitzwilliam,' he said, his voice low, but not exaggeratedly so. 'The major does realize,' he went on, 'that in view of the circumstances of his father's death, that there will be certain enquiries that the police will be, quite rightly, making about the late Mr Fitzwilliam's financial circumstances and about the distribution of his estate. He feels in that case it might be just as well for you to attend the reading of the will, which will take place at the house, at two o'clock and to ask any questions of me after that has taken place. The major and his family are quite happy to have you in attendance.' The voice was smooth, but the man's eyes were sharp.

Patrick nodded. 'I see,' he said in neutral tones. Why did the major want him present at the reading of the will? To stop the police from asking any awkward questions of the lawyer? Unlikely. The major would know better, would fully realize that the solicitor would have to answer any police questions either sooner or later. And that Patrick could easily pop around to the office on the South Mall later on if any more information was needed. No, he thought, if what the superintendent had said were to be true, then the major, an unexpected heir of his father's business, was doing this in order to prevent an outbreak of fury among members of his own family. The presence of the police would be enough to stifle protests and accusations.

'Quite soon after the funeral meal,' said Mr Murphy. He gave a quick glance at his watch. 'I've told Major Fitzwilliam that I will arrive at the house at two o'clock. Now I must leave you. There are some affairs that I have to deal with at the office before then.'

A neat way to escape the funeral meal, thought Patrick and wished that he could make a similar escape.

Patrick reluctantly returned to the Queen's Old Castle once the ceremony in Brunswick Street had been completed. He had a lot of work waiting for him, but as inspector in charge of the investigation he felt that he should attend the traditional meal. He had received an invitation, not a particularly warm one, but an invitation, nevertheless, from the dead man's younger son, though not, he noted, from the older brother nor from the wife or daughters.

'Thank you, major. It's very kind of you.' Patrick overheard that said quite a few times as he passed the crowd clustered around the major. He watched surreptitiously to see how many of those who had attended the burial would accept the invitation and now go on to have a meal with the mourning family. Not many, was his impression.

And, of course, it was an odd idea to hold it in the shop. Made one think that the reasoning behind the choice was that since the shop had to be closed out of respect for the death of its owner, then it might as well be used. Also, of course, it probably saved a certain amount of money. 'Food sent over from the Metropole!'; 'Did you ever!'; 'Who on earth thought of that!' He heard these words uttered by many as he walked rapidly down the street.

Whoever *had* thought of the idea, it had not been a popular decision, was Patrick's opinion when he arrived at the shop. The food was placed on the counters, and most people helped themselves from there and ate standing up, although eyes continually went up to that eyrie-like office, perched forty feet above floor level and even those who had not been present had little difficulty in picturing the body falling down and hearing the tremendous crash as the body landed. Patrick himself did his best not to look upwards, but found, nevertheless, from time to time, that he was speculating about those change carriers, wondering whether it would have been possible for an innocent party to send the fatal gas barrel up by mistake. Unlikely, he decided. The counter staff were all old hands, had all worked since their childhood in this shop. It would all have been automatic to them, that process of taking the customer's money, filling in the docket with name and price of the item to be purchased and then inserting the canister into the lightweight barrel, pulling the rod and sending it on its journey up to the sky-high office. Joe had checked the receipts on the dead man's desk. Five of them; five neat little piles: receipts and change for a pair of curtains from Michael Dinan's counter; six spools of thread from Kitty Fitzwilliam at the Haberdashery department; four pillow cases from her sister Monica's Household Linens; one straw hat and a pair of ladies' slippers sent up by Miss

Maria Mulcahy at the Ladies' Shoes department. Five receipts, but six barrels. The deadly contents of one of those six barrels was now sitting on his office desk, still with a faint smell of gas about it. Joe and Patrick had been over those barrels again and again, checking that the docket and the payment would have fitted in the barrel, outside of the inner canister. In fact, Joe had guessed that originally the barrels may have been meant to be operated without that inner canister. That may well have been an invention of Joseph Fitzwilliam himself, a double security for the money. It would have been still quite possible for the money and the docket to have accompanied the gas barrel, though it seemed slightly more likely that the gas container had come from the Men's Shoes counter. That empty department and the idle barrel standing ready to be despatched would have been a great temptation to any passing boy or a bored child, accompanying his mother while she shopped. Joe and he had confessed to each other that the flying barrels had always tempted them when young. Patrick gave a long speculative glance at the contraption. Odd to think that if Mr Joseph Fitzwilliam had trusted his employees a little more, that he might now be alive.

The Metropole Hotel had done its best for the funeral feast, had sent over trays of food, stacked high within vans, and had delegated some of its aproned waiters to dish out the goods. Nothing much to drink, though, thought Patrick, or at least nothing that anyone going to a Cork funeral would have regarded as real drink. Yes, there were soft drinks in plenty. There were also urns of tea, and one small bottle of whiskey which Robert Fitzwilliam added to the coffee or tea of those who had the courage or the nerve to demand it. Most of the counter hands and the apprentices contented themselves in eating vigorously, devouring the sandwiches, and bringing back their plates for fresh helpings of cake. Major Fitzwilliam did his best, conversing easily with the Reverend Mother and Dr Scher and then moving on and going from one figure to another. Most tried to say something nice about his father and he welcomed these efforts with a nod of his head at the beginning and a bow of acknowledgement when the speaker had come to a faltering end.

'Another sandwich, inspector. Or could I get you some more tea?' The offer took Patrick by surprise and he spun around. This man was not one of the family.

'Nothing, thank you,' said Patrick. 'I must be getting back to the barracks.' Why was this man acting as host? Not a suspect, or probably not, he added, mentally reminding himself that at this stage of the enquiry it would be unwise to rule out anyone with even the slightest connection to the murder scene or to the murdered person. Séamus O'Connor, counter hand for the Men's Shoes department. The man who had been absent from his counter, had been down in the storeroom when his employer had fallen to his death.

'I'd like to have a quick word with you, if I could,' O'Connor said then, blurting the words out as though afraid lest his courage should evaporate if he hesitated.

'Certainly.' Patrick was annoyed with himself. He should, by now, be well used to the way in which people came sidling up to him on various pretexts, looking to pass information. Without hesitation, he picked up a plate, looked around for a napkin, but there were none and so he led the way behind the tall counter and pretended to examine the array of cake slices spread out on cheap tin trays, while making sure that no one could overhear. 'Yes, Mr O'Connor . . .' he said, without looking at the man.

'I just wanted to have a word with you about Michael Dinan,' said Séamus O'Connor.

'Yes.' Patrick bent a little lower and examined a chocolate slice. He was tempted to indulge himself, but he had made it a rule neither to eat nor to drink anything belonging to a possible suspect while he was on a job. There were still very strong feelings against the present government and the treaty that had been botched up with Britain. And their employees, the police and the army, were very open to suspicion and easy targets for accusations of bribery. Accept nothing from potential criminals, was a good rule. In any case, he thought ruefully, I'm putting on weight for the first time in my life. 'Michael Dinan?' he queried.

'He's in charge of the curtain department; just for the next few days. Got a week's notice a few days ago.'

'I see.' Patrick tried to make his voice sound neutral. It was not for him to say that he knew all of this already, but Séamus O'Connor rounded on him with a certain nervous fury.

'Easy to say that!' The words exploded from him although he kept the tone down. 'You don't see, inspector. You don't know how we live our lives here working in these shops. The boss is always right and the worker is always wrong.' The man sounded in a state of nerves, but none of the employees looked happy. If rumour was correct the shop might be up for sale and then all of the jobs could be in jeopardy.

'Was Mr Dinan accused of something?' Patrick kept his voice very soft, both to defuse the spark of temper and to avoid calling attention to them. He left the tray of chocolate cakes and moved on to look at the buttered scones.

'He was accused of giving the wrong change. No evidence. No complaint from the customer.' Séamus O'Connor also bent down over the scones, his head very near to Patrick's. 'You know how it works here, inspector. None of us is trusted to give change. And the old man, I mean Mr Fitzwilliam, well I won't speak ill of the dead, and in his own way he was a straight man, but he would wrap the docket around the change, twist it around the coins or the notes so that nothing could fall out.'

'But this time . . .' Patrick began to guess what was coming.

'This time, Mr Robert came along just as Michael was digging out the docket and he grabbed it from him, accused him of trying to palm a half-crown, made a big fuss about it, apologizing to the customer, telling her that he would deal with the matter, insisting on spreading the change out on the counter and checking with the bill and making her feel that she had just been saved from being cheated. Everyone in the shop could hear him.'

'And what happened next?'

'Well, Michael was stupid. Hasn't got too good a hold on his temper. Should have just pretended that something had slipped, or just kept quiet, done what we all do, say, "Yes, sir, no, sir," and so on, but Michael is not like that. Nothing would do him but to shout out that he was wrongfully accused and that Mr Robert was the one who slipped the half-crown from the bundle in the first place. He even went so far as to accuse Mr Robert of trying to get him into trouble.'

Not clever, thought Patrick, but he waited for the rest of the story.

'And so, Mr Robert sacked him. Gave him a week's notice.'

'I see,' said Patrick.

'But that's not all, inspector. You see, when I spoke to Michael afterwards, I told him that he had been a fool and that he should know by now that the boss is always right. And I advised him to try an apology even now and see if that worked.' Séamus stopped abruptly, put a scone on his plate and moved rapidly away as Robert Fitzwilliam approached.

'Have you got everything that you need, inspector? Can I fetch you anything? More tea?'

'I'm trying to resist temptation,' said Patrick. A year ago a situation like this would have left him tongue-tied, but now he had a score of little phrases memorized for occasions like this. 'Putting on weight,' he said with a sigh. 'Too much paperwork these days. Used to get out on the push bike a lot, but now I'm tied to the office most of the day.'

Time for me to go, he thought. He took his watch from his pocket, said loudly, 'Is it twelve o'clock already? Well, thank you for your hospitality, Mr Fitzwilliam, but I must get back to the office now.' Robert Fitzwilliam didn't pick up on the theme or even make any reply. An odd man. Young Mr Robert, he was called, but, of course, he was not young. Would be about fifteen years older than myself, thought Patrick. He put down his plate, went across to shake hands with the rest of the family and to repeat his condolences. Mrs Fitzwilliam was slumped in a chair; her head was on her chest and she appeared as though she might be sleeping. One of the daughters was in earnest conversation with the Reverend Mother and he didn't want to interrupt that. And the other daughter avoided his eye when he looked towards her. He made his way towards Major Fitzwilliam who was whispering in the ear of a property auctioneer and who thanked him perfunctorily for coming and then resumed his story. Patrick made for the back door, leading into Brunswick Street. He had retained his coat and so did not have to pause while someone fetched it. He had needed it, he thought as he made his way past empty counters: Household Linens, Haberdashery, Millinery, Curtains, and Ladies' Shoes. All of those names bore a significance for him now. From one of these counters that deadly barrel of gas had gone whizzing up, concealed within the change barrel and ready to be opened by the owner of the business. What was it like to die of gas poisoning? Quick anyway, but not pleasant, he thought. He felt a shiver go down his spine and rubbed his hands together vigorously. The shop was freezing cold, making him wonder what it was like to work there. Still, at least the employees were having a magnificent feast today. The lack of outside presence meant that they had more than double of what would have been allocated to them in the normal way. In fact, when he came in first, they were lined up behind tea urns and had napkins over their arms as though they were intended to be waiters. The young apprentices, he had noticed, were then busily carrying chairs out for the visitors. They were now carrying them back to some store, but he was glad to see that most of them had cheeks distended with lumps of cake.

'You'll remember me to your mother and sisters,' he said to Mr Robert who had hurried after him as though to make sure that he was really leaving. He shook hands with him, also, while wondering whether that had been the right thing to say. He would have to think about that, would have to memorize some more phrases – something conventional about condolences – as the superintendent was a Protestant, a lot of Patrick's time seemed to be spent in going to funerals. Terrible waste of time unless the deceased had been murdered, he thought as he made his escape into North Main Street. When that was the case, however, then every opportunity to study the relations and friends was valuable. And often, the most interesting disclosures came just after he had left the scene.

He was not surprised, therefore, when, after three or four minutes, a voice from behind him said, 'You haven't got your motor with you today, inspector.'

'It's more belonging to the superintendent than to me,' said

Patrick cheerfully. Séamus O'Connor would have made sure
that he was not followed before opening conversation here
with him on the busy street. 'More trouble than it's worth;
that car,' he added in order to keep the conversation going.
It was true, of course. Cork's medieval centre had struggled
enough with horse-drawn traps and with donkeys and carts,
but the advent of cars was rapidly bringing everything to a
standstill.

'Quicker on your feet most of the time,' agreed Séamus.
He had moved a little closer to Patrick and was now shoulder
to shoulder with him. When he spoke, it was almost into
Patrick's ear. 'I thought that you might like to know this,
inspector. The real reason why Michael Dinan was sacked was
because he overheard something that he should never have
heard. I know that for a fact. You should ask him about it,
inspector. You would be interested to hear what Michael has
to say. Well,' he added, still in very low tones, 'this is where
I say goodbye.'

And when Patrick turned to look over his shoulder a minute
later, there was not a sign of Séamus O'Connor. He knew
the procedure, though, and walked steadily on, down the
narrow street until he reached the bridge. Even then, though,
he did not pause, but advanced until he reached the centre.
He stopped, leaned over to gaze into the murky depths of
the River Lee and waited. It took a few minutes, but not long
really. He was beginning to feel slightly tense when a voice
spoke in his ear.

'My grandfather used to talk about salmon coming up here,'
said the man beside him.

Patrick did not move a muscle. He did not turn to look at
the speaker. 'Is that a fact?' he asked in uninterested tones.

'It is, indeed,' replied the man, almost as though they were
both taking part in some sort of play.

A nod. That was all that was needed now. Patrick's nod
paid tribute to the grandfather, though he doubted the veracity
of the memory. Surely, even by then, sewage was pouring into
the river, making it a death trap for any self-respecting fish.
Only eels frequented it as far back as his own grandfather's
tales had stretched.

'Terrible place to live, this city of ours,' continued the voice. And Patrick gave another nod. 'You might as well throw yourself into that river once you lose your job.'

'Tell me about it; tell me about how you lost your job,' said Patrick, abruptly tiring of this oblique conversation.

'I never had any thought or intention of stealing that half-crown, of cheating that woman.' The voice was impassioned, now, but the tone was still low and the head, beside his own, ceaselessly turned from left to right. He, himself, took a quick, surreptitious look around. No one that he could see who might be remotely interested in the conversation.

'I'm listening. Tell me what you think,' he said. 'That accusation against you. It was trumped up, you imagine. Is that it? But why? Why should anyone want to get rid of you?'

'Because I overheard something that I shouldn't.' The reply shot back almost instantly. The truth? Or a well-practised retort?

'Want to tell me about it?' Patrick made his voice sound indifferent. The man beside him was wound up, taut, on the verge of explosion.

'I went down to the basement,' said Michael Dinan. 'I wasn't spying or anything. I just went down because I remembered that one of the rolls of curtains were down there and I seemed to remember that it had been badly damaged in the flood. I had a feeling that it was something that should be sold off in the sale.'

'And when was this?' Patrick introduced a note of impatience. This story was going to go on and on if he didn't pull the man up. Sooner or later someone would stop to listen and he would be in trouble for not immediately inviting the man to come up to the barracks and to tell his story there.

Michael Dinan seemed to feel the force of this. He gulped a little and then began to speak rapidly. 'I overheard Mr Robert ask young Mr O'Dwyer for some more time to pay the bill. You see, inspector, it's usually the old man who pays all of the bills. On the first of the quarter. That's the day that all the suppliers come for their money. They always use the basement. No room in that little office up there. So one of the big trestle tables that we use for cutting cloth, that is spread out with all the heaps of coins and wallets stuffed with notes. But on this last quarter day the old man had to go to a funeral and so he got Mr Robert to do it for him.'

'And?'

'I think that Mr Robert skimmed a bit off everyone's bill, told them the firm were a bit short that month,' said Michael Dinan. 'It would be something that a lot of firms would do, you know, inspector. And Mr Robert had just bought himself a new car so he might be a bit short of money. He probably managed to pay off most of them when he got his own monthly salary, but, of course, O'Dwyer is the biggest supplier, all the haberdashery and the millinery comes from O'Dwyer so theirs would have been the biggest bill. He probably asked for a bit more time. I don't know, but that's what I would guess. Anyway, I was down there a week ago, sorting out some flood-damaged curtains and Mr Robert came in with young Mr O'Dwyer and they were having a conversation. And Mr O'Dwyer said that he would just give him another two weeks and if the money wasn't paid up then, well, he would have to apply to his father, to Mr Fitzwilliam Senior.'

'What did he say to that?' enquired Patrick.

'One of the rolls of curtaining slipped and Mr Robert came around the corner and saw me.'

'Did he say anything?'

'Asked me what I was doing and told me to get back upstairs. Pretended nothing was going on. But I was shaking in my shoes. And then, the next day, he set up a fake and said that I had been robbing a customer of half-a-crown and I was sacked. Given a week's notice.' Michael Dinan finished his story, but Patrick could feel the intensity of the man's gaze.

'Is that all you have to tell me, Mr Dinan?' he asked.

The man shrugged his shoulders. 'Not for me to tell you what to think, or what to do, inspector,' he said. 'But if I were you I'd be wondering who had a motive to kill the old man. Theft is a serious thing, not just for people like me, but for people like Mr Robert, too. His father wasn't the type to have any mercy on him if it was discovered. There's jail for the rich as well as jail for the poor, you know.'

It was a good story, and well-told, thought Patrick. It gave

Robert Fitzwilliam a motive. But what if the story was told just to disguise the murder by Michael Dinan. He, like the rest of the staff, had seen the use of these deadly little gas canisters, shaped as if to fit into the small barrels. If the owner of the shop died, then all would be chaos for a while. Everything, more or less, had been left to the major, that was the word on the town. And nothing, not a farthing, to Robert. It seemed as if old Mr Fitzwilliam had found out about Robert not paying the suppliers. That would have formed a good reason for his disinheritance.

But, of course, there could be another side to this story. Patrick was conscious that Michael Dinan sent furtive glances at him while pretending to watch the busy scene as the ship moved in to dock at the quay. Perhaps it was old Mr Fitzwilliam who sacked Michael Dinan. Surely that would fit more with his knowledge of the shop. Robert was floor manager, but seemed always to work under his father's directions, often shouted down from on high, and often, doubtless, embarrassing him in front of all the staff and customers. A fairly unpleasant old man. No terrible surprise that he was murdered. But who did it? A member of the family, or one of the staff? Patrick mentally checked through the list of those who had access. Mrs Fitzwilliam and her two daughters. And then there was Michael Dinan on Curtains, Miss Maria Mulcahy on Ladies' Shoes, and the possibility that Séamus O'Connor, though supposed to be organizing the damaged goods in the basement, might have slipped back to his own, unstaffed counter and sent the deadly gas canister up to the office. Did he have a reason? Not that Patrick knew, but he also knew that patient and meticulous questioning and investigation of every possible aspect might possibly bring something to light.

'Séamus O'Connor is a good friend to you, is he?' He asked the question in an idle fashion, but was immediately aware that the man had tensed.

'Not particularly.' The answer was very abrupt, almost angry, but a note of fear underscored the annoyance. And why should he object to that question? And why had O'Connor gone to so much trouble to set up this meeting between the inspector

and the suspect? Patrick kept his face tilted upwards, his eyes
fixed on a successful seagull who was being mobbed by the
other birds. But he was conscious that there was an unnatural
rigidity about the man next to him. He turned his head slightly,
still following the triumphant seagull as the bird dived down
to the river again. Yes, as he had thought, Michael Dinan was
casting sidelong glances at him. Wondering how much of
the story the policeman had swallowed. The Curtains counter,
he now remembered, was quite close to the Gentlemen's Shoes
counter. It would have been very easy and quite natural for
Séamus O'Connor to leave his work in the basement and come
up to his own counter on the pretext of fetching a pen, or a
pair of scissors. And if he had done this, then Michael Dinan
would definitely have spotted him. Were they going to give
each other alibis? Had the news about the inheritance leaked
out? If so, both men would be looking for a new job. I'll get
Joe on to this, thought Patrick. His assistant was excellent at
this sort of work, matching statement against statement and
drawing neat and detailed ground plans.

'Well, time for me to get back to work,' he said aloud.
'Can't spend the morning standing here and looking at the
seagulls.'

'I suppose that's what I will be doing with my time, come
next Monday,' said Michael Dinan. 'Mind you . . .' he said
and now Patrick discerned an unpleasant note coming into his
voice. 'Mind you,' he repeated with emphasis, 'I've had an
offer that I am considering, just considering, mind you.'

'Good,' said Patrick briskly and then he strode away. It had
been a threat, he recognized. It had to be the IRA who had
made Michael Dinan a proposal. No shop in Cork would
employ him without an excellent reference and he would get
no reference from the Fitzwilliams. No, he had been offered
a job and his words bore a veiled threat. The IRA were at
odds with the *Garda Siochána* and Patrick himself had rubbed
up against them a couple of times during the last few years.
If Patrick's life was the price of a recruitment to their ranks
of an able-bodied man with a good knowledge of the shops
of Cork, then the price would be paid without hesitation. He
shrugged his shoulders as he left the bridge and walked up

Barrack Street. He couldn't go around looking over his shoulder all the time. He had to trust to luck and to highly developed instincts which warned him of danger. He had a case to solve and he was determined to solve it as quickly as possible.

TEN

The Reverend Mother had persuaded Dr Scher to leave his car parked outside the church and to walk with her through the narrow streets and enter the shop by the back door to the Queen's Old Castle. He had thought it beneath her dignity to arrive on foot, but she persuaded him that she would enjoy the walk.

'Good to get some fresh air,' she declared. 'These stuffy churches always make me cough.'

'I hate these affairs,' he said, and the Reverend Mother looked at him with surprise. Dr Scher, she had always thought, was the most convivial of men. He met her look with defiance. 'Puts a terrible strain on the family,' he said. 'Not the time nor the occasion,' he said. 'If they'd only leave a month or so, then the family might welcome everyone talking about the deceased, but not now, not when grief is raw and emotions are churned up. This is the wrong time for neighbours and friends. Now is the time for the family to huddle together and to keep away from the outside world.'

'I see,' said the Reverend Mother. And she did see, but did not want to probe. He had his mind focussed on one member of the family, but that was not for her to question him upon. And so she added lightly, 'Well, make sure that you don't eat too much cake and then you will feel a lot better.' He was, she thought, worried about the effect of this very public affair on the fragile health of Mrs Fitzwilliam. Luckily there did not seem to be a large amount of people making the short journey from the graveyard to the back door of the shop. The shop assistants and their apprentices, the older ones well out-numbered by the young, had gone ahead of the mourners and their condolers, sent on their way, as far as she could see, by Robert Fitzwilliam while his older brother, the major, shook hands and gave some information about his father's life and career to the *Cork Examiner* reporter. Mrs Fitzwilliam was just ahead of them. She had a daughter on either side of her and appeared to lean heavily on both. She was dressed in black and wore on her head, well-pulled down over her eyes, a rather old-fashioned hat with a very heavy veil. It was almost impossible to see her face through the black netting, but her shoulders were slumped and she moved almost like an automaton. Each of the younger women had linked arms with her and they almost seemed to carry her forward on the way back to the church. The Reverend Mother looked a couple of times at Dr Scher, wondering whether she was keeping him from a patient, but she did not like to make any suggestions. He was, after all, a free man. He would, she was sure, know her well and know that the Reverend Mother had not the slightest objection to walking by herself and did so, as he well knew, very frequently. She quickened her step slightly and soon they were directly behind the three women and then the doctor seemed to relax slightly. It was a pity, thought the Reverend Mother, that someone had the strange idea of holding the after-funeral meal within the shop, rather than at the house. If poor Mrs Fitzwilliam could get to her own house, she could easily slip upstairs and lie on her bed with a couple of aspirins or even just a soothing cup of tea.

However, the woman soldiered on until some of the guests had begun to leave, most of them having left their cars outside of the church. Mrs Fitzwilliam watched them leave and then, quite suddenly and quite abruptly, she stood up and fumbled on the floor for her large handbag. Once she had it in her hand, though, she did not move. She appeared frozen. She stood very still and she gazed up at the small office perched almost at roof height on the wall. The sight of it seemed to paralyse her and she pushed aside the efforts that Kitty was making to get her to advance a little further. Monica had gone off and had just returned with another cup of tea when the woman suddenly drew in a deep breath.

'I can smell gas!' She said the words in a shrill, panic-stricken manner. Her voice rose up almost to a shriek, but then she sobbed and began to tear the veil from her hat. Both daughters took her arms and tried to seat her on the chair, but she resisted them, sucking in loud, sobbing gulps of air. 'Like a rat in a hole,' she seemed to be saying. The Reverend Mother looked across at the woman with deep concern.

'You'll be all right, will you?' Dr Scher addressed her in rapid, and concerned tones. 'Will you be all right, Reverend Mother? Can you get a taxi back to the convent?'

'Yes, Dr Scher, you go!' The Reverend Mother made a quick gesture of command and he left her instantly. He took the widow by the arm and urged her towards the door.

'Let's come out into the fresh air.' The Reverend Mother heard him speak softly in cajoling tones to the stricken woman and applauded his quick-wittedness.

Mrs Fitzwilliam, however, was not going to allow herself to be taken out quietly. 'I smell it, I smell it. There's gas in this place. Where's Robert? Break the roof, Robert. Go on, break the glass.'

'Janey Mack! She's gone stark, staring looney!' said Brian the apprentice, who had just appeared at the Reverend Mother's side. There was a slight undertone of huge enjoyment in his voice and the Reverend Mother hoped that none of the family would hear that. Adolescents, girls as well as boys, lived in their own egocentric world. She had decided that a long time ago, had become completely reconciled to it, but knew that parents and employers were everlastingly surprised and horrified by displays of selfishness or inappropriate mirth. She looked at the bright, cheerful face beside her own and decided to ignore that last remark. Dr Scher was now talking soothingly to Mrs Fitzwilliam and one of her daughters – Monica, she thought – had proffered a cup of tea which her mother gulped down, though still looking around in an apprehensive way. The Reverend Mother decided that it was time for all wondering eyes to turn away from the unfortunate woman. Dr Scher, she noticed, had quietly taken a bottle of pills from his attaché case. Time to distract attention from the unfortunate woman.

'Do you think that you could find me some tea, Brian?' she asked in loud, clear and cheerful tones, designed to assure everyone that the Reverend Mother could smell no gas in the chilly atmosphere. 'And some cake,' she added. She didn't particularly want any cake; she had no liking of sweet foods, but guessed that he would relish some. She moved towards the centre of the shop and watched with amusement the eagerness with which he sped off and the care that he took over the selection, sometimes choosing and sometimes putting a slice back, rejecting a solid-looking piece of fruit cake in favour of a cream-filled chunk of sponge. In the meantime, the Reverend Mother commented on the weather to anyone within reach and they, like all good citizens of Cork city, responded with various platitudes and stared upwards at the glass roof high above them. Robert, finding that everyone was looking upwards, went around and switched on the gas lamps and Brian took the opportunity to make a close study of all of the cakes and sweetmeats laid out on the counter tops.

It was quite some time before he made a final selection. The sky was getting very dark overhead and less light came through the glass roof, allowing the gas lamps to illuminate, in a more individual way, the faces which passed beside the copper pillars. The Reverend Mother studied the members of the Fitzwilliam family as she waited. Lucy was right, she thought. The major would probably be a great success with the female population out in Palestine. He had an aristocratic set of features, very black eyebrows and hair, a touch of grey at the temples, but still almost Spanish dark. Good hair, she thought, hair that had a hint of a wave which allowed it to spring from his forehead and stay tidily clasped to his head. His aquiline nose was perfectly balanced by a pair of prominent, wide cheekbones, which gave an aristocratic shape and form to his face. That same family nose, however, made his twin sisters appear plain and turned the heavy-jawed, plump face of his brother Robert into a mask-like visage. Not one of the four had inherited the delicate features of their mother who, in her youth, fifty years ago, had been a very pretty woman. She must be a good five or six years younger than I am, mused the Reverend Mother, but the woman's skin was as lined and her eyes as drooped as some of the ninety-year-old sisters in the convent. A hard life, perhaps, but for some women it might have been a rewarding one, working side by side with her husband to build up that small and almost useless share of the family inheritance into a prosperous business. The ancient ruin, which she could remember as a child to be lying empty and derelict, had certainly been turned into a useful space.

'Going to rain,' said Brian, reappearing at her side. 'It's great when it rains, here, Reverend Mother. Look, look up there, up next to the roof. Our dormitory is up there. You should hear the rain on a wet night. Bangs down on the glass roof. Blows your ears out.'

That did not sound a very desirable state of affairs and the Reverend Mother cast a worried glance upwards at the darkening sky. In a moment she was joined by Dr Scher.

'It's going to rain; I'm going to fetch the car,' he said. 'I'll park it outside the front door on Tuckey's Quay. Don't worry. Major Fitzwilliam will take his mother home. She's fine now. You stay here until I get back.' And then he was gone.

'I think you'd better help me with all that cake, Brian; Dr Scher sounds as though he is in a hurry.' The Reverend Mother had her eyes fixed on Mrs Fitzwilliam. She had swallowed her tea, and presumably a pill and was now standing alone, and without her family, just beside the Millinery counter. The poor woman was, like Brian, looking up every few minutes at the darkness overhead.

'C'mon, c'mon,' said Brian thickly, through a mouthful of cake. 'C'mon, let it down, let it down, let it down! That's what we all, all of us apprentices say; it's like a sort of magic spell,' he explained when she looked at him with surprise. 'The rain, Reverend Mother,' he explained. 'It cleans the roof. Otherwise, first thing every morning, we have to go out there, with a cloth and wipe that glass. The ole fog gets it filthy and the boss makes us crawl out with wet sponges. Can't take a bucket, neither, might crack the glass. Have to keep going forwards and backwards. It's no fun,' said Brian, taking an enormous bite of the chocolate slice.

No, not much fun, and very dangerous, thought the Reverend Mother picturing a crack in that glass overhead and the lethal injury that could be caused to a boy who fell through. Were there any laws about how apprentices were treated, she wondered, and looked up again. Yes, Brian's wish was going to be granted. The first large drops had begun to fall and she hoped that Dr Scher had by now reached the shelter of his car.

The large shop had been filled with the buzz of voices, but now nothing could be heard but the thundering of the rain, crashing down upon the glass roof. Only the few visitors, such as the priest, herself and Tom Murphy, owner of a nearby shop, gazed upwards at the thunderous onslaught. The counter hands of the Queen's Old Castle shop and the lowly apprentices did not take much notice but helped themselves liberally to the cake. The major, noticed the Reverend Mother, unlike his brother and his two sisters, was amongst those who gazed upwards. That glass, which in fine weather seemed to be such a good idea, such a source of light within the cavernous shop, now became something threatening. The employees and workers, however, were used to it and Brian took the opportunity to make another raid upon the fast diminishing slices of chocolate cake which were displayed upon the Millinery department counter.

As he did so, he came within sight of Mrs Fitzwilliam and this time her scream was loud enough to surmount the noise of the rain beating down on the glass roof. For a moment, it was only a scream, high-pitched and piercing, but then it dissolved into a flood of words.

'That boy,' she screamed. 'It's that boy. He was the one with the gas canister. I saw him.'

Brian stood, looking aghast, his fingers still hovering over the slice of chocolate cake, his pale green eyes large and fixed with terror upon the woman's face. The Reverend Mother moved over towards him protectively. He was, after all, not much more than about thirteen years old, she thought. Despite his usual cheerful air of confidence, he now looked stunned and horrified. This accusation had been shouted too loudly to be ignored or be treated as a joke. He looked wildly around, the freckles standing out prominently on his winter-pale face. But before the Reverend Mother had reached the woman's side, the major also had moved, more swiftly than she. He had his arm around his mother and half-lifting, half-dragging, he was moving her out from behind the shelter of her counter.

'Come along, Mother, you're tired and overwrought. This is all too much for you. Robert!' The last word was said in quite a different tone, was whipped out in an authoritative note that sounded as though it were a parade ground order. Robert left his tea and his cake and his conversation with Tom Murphy and came over reluctantly and took his mother's other arm. The Reverend Mother stood in front of Brian, blocking the sight of the boy from the unfortunate woman. She wondered whether Mrs Fitzwilliam was deranged or whether she had this new-fangled illness designated as a nervous breakdown. Whichever it was, it did not appear as though her family, with the exception perhaps of the major, were in any way sympathetic to her. Neither of the daughters came forward. Both had retreated behind their counters, the Haberdashery and the Household Linen counters and both were looking more embarrassed than worried. And Robert had a sulky and quite impatient look on his face as he hauled his mother along.

'I never!' said Brian. His denial was addressed more to his fellow apprentices, than to her, but the Reverend Mother chose to be the one to answer.

'No one is suspecting you, Brian,' she said calmly. 'Now, finish your cake, like a good boy, and then go to the front door and look out. Come back and tell me if Dr Scher's car is parked outside. It's a . . .'

She looked distractedly around, wondering whether Mrs Fitzwilliam had been taken away. The sons, she hoped, would take their mother home. She would have Dr Scher to herself. She would, she thought, tell of the accusation hurled at Brian. It probably would be best if he forbade Mrs Fitzwilliam from going into the shop until she began to regain her equilibrium; that was what she would suggest to him.

'I know it. A Humber; an old Humber with a few bashes.' Brian regained his cheerfulness, posted the last chunk of chocolate cake into his mouth and went rapidly down the middle aisle, between the banked rows of counters. Everyone was looking at him, though; especially his fellow apprentices.

A scrap of a sentence came to her ears. It was uttered in the uncontrolled voice of an adolescent, still not used to his rapidly deepening voice, and so there was little chance of it being overlooked. 'He kept on saying he was going to do for him and now he's done it,' said a tall boy with an outbreak of pimples on his face and neck.

'You get those cups washed and keep your voice down in the shop, McGrath,' snapped Kitty and the Reverend Mother looked at her with interest. This daughter, this Kitty, had an efficient way about her.

The Reverend Mother moved across to her and introduced herself. 'Brian was a pupil of mine once,' she observed. An explanation was due as she had sent the boy on an errand without asking his masters or mistresses. 'Your father, may God grant him eternal rest, was kind enough to offer me his services when I was collecting the goods that he donated to our charity.'

'Oh, that's all right, Reverend Mother. Make as much use of him as you wish. An idle young wretch, but, sure, they're all like that. Their one aim in life is to get out of doing anything that might seem like hard work.'

Kitty sounded assured and had made no reference to her mother's accusation. A balanced woman, confident and self-possessed. The Haberdashery counter was in very neat order, thought the Reverend Mother. The innumerable small drawers, with their brass knobs, were all well-polished, and a collection of representative items was grouped on the counter, displayed under glass covers and with the prices neatly inscribed on glossy white tickets. The counter had a more modern look than the rest of the shop and was well lit with a gas lamp angled on it from above.

'I'm sorry that your mother is so upset,' continued the Reverend Mother. 'Your father's death in those circumstances must have been a terrible shock for all of you.'

'Not made any easier by the presence of the police at the funeral,' said the woman grimly. The remark was probably meant to be carried back, but the Reverend Mother did not waste any time in defending Patrick's presence at the funeral. There was no doubt that murder put a great strain on the family of the victim, but, on the other hand, there was no way of avoiding an investigation. 'All right for them, going around asking questions,' continued the woman. 'How do they think that makes us feel? Can't they imagine what an effect something like this has on a wife?'

'And on the sons and daughters?' The Reverend Mother watched the effect of that remark. What would be the reply to it?

Kitty Fitzwilliam almost shrugged. There certainly was a twitch to the heavily padded shoulders of the rather ill-fitting costume which she wore. Black, with a skirt which was neither long nor short, but which dipped uncertainly around the region of the calves of her legs and a jacket which, though of the same colour, seemed to have no real relationship to the skirt and to be made of a different material. She still retained the ugly black straw hat that she had worn in the church. It was squashed down over her eyebrows, and all in all, she presented the appearance of a woman who had snatched a few items from the Ladies' Millinery counter and had decided that they would be appropriate for a funeral. Monica, though of the same age, was considerably better dressed. The Reverend Mother wished for the companionship of her cousin Lucy who would immediately be able to match an outfit to a shop, but even without that aid, she would be prepared to put a bet on her conviction that Monica's rather smart, black, fur-trimmed costume had not come from the stocks of the Queen's Old Castle.

'My mother gets easily upset,' said Kitty. She did not, noticed the Reverend Mother, comment on the notion that her father's death would be upsetting for her or for her brothers and sisters. It seemed to point to poor relationships all around, but it may just be something to do with a laconic and inhibited personality. It must be odd to have the role of father subsumed into the role of employer. It was very possible that this dual relationship would weaken natural ties and that here in the shop, Kitty's grief for a father was buried beneath the needs of the business.

The Reverend Mother found her eyes going to the wires which sent the change barrels zooming up through the empty space of the old castle until they reached the small office high up on the side wall.

'I suppose the boys have great fun working these,' she said impulsively.

Kitty surveyed her with the air of one who was used to

dealing with senile old ladies. There was a palpable sigh, and a patient attempt at a cold smile. 'The apprentices are never trusted to handle money or to work the change barrels, Reverend Mother,' she said emphatically.

'Oh, I see,' said the Reverend Mother.

'That's the rule, Reverend Mother,' said a man's voice from behind her. 'But of course, some of these boys are a law unto themselves. Especially young Brian. A very headstrong boy, unreliable, not very satisfactory in many respects. In fact . . .' The voice trailed off and the Reverend Mother turned around. Robert was back from escorting his mother from the premises. Gone home in the major's car, no doubt. What, she wondered, was he implying?

'Was your father not satisfied with him?' She allowed a note of surprise to enter her query and Kitty looked quickly from one to the other.

'Some of them take longer to settle to steady work than others,' Kitty said. It had the air of being an excuse for Brian, but her anxious eyes were fixed upon her brother. Robert did not respond, did not look at her, but continued to look across at the front doors where Brian, beckoning enthusiastically, had appeared. After a minute he said curtly, 'I think that young Brian is signalling to you, Reverend Mother. Dr Scher must have brought his car around. What a pity that he was not here when my mother's nerves broke down again. He has been her medical attendant for many years, been paid well for his trouble, too.'

An unpleasant man. A thoroughly unpleasant man. His tone implied that Dr Scher had fallen down on the duties that he had been paid for. The Reverend Mother said a few last farewell words to Kitty and went towards the front door, to where Brian was waiting. She felt rather sorry that she could not take him with her. In some way, she had an uneasy feeling about him. There had been a note of malevolence, not just in the screamed words of the distraught widow, but also in the measured cadences of the middle-aged Kitty, whose youth had mouldered in this damp, cold shop. And in the irritable words of Robert Fitzwilliam who had, if Lucy was correct, been denied his inheritance.

This custom of apprenticeship, a leftover from English law, was one that favoured the well-off by providing them with cheap labour and a source of income as the parents of the apprentice had to pay a fee – in many cases a fee which they could ill afford. And a practice which reduced the children of the poor to a status of almost slavery. The boy, Brian, was the possession of these unhappy and disappointed people. Brian Maloney's mother had arranged his apprenticeship, had gone back to her own people on a farm outside Mallow. He was on his own, was without any adult protection and at the mercy of those who employed him.

As Dr Scher escorted her to his battered old Humber, she reflected upon Brian and hoped that the boy was not in any kind of danger of losing his position as an apprentice and finding himself destitute and homeless in the city of Cork.

Or, perhaps, in even greater danger. If he had been a witness of anything, of anyone inserting a suspicious canister into a change barrel; if he had seen anything like that as he had darted, agile as a young puppy, around and through the counters of the Queen's Old Castle, well, then, Brian Maloney might be in grave peril.

ELEVEN

P atrick left the barracks in good time to attend the reading of Joseph Fitzwilliam's will. He thought that he would walk there. The Fitzwilliams' house was in Glenville Place, just overlooking the river, only about twenty minutes from the barracks. And about ten minutes' walking time from the Queen's Old Castle shop. Not somewhere that I'd particularly want to live, thought Patrick, as he rounded the corner onto the quay. A tall, thin, four-storey house with some windows on the steep roof showing that a fifth storey was accommodated behind the slates. A bedraggled maidservant opened the door to his knock and indicated, wordlessly, a door on the left. Patrick hesitated for a moment, but the maid had disappeared down some stairs to the basement area of the house and so he put his hat on the hat stand, tapped on the door and pushed it open.

No refreshments here, but the family were gathered and he had, he decided, come to the right place. Mr Rupert Murphy, flanked by a middle-aged clerk, was leafing through the contents of his attaché case, rather more in the fashion of one who was killing some time, than as if he were really looking for something. The clerk had arranged some papers neatly on the small table in front of them and Patrick caught a glimpse of the words 'Last Will and Testament' on the top of a page. When Mr Murphy saw Patrick, he came forward immediately and held out a hand for him to shake.

'Ah, inspector, come in,' he said in a genial, host-like fashion. 'Come and sit down. This chair comfortable enough for you? Haven't got the light in your eyes? Warm enough?'

'I'm fine.' Patrick felt somewhat embarrassed. The chair was in an ideal position, well away from the lawyer and his clerk, away from that focus of attention, but it gave him a perfect view of the family grouped to one side of the fireplace. He sat down quickly and in turn fumbled through the contents of his own attaché case. They were all there, all grouped on one side of the fire. Old Mrs Fitzwilliam was slumped on a long sofa, with her two daughters, one on either side of her.

Monica, he noticed, was very smartly dressed. She had taken off the warm woollen coat which she had worn for the funeral and was now wearing a slim-fitting, black, silk dress with a necklace of pearls around her neck – three rows of them, he noticed, fitting around her neck like a glittering collar. He didn't know enough about pearls to be certain that they were real, but he knew that they looked expensive. And that, twins or not twins, she looked years younger than her sister.

The major had ensconced himself on a broad upholstered easy chair, his well-polished boots were placed on a matching upholstered stool and by his side he had a small round table with a glass of brandy or whiskey standing on it and an open box of cigars placed ready at his hand. Robert, however, in stark contrast to his brother, was sitting on a hard, upright chair and staring fiercely ahead.

'Well, yes,' said the solicitor. He cast a quick glance around the room and then embarked upon a few minutes of legal jargon while the family of the deceased, except for the major, eyed him with distrust. And then the will was read. The house at Glenville Place and some shares were left to the wife. Both daughters got two thousand pounds each. Patrick could see how their faces fell at this. The major puffed at his cigar and sipped his brandy and showed little interest in the proceedings as the solicitor said the words: 'and all the residue of my estate to my eldest son, Major James Fitzwilliam'. No one moved or said anything as the solicitor read out the long list of all of what the dead man had possessed. It was only when he came to a full stop with the conventional words, 'This is the last Will and Testament of Joseph Thomas Fitzwilliam' that it seemed as though full realization dawned.

'He left me nothing,' said Robert and the words jerked out from him as though he was an automaton.

'The shop, everything to James; he must have been mad!' Kitty, thought Patrick, looked as though she were about to explode.

'The will was made by me and it appeared to me and to

my clerk that the late Mr Fitzwilliam was of sound mind,'
replied the solicitor. 'And I do understand that Mr Fitzwilliam
informed you of his intentions in advance.' His tone was
measured and unemotional. Probably used to a fuss at the
reading of wills, thought Patrick.

'But that's rubbish,' cried Kitty. 'Nobody believed him. He
was always doing that sort of thing. Nobody thought that he
would actually do it. He was always talking about changing
his will. We never thought that he would do it so quickly,
that he would go off on the—'

'That's enough, Kitty,' said Robert. He spoke in an undertone
but there was a vicious sound to his words.

Never thought that he would do it so quickly. The words
echoed through Patrick's mind. Quite a motive for murder on
the part of Robert, but also of the two sisters and of the widow.
He sat very still and avoided drawing attention to himself.

'Let me see the date on that will.' Robert almost snatched
the piece of vellum from the solicitor's hand. 'Yes, the very
morning after,' he said almost to himself. 'He went to the
solicitor the morning after and made a new will. You knew
about that, did you?' He glared at his brother.

'He told me, yes.'

'And that's why you came back?'

'He wrote to me beforehand,' explained the major. 'Asked
me to come home. Said he felt worried and that he felt he'd
like to have me with him.'

Not quite an answer, thought Patrick.

'Worried!' sneered Robert.

'And now I'm afraid that I must leave you all. I have an
appointment with another client.' The solicitor got to his feet
and firmly packed the will into his leather attaché case. The
clerk was on his feet also and with a quick look at his master,
he left the room after a muttered farewell. No one took any
notice of him. All eyes were on the solicitor and he responded
as one who had dealt with this sort of situation many times
during his life as solicitor to the moneyed of Cork city.

'You will all receive a copy of the will, hopefully by
tomorrow's post, if my clerk has time to type out the copies
this afternoon,' he said. 'If not it will certainly be with you

on the following day. May I drop you off near to the barracks, inspector? I am going your way.'

There was little chance of declining that invitation, but Patrick felt that he might have preferred to stay. It was interesting how money and bequests brought out the worst in people. Still, he had heard enough to give him food for thought. And there was a question that he needed to put to the solicitor.

He waited until he was safely ensconced upon the luxurious leather seat and that all doors were closed before he put it to the solicitor. 'And the date of the will?'

'Friday the first,' said the solicitor, not looking at Patrick, but carefully turning his expensive car around the sharp corner.

'And the major came home?'

'I believe it was the Sunday before,' said the solicitor cautiously.

'So,' said Patrick, 'the major comes home, shows himself to be very useful in the aftermath of the flood, brings these gas cylinders, I understand, organizes the fumigation of the damaged goods, perhaps helps with the planning of the sale and then old Mr Fitzwilliam has a great row with other members of his family . . .'

'I understand that the major was absent, meeting old friends on that occasion,' said the solicitor, smoothly braking in order to allow a suicidal messenger boy, his bike almost touching the car's bonnet, to swoop across the road.

'So the row with the rest of his family occurs on a Thursday when he tells them of his intentions to change the will and then old Mr Fitzwilliam goes into his solicitor on the following morning and makes a new will, leaving almost all of what he possessed to his eldest son, Major James Fitzwilliam, nothing whatsoever to his younger son and probably what they would regard as a pittance to his daughters. Oh, and just enough to maintain his wife.' Was that last of importance, or not, wondered Patrick, but they were now crossing the bridge and he knew that he had not much more time, here in this enclosed space, with a man who was reputed to know most of the secrets of the well-off families of Cork.

'Of course, there are some people who are for ever

making wills,' said Patrick endeavouring to make his voice sound indifferent and to adopt a tone of one who is making conversation to fill in an idle moment.

For a moment, he thought that he saw a smile twitch at the lips of the man beside him, but then the smile faded. 'As a police officer in charge of an investigation into a suspicious death, if you ask me a question I am bound to answer it,' said Mr Rupert Murphy in the tones of someone quoting from a textbook as he cast an expectant glance over his shoulder before refocussing on the road ahead.

Patrick thought about that for a moment and then asked the question. 'How many wills had Mr Fitzwilliam made?'

'Ten. I counted them up yesterday. Had a little bet on with my chief clerk about it!'

'And each time he had announced it to his family?'

'I believe that you are right.'

'And so . . .' said Patrick seeing his destination getting closer and fumbling for the right words, 'it might have been expected by all parties that this will might have been changed yet again.'

The solicitor drew his car to a smooth halt outside the police barracks. 'True,' he said. And then as Patrick reached for the door handle, he added thoughtfully, 'Mr Fitzwilliam was fortunate, or perhaps unfortunate, enough to be able to see me on the morning when he telephoned. I had a cancelled appointment just before lunch time on that day.'

'Thank you,' said Patrick. He got out of the car, but he did not go into the barracks straight away but walked up and down, thinking hard. It was only when he saw old Tommy who had left his place on the desk and was now standing at the window peering out at him that it dawned on him that he was behaving in an eccentric fashion. He gave one last, face-saving glance at the sky and then went into the barracks, rubbing his hands as he went.

'Going to be a cold night tonight, Tommy,' he said before the man could ask him what he was doing. 'You look at that sky out there.' And then, very quickly, before any reply could be given, he asked, 'Joe in, is he, Tommy?' And then he went down the passageway, clicking his heels against the wooden flooring and walking in a very erect way. He would solve this murder, he swore it to himself.

'The trouble with this man, old Mr Fitzwilliam, Joe,' he said opening the door to the sergeant's office and then closing it firmly behind him in case Tommy followed him down the corridor with a verdict on the weather. 'The trouble with him,' he said once he was safely inside, 'is that he was a most dislikeable fellow. Everyone wanted to kill him and that's making it jolly hard for you and for me.'

'You're in a good mood,' said Joe eyeing him with amusement.

'Wait until you hear about the wills,' said Patrick, taking off his coat and sitting down on the windowsill. 'The man made ten of them, probably a will every couple of months. Had fun with them, too, I gather. Anyway, let me tell you of his last will and testament.'

TWELVE

Dowden's shop was by far the most expensive shop in the city of Cork. The wives of the wealthy shopped there for their dresses, coats, costumes, hats, gloves and silk stockings. Its small neat van could be seen traversing the streets of the moneyed citizens who lived on the slopes of Montenotte or in the mansions by the river at Blackrock. Dowden's was immensely accommodating and always happy to send out a selection of newly arrived two-piece costumes or coats, 'on apro.' so that their customers could try out the goods in the privacy of their houses.

Eileen had always loved wandering through Dowden's, imagining what she would buy for herself and for her mother once she had made her fortune. On one of these wanders she had an inspiration. 'Shops like Dowden's should send out leaflets to their customers. Half of those women are too lazy to come in and shop for themselves,' she said to Jack as she watched him slot letters, at lightning speed, into lines of type. 'I hear the assistants on the counters, phoning them up and saying things like: "Oh, *Modom* will love those new suits that we've just got in. We've got one that's the very thing for *Modom*. It's just *Modom's* colour. A true duck egg blue. And in *Modom's* size. Just let me send out one for *Modom* to try on".'

'And what if *Modom* doesn't like it?' asked Jack, neatly picking up a pair of the letter 'e'.

'Well, it gets sent back, of course,' said Eileen impatiently. 'But, you see, these sales ladies will only offer them the sort of thing that they have bought in the past. What if Dowden's have leaflets printed with descriptions of the new clothes for the season and have little drawings of them? You could do the drawings, couldn't you, Jack? You are excellent at that.'

'You'd better have a word with the boss,' said Jack. 'But I think it's a great idea,' he added generously. 'And where

Dowden's lead, others will follow. The boss will love you for
that, Eileen. Nice steady source of income. And with a bit of
luck the shops will have drawings of the clothes already. The
manufacturers are bound to have done those.'

And so, on a cold spring morning, Eileen sat down in the
back room of Dowden's and inspected the spring collection
of costumes that were being unpacked. She didn't think
much of the drawings, she thought Jack would have made
a better job of them, but then told herself that it gave all the
more scope to her pen. She took out her notebook and noted
the good points of each piece of new clothing. And colour.
Colour was something that could not be printed in the leaflet
so she would have to describe it well. *Bay leaf green, glowing
amber, softest camel, bright clear azure, gentian shading
into purple* . . .

By and by, from the fitting room across the passageway,
she heard the words '*eau de Nil*' and she made a quick note
of it. It was the voice of the principal saleswoman, a very
well-spoken lady, talking to a customer. 'That *eau de Nil* colour
suits you so well, Madam.' Eileen giggled to herself. How
could the woman say things like that and keep a straight face?

And then she heard a different voice, a man's voice, slight
English accent, quite posh, and uttering a name that attracted
her attention. 'Oh, for goodness sake, Monica, that's the fifth
thing that you've tried on. Can't you make up your mind?'

And then the saleswoman, sweet as pie. 'Could we offer
you a cup of coffee, Major? Maureen, run and get the major
a cup of coffee and the *Cork Examiner*.'

Eileen peered through the curtained doorway. She couldn't
see the occupants of the fitting room, but the table outside
was piled high with neatly folded luxury garments. 'Maureen'
had abandoned wrapping a couple of silk dresses in soft tissue
paper and rushed off to get the cup of coffee and the *Cork
Examiner*. Major Fitzwilliam came back from the window
overlooking Patrick Street and threw himself impatiently into
a comfortable armchair. A moment later, Miss Monica
Fitzwilliam came out wearing a blue-green costume with a
nipped-in waist and a surprisingly short skirt. So that was *eau
de Nil*. Subtle shade, noted Eileen.

'What do you think, James?' asked Monica as she walked up and down and admired herself in the mirrors which lined the passageway.

The major grunted, but didn't reply. The saleswoman glanced from one to the other, appraising, thought Eileen knowingly, the size of the purse of the one and greed of the other.

'Of course, this is cashmere, and cashmere is, I have to admit, just that teeny weeny bit expensive. I might just be able to find a similar colour in a plain wool,' she said, and Eileen had to stop herself giggling at the disdainful way in which she pronounced the words 'plain wool'.

'Oh, no,' said Monica with a shudder. 'Not plain wool. Cashmere feels so soft to the skin, but, of course, I will need something warm when I am on board ship. Will cashmere be enough? It feels so deliciously light, but . . .'

'I've got just the thing,' said the saleswoman enthusiastically. 'Just come in. A Coco Chanel jersey with a high neck. Will slip under that costume as easy as anything. Beautiful cashmere in just that subtle shade of buttermilk that will really light up the *eau de Nil*. Not everyone can wear these colours, but with Madam's complexion . . .'

Eileen noted down 'subtle shade of buttermilk' into her notebook while the saleswoman bustled off to get the selection of Coco Chanel jerseys. There was going to be pink and white and grey as well as the buttermilk cream, she had said before leaving, but Eileen, taking another peep at the strands of grey in Monica's dark hair, decided that if she were the saleswoman she would persuade her into buying the cream-coloured jersey to go under her *eau de Nil* costume.

And then she stopped thinking about clothes. The major had waited until the woman had disappeared, and then spoke in an undertone, but in a voice full of irritation.

'Come on, now, Monica, I'm not made of money, you know.'

Monica responded in the same low voice, but Eileen, peeping through a slit in the curtain saw that there was a slightly unpleasant smile on her face as she said, 'You forget, my dear brother, the events of the last few days. You were the one who was left a fortune, weren't you?'

'Not a fortune,' he said with a shrug. 'And I have other uses for it than wasting it on silly clothes. You should see the size of my debts.'

'Nevertheless, you have to admit that it was a very fortunate occurrence for you.' There was a pause after Monica said that, and then she added, 'That's if *fortune* came into it.'

There was a long silence after that. Eileen peeped out through the crack in the curtains. She felt an excitingly cold thrill run down the back of her spine. Was Monica going to accuse the major, her brother James, of the deliberate murder of their father? But, thought Eileen, he had come in the front door just after the man had fallen to his death. She had seen that, herself. She thought about the Queen's Old Castle and began to wonder about other entrances and exits. But the man would have been so noticeable in that fancy uniform that he wore to impress the citizens of Cork.

And in any case, it was the major who was staring at his sister with a look that seemed to be of utter horror.

Eileen's eyes widened. What had happened on that morning?

To her irritation, she heard the click of heels that signalled the return of the sales assistant, accompanied by another assistant bearing coffee, cake and the *Cork Examiner* for the entertainment of the man who was paying for this enormous heap of expensive clothes. This, she thought, would put an end to the intriguing conversation between brother and sister.

Eileen kept her ears open for undertones as she worked on diligently, studying the catalogues, writing down a sentence or two about each of the new arrivals, trying to make it sound as though she were a fashion expert, checking all of the details and then reading through everything with a critical eye. But apart from a murmur of voices, no more was said from outside until after Monica emerged once more from the changing room, saying dramatically, 'I just can't make up my mind, James. What do you think, the buttermilk cream or the soft black? Mrs Harrington loves the cream, but I must say that I think the black is very smart.'

He did not hesitate. Eileen, peeping through the curtain again, saw that he did not lift his eyes from the middle pages of the *Cork Examiner*. 'Why don't you have a pair of both and that will see you through the chilly mornings on board ship,' he said in indifferent tones.

And Monica's smile was not just a smile of pure pleasure; it bore more resemblance to a smirk of triumph. She handed over the jerseys to Mrs Harrington. And when the pair departed, she led the way like the victor.

Eileen left it a good ten minutes after their departure before she emerged from the back room and went in search of Mrs Harrington. The woman was in a wonderfully good humour after having given instructions to the van driver about the delivery of all of the parcels to Glenville Place. She read through the description of the spring goods with several approving nods. Very knowledgeable, too, thought Eileen. She herself thought that the price should go at the top of each item, but Mrs Harrington shook her head firmly.

'I like to get them in here, my dear,' she said. 'If the price is on the item, they might decide it's too expensive. It's the same thing when the goods are sent out on "appro." – well, they might buy it, or their husband might turn up his nose at it, say it's very dear, or that they have something else in their wardrobe just like it, but if they come in to enquire about the prices or to have a look around, you'd be surprised how much they will buy and how much more satisfied they will be. I like to show them what suits them.'

'I bet,' said Eileen. And then, taking a chance, she whispered, 'You were right, the buttermilk cream suited her better than the black.' And then fearing that she might have overstepped the limit, she said impulsively, 'When I make a fortune, I'll come straight to you and you'll choose me a lovely outfit.'

'Well, I hope you do make your fortune, my dear,' said Mrs Harrington. 'Now, let's come and have a look at the ladies' shoes. You've done a very good job there,' she said with a nod at Eileen's notebook. 'I can see that we will get along very well together.'

'Oh, thank you,' said Eileen, but already her mind was busy. She looked up at the clock. Almost half-past twelve, nearly time for lunch hour. She wouldn't, she thought, go straight back to the printing works. She would take one of the Patrick Street buses that would drop her at the foot of Barrack Street.

Patrick, she thought, might be interested in the conversation that she had overheard. *Poor fellow,* she said to herself, *he needs a bit of help from someone with brains.*

Patrick was hastily concealing a sandwich beneath his desk when Joe showed her in.

No human weaknesses must be revealed, she said to herself, and then, aloud, she said, 'Ah c'mon, Patrick, g's a bite.'

And by a miracle, he grinned. Not quite so stiff as usual, she thought. He put the sandwich back on the table, wiped a wooden ruler with a piece of blotting paper and meticulously halved the sandwich with the sharp edge of the ruler. She took it from him as he was looking around for something to serve as a plate, and she sank her teeth into it and chewed vigorously.

'Not bad,' she said. 'Did you make that yourself?'

'No, Joe's mother. We're very busy today. No time for lunch. What brings you here, Eileen?'

'Some people,' she said, aiming her remark at the window, 'would take that for a brush-off.'

He was taken aback at that. No concept of humour, she thought. Still, he had spent his teen years in that awful North Mon. school where the boys were flogged into high examination results in the civil service and university scholarship performances. And no fun afterwards as straightaway he had joined the police. No decent human society, no banter between boys and girls, no flirting, nothing. She smiled at him forgivingly.

'I've overheard something of interest to you about the Queen's Old Castle murder, Patrick.'

He put down his sandwich. 'Really?' he said.

'I was in Dowden's and I overheard Monica talking with her brother, the major.'

He had raised his eyebrows at the word 'Dowden's', had not expected her to frequent the most expensive shop in Cork, but at the mention of Monica and the major, his face grew serious. 'Tell me,' he said.

'He was buying her tons of really posh, really expensive clothes,' said Eileen briefly. She thought of mentioning 'Coco

Chanel' but decided that he might well not have heard of the famous designer. 'He's taking her out to Palestine with him,' she added. 'Buying her outfits to wear on-board ship, and silk dresses for the parties out there.'

'A good brother,' he said, almost flippantly.

'What about Kitty?' she asked. 'And the stuff he was buying would be a year's salary for me. And that's not all. Wait till you hear.' She took another bite from the half sandwich and chewed it. Let him wait, she thought, noticing that he was no longer eating his own sandwich.

'Good point,' he said after a minute. 'So go on, tell me all.'

'Well, he quibbled a bit once, told her that he wasn't made of money. And she said: "Nevertheless, you have to admit that it was a very fortunate occurrence for you." These were her very words.'

Patrick looked up sharply. 'Fortunate?' His voice held a query.

'Well,' said Eileen, 'there was a bit of a pause after Monica said that, and then she added, "That's if fortune came into it".'

'And these, again, were her very words?'

'Cross my heart and hope to die,' said Eileen flippantly.

'And what do you think that she meant by that?' He spoke, almost to himself, and she understood that he was not really asking her. She said nothing, just chewed the crust of her sandwich. Nice bread, homemade, she thought. Joe's mother must be a good cook. She wondered whether Joe had a sister. Joe's mother might start by making sandwiches, but soon there would be an invitation to tea. He would be seated beside the sister. A good match. A young inspector of the police might even be a superintendent before he was thirty. Eileen resolved to have a chat with Joe to see whether he did have a sister.

After a minute, she was bored with the silence. 'Well, it's obvious, isn't it?' she said impatiently. 'After all, the major inherited all of his father's business. Surely he is the one who had the most reason to bump him off. And I heard him say that he had debts. Don't forget about that, Patrick.' She looked at him impatiently. He was just the sort of person to stick to facts all of the time, she thought. Of course, the major was in the clear if you looked at the bare facts. He had only just come into the shop when his father fell from on high. 'He might have been in earlier on,' she said aloud.

Patrick shook his head. He opened his notebook, looked through it and shook his head again. 'He left the house in Glenville Place only five minutes earlier. One of the maids served him a three-course meal after the other five had left to go to the shop. Orange juice, oatmeal porridge, rashers, egg, fried bread and coffee. And after that he sat in the dining room and smoked a cigar.'

'I see,' said Eileen. It did sound rather conclusive. 'Perhaps he bribed the maid,' she said hopefully. 'He looks a bit of a lady's man. He was being very charming to the saleslady in Dowden's.'

'Perhaps,' said Patrick, but he said it rather sceptically.

And then suddenly Eileen understood it all. '*She* did it! Monica did it! She mightn't have told him that she was going to do it, but she probably relied on him feeling generous. Perhaps they were always good friends, the two of them. He might even have invited her to come out to Palestine with him before any of this happened. She might have accepted and then, listen Patrick. It all makes sense. Monica might have thought how much nicer a time the two of them would have if James inherited a fortune. And so she bumped off the old man before he could change his will. I've heard that he was always quarrelling with his family, always changing his will. A man that I work with told me that. Come on, Patrick, it's a good idea, you have to admit.'

He stayed very still for a while. She gazed at him hopefully waiting for him to speak, waiting for him to congratulate her. Everything was so quiet that she could hear the clock ticking.

And then he rose to his feet. 'It was extremely good of you to come over here in your lunch hour,' he said stiffly.

She got up, also. 'Do you practise saying these things, Patrick,' she asked and then was a little sorry when she saw him redden. 'Well, good luck, Patrick,' she said, as he politely opened the door. She doubted whether he had the brains to solve this strange murder, but then told herself that it was none of her business. She should get back to the printing works and start the layout of the Dowdens' Spring Fashions leaflet. Two hundred copies. That was a nice little piece of business that she had brought to the printing firm. She should keep her mind on her own job, she thought, and let Patrick get on with solving his own problems. 'Say thanks to Joe and to his mother for the sandwich,' she said. 'Oh, is Joe an only child, or has he any sisters?'

'Three of them,' said Patrick looking slightly bewildered.

He always did find it hard to keep up with the working of her mind, Eileen told herself pityingly. 'I thought so,' she said gently and was pleased to see that he looked even more puzzled.

THIRTEEN

P atrick leaned back in his chair and fixed his eyes on the ceiling. He stayed perfectly immobile but his mind was active. Joe had drawn a neat ground plan of the Queen's Old Castle shop, with each one of the counters labelled with its name and now, within his mind's eye, Patrick went from one counter to another. Curtains: Michael Dinan (the man who had been dismissed) and his apprentice Con Meaney. Fourteen years old and scared of Michael Dinan. Gents' Shoes (That was Séamus O'Connor's counter, but he was not there, had been busy stock-taking). His apprentice was Brian Maloney who had been under the Reverend Mother's eye, kept busy filling her basket with flood-damaged goods. And then there was Haberdashery: Miss Kitty Fitzwilliam, a very direct lady, plenty to say for herself. Significantly her apprentice, seventeen-year-old Henry Spiller, had been sent down to the basement to get more needles and had only just returned to see Mr Fitzwilliam fall from the balcony. Joe had questioned Henry Spiller and there was a note opposite to his name: *sharp lad. On the ball. Knows which side his bread is buttered on.* Not exactly the language advocated in the police manual on questioning witnesses, but Patrick knew exactly what Joe meant. Henry Spiller had already done five years of apprenticeship. He would be hoping to be taken on as a permanent worker. He would definitely not give evidence against a member of the shop owner's family, but he may have betrayed something inadvertently. And so he was sent on an errand. Yes, Miss Kitty would not have been observed if she had substituted a gas canister for the change barrel. But why would Miss Kitty want to kill her father? How much had she been left in a former will? More, he guessed. Was she sick of the shop? Or could she have come to some sort of unspoken agreement with her older brother? According to Eileen MacSweeney, one of the sisters might have been trying to get a bit of money out of him, so why not the other. After all, the major was an unmarried man. Perhaps he would take both sisters out to Palestine to keep house for him? Unlikely, thought Patrick, Kitty didn't seem the type, but worthy of consideration. But then, none of the family, except perhaps the major, knew that the new will had been made on that dinner hour three days before old Mr Fitzwilliam had been killed. Still, they had been told that the major would inherit so they might have taken a chance on it. Or else have ways of keeping track of their father.

And then there was Household Linens. The other daughter, Miss Monica Fitzwilliam, was in charge there. She said that the apprentice, Tom Donovan, had loaded the change barrel and sent it off on its journey. The apprentice, remembered Patrick, had not contradicted that, but had looked scared and uneasy while being questioned. And Patrick, himself, had questioned the lad. Not a confident type. Very thin, very pale face, hollow chest, bent over like an old man. And Miss Kitty had stated loudly and positively that apprentices were never allowed to touch the change barrels. Had looked accusingly at her sister. Not much love lost between them, had noted Joe. So why, if the truth had been spoken, had it come about that on this occasion Tom Donovan had been entrusted with the task – or had he? Patrick made a mental note to see the boy again. He couldn't ignore Eileen's story, but he always suspected her of exaggerating.

And then there was Millinery: Mrs Agnes Fitzwilliam. Well, she was in a right state. Impossible to question her properly. He had talked with the apprentice, but the boy had just repeated 'Dunno, sir' over and over again. Patrick inserted a mental question mark about young John Joe Burke's evidence. Was the boy stupid, or was he just frightened? The latter, probably. The city was full of bright lads, all looking for the prospect of a permanent job, plenty of them available for an apprenticeship. From what he had heard of Mr Fitzwilliam, he would have been unlikely to take any boy who didn't have a good reference from his school and didn't appear to be bright as well as willing. A boy as stupid as John Joe Burke appeared to be now, would never have got an apprenticeship if he had been like that three years ago. More likely the boy was frightened. He wondered whether he could see those apprentices again in a more private setting. He made a note about that. 'Word with Joe', he wrote.

And then there was the Ladies' Shoes counter: Miss Maria Mulcahy. Her apprentice was a new boy, Christy Callinan. Twelve years old. A nice little boy, blond curly hair, blue eyes and a mouthful of large, rather buck teeth. Christy had been the chattiest of them all and still new enough to be fascinated by those change barrels. He said that Miss Mulcahy had explained everything to him. She seemed a kind, almost motherly woman. Shame if someone didn't marry her before she became too old to have a child of her own. He thought about Séamus O'Connor and then about Robert Fitzwilliam, which one of the two did Miss Mulcahy favour? That was an easy question to answer. It was obvious that Robert would be the better match. But then, he said to himself, Séamus O'Connor would be much more likely in the end. Robert was not the type to take a chance on infuriating his father. He dismissed the matter from his mind and went back again to the problem of the gas canister.

Six barrels queued up and awaiting change and receipts. These had been all sent up within minutes of each other. And five of the six were innocent, but the sixth carried death. How was it not spotted that one barrel carried a different canister.

After all, there was an apprentice at each counter. That was the shop's practice. But, of course, apprentices were continually sent to and fro with errands, or occasionally told to escort a customer to the door, to carry parcels to a waiting car or taxi. The pages of notes that he had accumulated had convinced him that any one of the five counters: Ladies' Shoes, Household Linens, Curtains, Millinery or Haberdashery could have sent the fatal barrel.

And one of those six counters, Séamus O'Connor's Gents' Shoes, should have had no one there as the man himself was busy in the store room, and his apprentice had accompanied the Reverend Mother as she filled her basket full of gifts for the poor and the needy.

The most likely thing was that the gas canister was sent

from there as no one had admitted sending something from the Men's Shoes' counter.

Patrick looked at the clock on the wall and compared it with the watch that he had taken from his pocket. Abruptly he got to his feet, took down his coat, cap and umbrella and proceeded.

'I'm going out, Joe; be back in an hour,' he called through Joe's open door as he went down the corridor.

'Yes, sir,' said the well-trained Joe, hardly raising his eyes from his desk.

'Going out, Tommy, be back in an hour,' he said to the man at the entrance desk.

'Where shall I say that you are going, inspector, if anyone asks' said Tommy as Patrick made for the front door.

'Say you don't know,' said Patrick. But he said it very low and was out of the door before Tommy, who was sensitive about his deafness, could make up his mind whether to ask him to repeat his answer or not. Tommy could be a dangerous enemy; very well in with the superintendent. Both of them Protestants, and Protestants tended to stick together in the city of Cork.

In any case, he was a bit ashamed of himself. Not for anything would he have told the inquisitive Tommy where he was going. Why, on earth, should an inspector want to consult with an elderly nun?

'Just wanted to check on a few matters, Reverend Mother,' he said ten minutes later. And then wondered what he had wanted to ask. He was a bit disconcerted to discover that Dr Scher was there also. For form's sake, he pulled out his notebook and made a pretence of looking through it. There was the Reverend Mother's evidence. All very clear. He tried to formulate an intelligent question, but his worries kept intruding into his thoughts.

'Join me in a cup of tea,' said Dr Scher hospitably. 'They make it very well here. Best place in the whole of Cork. And look who's here now! Come in, Sister Bernadette, come in. Ah, thank you, Sister Bernadette. You're an angel. Look at that, Patrick! Fresh tea and some more cake. Enough for all. Didn't fancy those cakes at the funeral. Not up to your standards at all, Sister Bernadette.'

Patrick put away his notebook, sat back, relaxed and waited until Sister Bernadette had left the room.

'I've been listening to the reading of the will,' he said then, sipping his tea.

'Stale news, lad, stale news,' said Dr Scher. 'The major gets it all. The whole of Cork knows about the will.'

Patrick hesitated for a moment and then told himself that the information about the other wills would soon be all over Cork. After all, wills were public property once the man or woman was dead.

'The *latest* will. He made ten wills,' he said mildly. 'This was number ten.'

'And told his family about it every time, I suppose,' said Dr Scher. 'That type always do. Keeps the family on their toes. What a pity that I don't have a large family gathering around me, each and every one of them hoping desperately to inherit my collection of Cork silver. What fun I would have, changing my will every month or two. What do you think, Reverend Mother? Would you like a mention in my will? I could leave you a Georgian silver teaspoon.'

The Reverend Mother smiled discreetly, but said nothing. Patrick felt her eyes on him, full of interest and waiting for what he had to say.

'I'm not sure who were the earlier beneficiaries,' he said, feeling somewhat comforted by her belief in him, 'but I can tell you that the two daughters appeared to be very upset to be left only a couple of thousand pounds each, so I would imagine in the past that they had received much more. However, I think that the most interesting thing that I learned today was that old Mr Fitzwilliam rang his solicitor for an appointment on Friday and unexpectedly, because of a cancellation, he was able to come straight in on that very morning, whereas in the past he would usually have had to wait for a few days, or even a week.'

'So,' said the Reverend Mother, 'when he announced to his family that he was going to change his will, it would be expected that it wouldn't happen immediately, at least not for a few days. And if there was a murderer among them, they would think that they had to act relatively quickly while the old will was still valid.'

'Or, on the other hand,' said Dr Scher, 'my friend the major, having been told that he was to inherit, and perhaps knowing that his father had gone to see the solicitor . . . who knows he may even have driven him into the South Mall, they appeared to me to be on excellent terms when I met them in the Imperial Hotel at lunch time last Friday. As I say, the major might think, Well, if my father drops dead over the weekend or even on Monday morning, then I inherit a fortune, but then, by Tuesday Robert and the girls might be back in favour again and I will be out there in Palestine with nothing but my salary to live on and I will have an old age of living on an army pension. Can't you hear him saying that? Well, I can. These army fellows. Life is cheap to them.' Dr Scher sat back and looked defiantly from the Reverend Mother to Patrick.

Patrick nodded. 'He might even have told one of his sisters. He seems to be very close to his sister Monica. The will seems as though it was the important factor in this killing. I can't see what else could have motivated anyone to kill Mr Fitzwilliam.' Patrick mused through his recollections of the notes in the policeman's handbook. *Greed, Anger, Lust, Fear, Blackmail* . . . 'Though the man Dinan,' he said aloud, 'the man who was sacked, might have hated him, but somehow I can't see that he would have killed him. And I think that he blamed Robert more than he blamed old Mr Fitzwilliam. But I have had an informant who tells me that she thinks one of the sisters, Miss Monica Fitzwilliam, was blackmailing the major into buying her a large amount of clothes in Dowden's. According to my informant it would have cost her a year's salary to buy these garments.' Patrick looked at both elderly faces and saw interest, but not surprise.

'Her?' hinted Dr Scher.

'Eileen, I suppose,' explained the Reverend Mother and Patrick felt himself flush with embarrassment.

'She has a theory that Miss Monica might have been the one to kill her father in the hope that her generous brother would reward her.' Patrick shrugged his shoulders.

'What about Robert Fitzwilliam?' asked Dr Scher and Patrick nodded with relief.

'Yes,' he said. 'Somehow he fits the picture, better, although he did not, in fact, benefit, he may have hoped to. And certainly he had opportunity, whereas the major certainly had none.' He went into some detail about the evidence from the parlour maid at Glenville Place and the major's breakfast and the evidence from all at the Queen's Old Castle that the major had barely arrived through the door when his father fell from on high. 'So all in all, if it were one of the family, I would favour Robert, but he did not benefit from the murder. He had been disinherited completely. Not a penny left to him.'

'But then we can twist it in another direction,' said Dr Scher, 'and say that Robert says to himself, "My father is talking of changing his will. It will take him a week or so to do that and I cannot afford to allow him to leave me destitute. I just have a few days to act. How do I do it? Well, what about one of those gas capsules that my big brother has brought back from the war. If one of those is used, then he will be the one to be suspected." What do you think, Patrick? Sounds possible, doesn't it?' Dr Scher sat back with an air of one who has successfully acted a part. He looked from one face to the other. The Reverend Mother pursed her lips, though Patrick nodded, but then glanced through his notebook again.

'I'm not just thinking of the family, though,' said Patrick. 'There were a lot of people in the city who disliked old Mr Fitzwilliam. As I mentioned before, certainly one of his employees, the man who was facing the sack at the end of the week, the man called Michael Dinan, he would certainly bear a grudge. And there may be others among the counter staff, or even the apprentices who hated the man. He was not, by reputation, a pleasant man to work for.'

'It was an unusual way to murder anyone,' said the Reverend Mother thoughtfully. 'And unless the person was witnessed deliberately inserting the gas canister into the change barrel, it would be almost impossible to pin it on anyone. It is also, perhaps,' she went on, 'an easy way to murder someone. Quite unlike sticking a knife in someone, or hitting them over the head with an iron bar, or even emptying a revolver into a man's heart. But there is something else to take into account. This sending up of a gas cylinder would have a strong element of chance in it. After all, Mr Fitzwilliam could have spotted the difference, could even have recognized one of his son's gas canisters. He could, in fact, have gone straight to the door, thrown the cylinder away and allowed the gas to float harmlessly away in that huge building. It must be about forty feet high, at least. According to the young apprentice who helped me, all of the staff had witnessed these gas cylinders being used to take the smell of damp away from the goods in the shop. I think that the murderer could not have been sure that it would have worked, even if opened.'

'Or else old Mr Fitzwilliam might have recognized it for what it was and simply not opened it. After all there was a shelf load of these things down in his cellar. He must have been familiar with its appearance. Apparently he took a great interest in these gas cylinders, actually asked the major to bring some back with him as they had so many flood-damaged goods. Yes, you are right, Reverend Mother. It was a very chancy, very unsure way to murder someone. And though it looks most likely that the change barrel was sent up from the unmanned counter, that's not certain either. One of the apprentices might have been passing and been unable to resist the fun of whizzing one of these things up. I know, when I was a boy, I used to think that I would love to do that,' said Patrick, looking rather embarrassed as he confessed to such wild ideas in his boyhood.

'Oh, I meant to ask you whether there were any fingerprints on it, Patrick?' asked Dr Scher. 'I thought of that, you know, thought of it immediately and I picked it up with my handkerchief,' he said proudly to the Reverend Mother as he helped himself to another piece of cake. 'I'm a great fan of the Sherlock Holmes stories. Have you ever read them, Patrick? No, well, you should. I'll lend you some. The *Sign of Four* has a lot about fingerprints. You'll enjoy that.'

Patrick thought about his usual daily work. He thought about the overnight shop raids, the drunken fights down the quays, the wives with broken arms, the terrified children where both parents were almost permanently drunk, the ever-present threat from the IRA. And he thought about his biggest worry at the moment, the gang that managed prostitutes and were reputed to be actively recruiting twelve-year-olds of both sexes. He reviewed his daily workload which often stretched well into the night, sometimes almost to midnight, and could not see himself sitting by the fire with a novel about an amateur crime investigator in his hand. And he did not think that Sherlock Holmes's methods would work well in the troubled city of Cork. Nevertheless, Dr Scher meant well, so he nodded and smiled and hoped that the doctor would forget about his offer.

'And the fingerprints?' Dr Scher leaned forward eagerly.

'Well, I'm afraid that we couldn't get too far with them,' said Patrick apologetically. 'Joe had a go with this powder that we got from Dublin. Sprinkled it all over the canister. But, to be honest, you couldn't see much. It was all messed up, loads of different fingerprints, different sized fingers, I'd say. Looked as though half the shop had handled it.'

'They would have been a great novelty when the major brought them into the shop,' said the Reverend Mother thoughtfully. 'I understand that he brought a suitcase full of them. They would have been passed from hand to hand. The young apprentice, Brian Maloney, spoke to me very enthusiastically about them and how they got the smell out of the river-damaged goods.'

'They had a shelf load of them in the basement,' said Patrick. 'All standing up there, ready for anyone to help themselves. Of course they weren't considered particularly dangerous. And they wouldn't have been if Mr Fitzwilliam had any ventilation in that office of his. But he didn't. He was a man who felt the cold very much, according to his son. My sergeant, Joe, said the place was very hot and airless, even though Robert Fitzwilliam had turned off the gas fire by the time that he had got up there.'

'And so,' said Dr Scher thoughtfully, 'we might get a picture of our murderer. A man who grabs an opportunity.'

'Or a woman,' said the Reverend Mother. 'Remember this murder took no strength, no special knowledge, and probably could be done with very little risk to the murderer. You may not get a conviction with this, Patrick. It's possible that the murderer will go undiscovered and unpunished.'

Dr Scher shrugged his shoulders. 'Would that be a bad thing? After all he wasn't a particularly pleasant old man.'

'Murder, the deliberate taking of human life, is a very bad thing, Dr Scher,' said the Reverend Mother severely. 'And once someone, whether man or woman, has successfully committed one murder, he or she may commit another one. It may become a habit, an easy way to get rid of an enemy, to get rid of someone whose death will benefit you. No, Patrick, I don't think that you should accept that the murder may be unsolvable. Or, indeed, that it may be desirable to leave it unsolved. That's dangerous thinking. I am just warning you that it may be very difficult.'

There was, thought Patrick, an unusual atmosphere in the Reverend Mother's room. Almost as though she and Dr Scher were at odds with each other. Usually they were the best of friends and the Reverend Mother, he knew, relied on Dr Scher for his friendship, for his common sense as well as for his medical expertise. And had there been, he wondered, a slight emphasis on the word 'woman' and on the use of 'he' or 'she'. For himself he did not really suspect either of the daughters and nor the mother either. In fact, one look at that poor woman would tell anyone that she would be totally unable to plan something like sending up a gas canister to her husband's office and if by any chance she did do that, well, then her sons would act quickly and she would find herself in one of those private mental hospitals before the police could even draw up a warrant for arrest.

And yet, Dr Scher had a worried look about him. The Reverend Mother, he thought, did not look very well. It was unusual for her to sit so closely to the fire. He saw Dr Scher shoot a few glances at her. And even when he spoke there was a slightly forced note in his voice.

'I think that I'll help myself to another one of Sister Bernadette's delicious cakes,' he said. 'Great cook, Sister Bernadette. She's a treasure to your establishment, Reverend Mother. Think of what those hotel cakes were like after the funeral. I just couldn't fancy them at all.'

'Not with all those hungry boy apprentices watching every move; not with that very thin child,' said the Reverend Mother. She had the air of one who is glad to turn the conversation. 'Did you notice that boy, Dr Scher? It's rare to see a boy of that age reduced to skin and bone unless he has tuberculosis or something like that. I wonder if he is worked too hard or doesn't get enough to eat for a growing boy.' Patrick noticed how she watched Dr Scher as she said those words. He waited with interest to see what the doctor said. It was apparent, from his nod, that he, too, had noticed that child. The boy who was an apprentice on the Millinery counter. John Joe Burke. Painfully thin. Frightened, also. He could bet on that. He had questioned him as carefully as he could, but had elicited little except that one word: 'dunno'.

'Name of John Joseph Burke,' said Dr Scher after a moment. 'So he said. I'm sure that he was a more worthy recipient of the slice of chocolate cake than I would have been. I had a feeling that all of these boys were too thin. Hungry, too, but I wouldn't take too much notice of that. Growing boys should be hungry, but that chap, scared stiff, poor young fellow. Had to force him to take it. To be honest,' he said looking slightly embarrassed, 'it did my heart good to see him swallow it down in a couple of bites. I swear that he looked brighter after it. I was only sorry that I couldn't take him home and give him a few square meals, but I suppose that there is a law about stealing apprentices. And I hope that there is a law about feeding apprentices? Is that right, Patrick?'

'I'm not sure. It's not something that I've come across. I must look it up, though nobody has ever asked about it. I suppose there are rules, aren't there? There must be,' said Patrick hesitantly. 'I suppose that the employers have to sign something to commit them to give their apprentices food and lodging, suitable food and suitable lodging.' He stopped then. The laws of apprenticeship came from England. Appropriate food and lodging in a prosperous English town might not work out to be quite the same thing in Cork. Standards were low amongst the poor of the city. He had seen a child fight a seagull for a mouldy slice of bread. Were the Fitzwilliams, a prosperous family, treating their apprentices correctly? It was not a question that had ever occurred to him.

He looked toward Dr Scher but the doctor was busying himself with the teapot and the cake knife and only said, almost mechanically, 'Ah, yes, Patrick, you could do a bit of questioning of those apprentices. Sharp-eyed at that age. See things that we old people miss out on. And while you are doing it, well, you'd be told a few tales about how they are treated, I'd lay a bet on that.'

Patrick accepted the cup of tea and welcomed the cake. Dr Scher had given him his opening. He could not waste time debating matters that were not his business. He had to solve the murder of a prominent Cork citizen. A murder that occurred within the man's own shop and in the full view of a couple of hundred of Cork's citizens.

'I wanted to ask you about young Brian, Reverend Mother, the apprentice who was with you, young Brian Maloney. Mr Robert Fitzwilliam brought up his name. Said that he was unreliable. I wondered what your impression of him was.' It wasn't quite a question, but he saw her eyes look speculative and knew that, sooner or later, she would answer that query. In the meantime he stirred his tea, nibbled at his cake and pondered over the difficulties of the case. 'If it was any other case, I'd be thanking God for having all those boys as witnesses!' The words burst from him with a vigour that made him feel slightly ashamed. He struggled to find the words that would explain his frustrations. 'You see, at that age they are as smart as paint and they usually see everything that is going on. You're right, there, Dr Scher. If this was a case of a murder down on the quays, or even on board a ship, they'd all be bursting to tell me what had gone on. But this is different. It's very different, Reverend Mother. These boys are probably terrified that they will lose their place if they say a word against their employers; that they'll be out on the street even if they say a word that their employers haven't already approved. So you see . . .' Patrick turned from the Reverend Mother to Dr Scher and then spread his fingers wide. He gave an exasperated sigh and said, 'So you see, I don't know whether to accept their evidence, to believe it, or totally disregard it. Five of them, five young smart lads, all standing at those counters that I am interested in, all of them ready to be sent on errands, eyes wide open, standing there, looking around them.'

'And, of course, a sixth who was with me, and who would certainly have had his eyes open,' put in the Reverend Mother.

'You think that they have been browbeaten, have been bullied; have been trained not to open their mouths unless they have been told what to say, is that it?' queried Dr Scher.

'I do,' said Patrick. 'And what's worse is that I don't know how to get them to talk openly to me. If I take them down to the police station, well, their employers could reasonably object to that. Could say that it disrupted the work of the shop. And, it was probably only in the stress of the moment that Joe got away with interviewing them by themselves. The employer probably has a right to be with them.' Of course, he thought, if it were true that the major was now the owner of the shop then he would be easier to deal with than his younger brother.

'I do see what you mean, Patrick,' said the Reverend Mother. He had the impression that she was reading his thoughts. 'There is, however, a third course. If I were you, I would ask the questions, whether in front of the employer, or when the boys are alone, and, Patrick, I would listen very carefully to the answers, but I would also evaluate what else was meant below the surface. I would ask myself what the boy's attitude conveyed, what was his reaction to a name or to the recollection of a procedure. And, of course, you would have to take into account the different personalities of the boys. Brian Maloney, as I remember him seven years ago, was a very confident, rather open, rather friendly sort of boy, very chatty and exuberant. That may now be overlaid with a layer of caution, but I would have thought that the basic personality is still there. Some of the other boys struck me as having a very different personality.'

The Reverend Mother, thought Patrick, appeared to be hesitant, just a little unsure. He opened his mouth to assure her that her views on Brian were of great use to him, and then he closed it. There was some more to come. He knew that. She was thinking it over. He waited, sipping his tea and nibbling the cake in order to satisfy Dr Scher.

'I think that if someone said to me that a boy was un-reliable, I would certainly check to see whether that was the truth, but I think I might also wonder why a man who employed the boy would have said such a thing. After all, he wasn't giving a reference; you weren't seeking to employ the boy and so "unreliable" was an odd word to choose, was it not?' The Reverend Mother sat back and looked meditatively into the fire.

'I suppose,' said Patrick hesitantly, 'that he might have been warning me not to take his evidence seriously.'

'And did Brian have any evidence to give?' asked the Reverend Mother.

Patrick looked through his notes. 'Very little,' he said. 'Nothing of any consequence. But, of course, Mrs Fitzwilliam did accuse him of being the one that had committed a murder.'

'And he was loose around the shop and could have gone to that Men's Shoes counter. And I suppose one of the other boys might just have sent up the gas canister when their superior had turned their back. Come to that, I suppose that I could have sent it up, myself,' said Dr Scher. He spoke hurriedly and almost as though he wished to turn the conversation from the accusation made by Mrs Fitzwilliam by bringing up remote possibilities for suspects. His concern for his patient was understandable and praiseworthy, thought Patrick impatiently, but he, Patrick, had a difficult and mystifying murder to solve and he needed any possible insights into this strange family. And Brian Maloney was a child with his life in front of him and no parent or family to support him. He, like Patrick, had been one of the Reverend Mother's pupils and now, he thought approvingly, she felt a duty towards the boy. It was very easy for the rich and the powerful to load their sins onto the shoulders of the poor and those without connections. Patrick felt that he could read the Reverend Mother's mind and he waited now for her to challenge the suspicion that had been voiced against Brian Maloney.

'I suppose,' she said firmly, 'that we all have it in our minds the accusation made by Mrs Fitzwilliam, when she said that Brian was responsible for sending up the change barrel with the deadly gas cylinder enclosed within it. Dr Scher is the lady's medical attendant and, I have no doubt, Patrick, that if it is a police necessity, he will be able to talk to you in private.' She stopped. She had, Patrick noticed, made it quite clear that she did not want anything to do with the business of Mrs Fitzwilliam's mental health. 'Brian,' she continued, her voice dispassionate and even, 'was with me for most of the time from the opening of the shop, right up to the time when I returned to the convent. He walked by my side, carried the basket and fetched articles which I pointed to. Normally, I understand, he would have been at the Men's Shoes counter and under the supervision of Mr Séamus O'Connor. When he left me, it was by my wish and he seemed to reappear with lightning speed. So I think that I can vouch for him. But that is not to say that he didn't disappear from time to time as he went to fetch me another towel or a child's gymslip. There would have been no reason, however, for him to go to the Men's Shoe department.'

'Nobody there at that counter when I picked up that pair of shoes for that poor one-legged man,' said Dr Scher. 'Don't know how reliable a witness I would be for things going on around me in the street, but I do know that I picked up that bargain pair of the largest shoes I could find and looked around to see if I could get anyone to take the money for them – and there was no one to take my money.'

'It wasn't supposed to be manned that morning,' said Patrick. 'Séamus O'Connor had been sent by Mr Robert down into the basement in order to deal with more of the flood-damaged stock. It was definitely Mr Robert who gave him that order, not Mr Fitzwilliam Senior, according to Joe. I checked on that.' He smiled a little at the approving nod from the Reverend Mother. 'I always do double-check on things,' he said, feeling slightly embarrassed. 'I find it saves a lot of time later on if I can be sure that I've done a double-check on everything.'

'Significant, that, isn't it? What do you think, Reverend Mother? I mean that Robert Fitzwilliam was the one who made sure that no one was on that counter,' said Dr Scher.

Patrick waited for her to comment but she said nothing. She wore a slight frown on her face and he wondered what she was thinking. After a few moments, he filled the silence after Dr Scher's comment. It did him good, he thought, to voice his thoughts aloud. Somehow to hear them said meant that he could assess whether they rang true. A clear, logical setting out of the facts was often a trigger to new thoughts. That had been his experience.

'There had been six change barrels up there on the desk in the office,' he said, picturing them in his mind as he spoke. 'Each one had been emptied of its canister when Mr Fitzwilliam fell to his death. One of them came up from that unmanned counter, but it is impossible to tell which one of them held the gas cylinder because all six barrels were empty. Joe smelled each one of them but could get no hint of gas from any one of the six. Understandable as the gas canister would have been closed when put in and only opened after it had been taken out of the barrel. More likely the cover was just on loosely and fell off when the canister was tipped out.' Patrick looked from one elderly face to the other and then got up impatiently and went to the window. Murder, he thought, irritably, was such an illogical business. No one committed murder unless they were a little bit mad and it was hard for a rational man with a plodding brain like his to delve into the mind of someone who was not quite sane.

'Unmanned, on purpose? If you think that, then you must think that Robert Fitzwilliam was the one who killed his father, or who planned it in any case.' Dr Scher returned his tea cup to its saucer with a decisive bang.

'Not necessarily,' said the Reverend Mother drily. Patrick wondered at her tone. Did she think that the doctor was distracting attention from Mrs Fitzwilliam and her daughters? It was possible that he was. An old-fashioned man, Dr Scher. Found it hard to think evil of women. Wouldn't mind putting the blame on Robert's shoulders. Did that, thought Patrick, mean that Dr Scher had suspicions of Mrs Fitzwilliam? Hope not, thought Patrick. I'd never get a conviction. That apprentice of hers is a bag of nerves. Never get him to be convincing in the witness box. And all Cork would be up in arms at the very thought of an elderly woman who suffered from her nerves being removed from her home, taken to the police station and from there to the gaol. It would be the end of his career if he made a mistake with this murder.

But I'm damned if they get me to fix it onto someone else who is innocent, he thought and then almost blushed as he saw the Reverend Mother's eyes on him.

'What do you think about Robert Fitzwilliam, Patrick?' she

asked and Patrick quickly averted his mind from that strange old woman and the sudden vision of her stuffing the gas cylinder into the change barrel. If John Joe Burke had seen her, well that explained why he was such a bundle of nerves, he thought, before replying to the Reverend Mother's question.

'It's quite understandable that Robert Fitzwilliam, as floor manager, had told Séamus O'Connor to leave his counter and to work among the damaged goods, sorting them out according to the degree of flood damage and saleability,' he said thoughtfully. 'On a Monday morning, it was unlikely that men, who had the money to purchase shoes, would be at leisure to visit the shop. But, of course, that meant that the Men's Shoes counter had no one standing there and . . .'

'Anyone could have seized the opportunity . . .' put in Dr Scher.

'I noticed, when I was there, how the light came and went in that shop,' said the Reverend Mother. 'It got quite dark when it started to rain. Anyone who worked there would have known that there would be a moment when no one would notice them. Our skies here are very rarely without clouds and, of course, fog can shut out the light almost as well as rain.'

Patrick made a note on the back page of his notebook. That, of course, he said to himself, was a good point. In fine weather and in daylight the Queen's Old Castle was mainly lit from above, through those sheets of glass, but rain fell in Cork city on two days out of three and fog filled many of those rain-free days. The shop had bright periods and then suddenly became full of shadows. Very easy for someone to wait for a cloud and then to quickly insert the deadly gas canister into the change barrel. Would anyone notice in a shop full of people? He doubted it.

'Patrick, who would have sent for Mr O'Connor if he had been wanted?' asked Dr Scher.

Patrick produced a neatly-drawn plan, folded and secured with a rubber band inside the back cover of his notebook and smiled a little as he noticed how the Reverend Mother nodded approval.

'I checked on that,' he said. 'It was Miss Mulcahy, Miss Maria Mulcahy. Séamus O'Connor had said that he left instructions at the Ladies' Shoes counter that he was to be called if anyone needed a pair of men's shoes.' After a moment, he said, 'The word is that they're doing a line.'

'Doing a line?' Dr Scher raised his eyebrows at the Reverend Mother.

'Walking out together, a Cork term for a sort of pre-engagement,' translated the Reverend Mother, adding tartly, 'goodness, me, Dr Scher, surely you know what "doing a line" means, after all the years that you have spent in Cork.' She turned back to Patrick. 'Would you have thought that she would connive at murder, though? She's a niece of Sister Philomena. She's often visited the convent. A fairly strait-laced young lady, I would have thought. Not so young now; if she and Séamus O'Connor did have an understanding, then it is time for them to get married.'

Probably meant that Maria Mulcahy would soon be approaching the age when she could no longer have children, thought Patrick, remembering that the same thought had occurred to him. And, he remembered, that he could not see much wrong with that. Cork was too full of children that no one was looking after, in his opinion. And the Church should stop forcing people to have children, he thought. The sailors down the quays were always selling rubber condoms brought over from England, but it would be a mortal sin for any church-going couple to use one of those. The only other alternative was for a man to wait until the woman of his choice was near to the end of her childbearing years. And that, he thought, was not a very attractive thought.

And then he was conscious of the Reverend Mother's eyes upon him and felt himself blush. He tried to shift the feelings of guilt from his mind, to sit up straight and to look competent and in charge.

'There was no sign of this young lady, or of her apprentice, when I went to the Men's Shoes counter,' said Dr Scher. 'I stood for a few minutes with them in my hand, holding them up high, in fact. I was looking all around and I wondered whether to go the Ladies' Shoes counter, but when I wandered over,

there was no one there except a young boy and he said that
he was not allowed to take money and he was told not to leave
the counter until Miss Mulcahy came back. So Miss Maria
Mulcahy, she who is doing a line, was not at her counter at
that moment, just a little apprentice.'

'Name of Christy Callinan.' Patrick checked through his
notebook. 'Did he look guilty, look as though he had been told
to keep a secret?'

'I must confess that he just looked bored,' said Dr Scher.
'Shame to have a young lad like that confined indoors from
eight in the morning until eight at night. Should be out kicking
a ball.'

Patrick looked slightly startled at that. 'He's lucky to have a
job and a future,' he said severely. 'But I wonder where Miss
Maria Mulcahy had got to.'

'I remember reading an old copy of a magazine at my tailor's
– called *The Tailor and the Cutter*. Anyway they had an adver-
tisement for staff and at the end of a long list of requirements
it said, invitingly: "The calls of Nature are permitted and
Clerical Staff may use the garden below the second gate." I
wonder whether Mr Fitzwilliam made any such provision for
his unfortunate staff,' mused Dr Scher.

'I should imagine, Dr Scher, that there could be many valid
reasons for Miss Mulcahy to be absent from her counter,' said
the Reverend Mother, a stern eye quelling the doctor before
he speculated any further and Patrick, feeling that blush creep
up again, busied himself with turning over the pages of his
notebook. 'Query: Miss Mulcahy missing from counter,' he
wrote and then read it aloud.

'And that would have been just a few minutes before Mr
Fitzwilliam fell to the ground, because I had gone off towards
the main door looking for someone to take my money when
I heard the crash,' said Dr Scher in placid tones. 'Well, well,
well, Reverend Mother. Sister Philomena's niece and all, as
they say here in Cork.'

The Reverend Mother, noticed Patrick, gave Dr Scher a
sharp look, but she said nothing, though her face when she
turned it towards him, bore an expectant look, as though
she expected him to challenge the doctor.

'Can't see why Miss Maria Mulcahy could have any reason to try to murder her employer,' said Patrick readily. 'Jobs are scarce enough in Cork and she was lucky to have her place. I don't think that Mr Robert Fitzwilliam, as floor manager, was particularly popular so there would be no reason to get rid of the old boss in the hope that the son would be any nicer. And at that stage, most people would have thought that Robert Fitzwilliam would go on managing the business after his father's death, just as he always did.' What an extraordinary business that was. To cut out the son who had worked in that shop for at least twenty years, or longer, in order to leave the whole business to the son who had hardly darkened the door during all the time that Patrick had known the shop.

'Would it be possible for Miss Maria Mulcahy to have known about the proposed change of the will?' asked the Reverend Mother. 'Presumably she knew that the shop had been left to Robert originally. It was probably the reason why she went to the cinema with him. It formed a second string to her bow and meant that she had matters of interest to communicate to Mr O'Connor.'

Patrick looked at her without surprise. Amazing how the Reverend Mother usually knew about all of those matters. She had heard about Robert taking the shop girl to the cinema. 'Mr Robert could have told her that he would inherit the shop, I suppose,' he said. Dr Scher, he noticed, was grinning. So he knew, also. Terrible place for gossip, this city, thought Patrick.

'Could have whispered it into her ear while the credits were rolling on the big screen,' said Dr Scher. 'They were very great together. So the word on the street goes, anyway.' Not a Cork man, but he had acquired the Cork love of gossip. He looked from one to the other of them, obviously waiting for exclamations.

'I'm sure, Dr Scher, that you don't mean that our police should listen to gossip on the street corners,' said the Reverend Mother tartly. 'Patrick is a man who deals in facts and in reliable information.'

Patrick smiled. He began to feel better. He sat back in his chair. So Michael Dinan was right. Well, well, well. He said nothing, though. And he would have laid a large bet on the certainty that the Reverend Mother knew all the facts about Robert, that he had been known to fiddle the books, and possibly that he had been to the cinema with Maria Mulcahy. *A wise man holds his tongue.* Someone had said that. Could it have been a quote from the Bible? And, of course, 'woman' could be substituted for 'man'. Wherever it came from it was a true saying. He cast a quick look at the impassive face opposite to his and then looked back at Dr Scher.

'Tell me all about it, doctor,' he invited and crossed his legs. 'What's the word on the street, then?'

'Well,' said Dr Scher with an air of huge enjoyment, 'lots of excitement about this. Everyone chatting about it in the university today. The way I heard it, Major Fitzwilliam would no more be interested in managing a shop than the man in the moon. The word is that the brothers will quarrel, Robert will go off; Blarney Mills have been advertising for a manager and so the major will have to have someone to manage for him and Séamus O'Connor is the senior man, so Séamus O'Connor becomes the manager and the major installs tills at each counter and gets rid of all of the paraphernalia of those change barrels whizzing up and down the shop. And then the major goes off, to Palestine, I've heard, leaving arrangements for the profits to be lodged in his bank. And so it might be a happy ending for Sister Philomena's niece, Reverend Mother. She can have her pick. Either Séamus O'Connor, or the new manager in the Blarney Mills. And, I suppose, that if Sister Philomena's niece helped the old man on his way, well, she can go and confess her sin to a priest and be forgiven.'

Dr Scher, thought Patrick astutely, was deeply worried. It was not like him to mock the religious ceremonies of the church, nor to try to rile the Reverend Mother like this. The Reverend Mother he saw was looking across at the man with concern. She, like Patrick, would have heard the note of pain in the doctor's voice. Mrs Fitzwilliam! There would be a strong relationship between a vulnerable patient and a caring doctor. Patrick had noticed how careful he was of her. And now he was very concerned to remove any chance of suspicion falling upon Mrs Fitzwilliam or upon her daughters.

Patrick got to his feet. He had a lot of new ideas in his head and his thoughts felt as though they had been sifted and were now sitting in orderly heaps ready for him to inspect them. He would walk along the quays for a while and then go back to his office. Efficient paperwork, meticulous checking of evidence, that was what would solve this murder case.

FOURTEEN

Sunday for the nuns and the lay sisters at the convent of St Mary's Isle was the usual day for visits from family and friends. Sister Bernadette in the kitchen always baked some cakes, and various parlours, as well as the recreation room, had fires lit and were available for the entertainment of the visitors.

The Reverend Mother usually walked around the convent for half an hour or so, available to all, looking in through open doors, ready to nod and smile or to exchange some words, but never intruding by opening closed doors or by interrupting any low-voiced conversations. However, when she approached the north parlour that day, she was arrested by a chorus of exclamations and by the words 'Queen's Old Castle'. Somebody was telling an exciting story, drawing it out, judging by the gasps. The Reverend Mother slowed to a halt and wondered whether to join the animated crowd, searching her conscience for an excuse. At that moment, Sister Bernadette came down the corridor trundling a heavily weighed trolley with a squeaking wheel; she might, if she lingered, be of use to her in opening the door. However, despite the sounds of questions and interjections from within the parlour, sharp ears had heard the sound and the door was thrown open by a young boy before she could lift her hand to knock politely.

'Goodness me, who is this new nun?' asked the Reverend Mother. The wit was feeble by any standards, but Christy Callinan, apprentice to Maria Mulcahy, was young enough to enjoy the joke. When he became older, thought the Reverend Mother, he might become self-conscious about those very protruding teeth, but now they added to the charm of his broad grin and hearty laugh.

'The Reverend Mother thought that I was a nun,' he called back to the group in the parlour and Sister Philomena got up in rather a flustered way, while her niece Miss Maria Mulcahy looked embarrassed. Amazing how all of those holy nuns were enjoying so intensely the story of that terrible death. Still, thought the Reverend Mother, most of their lives are fairly dull. This event, the story of the gas canister being sent up, hidden inside a change barrel, was, after all, an extraordinary one.

'How nice to see you again, Miss Mulcahy,' she said, coming into the room and shaking hands with the guest. It was good of the woman to bring the boy with her, she thought. It showed that she had a motherly attitude to her young apprentice. His accent was that of a boy from the country, it had the sing-song lilt of west Cork. Unlike Brian Maloney, he would not have school friends to see on his one day off and might well be bored and miserable unless a relative made the long journey into the city to see him.

'We've all been admiring his jacket. Look at that for smartness!' Sister Philomena beamed at the boy. 'Tell the Reverend Mother who bought that for you, Christy, won't you?'

'Miss Mulcahy,' said the boy. He did not, thought the Reverend Mother, say it with gratitude, nor even with a child-like pleasure, but with a certain measure of self-satisfaction, or was there even a slightly sly note in his voice. Not cheap, that jacket. Good wool. She felt it admiringly. A good Donegal tweed.

'Got it in the Munster Arcade, would you believe it?' continued Sister Philomena determined to display her niece's generosity. Not in the Queen's Old Castle, then, but in the much more expensive and more up-market Munster Arcade, in the heart of Patrick Street.

Interesting!

'Nothing for me, thank you, Sister Bernadette,' said the Reverend Mother, rising to her feet after a few minutes. 'I'm going to take a turn in the garden. Christy, would you like to come with me and see our hens?' It was the only thing that she could think of that might possibly interest a young boy on the convent premises, but the chorus of approval and of voices assuring Christy that he would love to see them gave immediate approbation to her suggestion. Christy, himself, didn't look at all convinced of this. Probably a country boy who had seen hens all of his life, unlike the city children of the school who had all been fascinated by the sight of those colourful creatures who laid tasty food for their benefit.

Nevertheless, she had enthusiastic backing for her offer. The convivial crowd in the parlour wanted to get rid of Christy. His novelty had faded. Now they wanted to question Maria Mulcahy without sharp ears listening in, and so Christy was told firmly that he would love the hens, was presented with a slice of cake by Sister Philomena and was ushered quickly to the door and told to be a good boy by Miss Mulcahy.

The Reverend Mother gave him a couple of minutes of peace to chew on the cake as she led the way towards the door to the garden. The river, she noticed, interested him more than the hens. He was from Baltimore, by the sea, and he wanted to be a fisherman, he told her, licking the crumbs from between his fingers. Didn't like the fish in Cork, not nice. Not fresh. He wished that he was back in Baltimore and out on a boat on a fine day like this. And his mam would fry up some fish with a bit of dripping that she got from the woman she worked for. He was knowledgeable about fish. Shrewd, too. Could see the problem of fish in Cork city. Too much filthy muck went into that river, he told her assertively, adding, 'You need to have fresh water for fish, Reverend Mother, and then when you catch them, you need to fry them when they are fresh. Fish do be going off awful quick.'

Half the time his father and his brothers couldn't sell their catch, apparently, before it started to go off. The locals caught their own fish, so they had to get them to the towns inland, or even to the city itself. Not an easy life, but there was a strong note of nostalgia in his voice.

'So what do you do if you can't sell the fish?' asked the Reverend Mother, pleased to have found a subject that interested him since her hens had failed so miserably to engage his attention.

'Well, we'd be smoking the mackerel on the beach,' he told her. 'You get tons of them in August. The sea do be black with them. Not a chance of selling them in August. Everyone catches their own. So we smoke tons of them and keep them to sell in the winter time. We eat them ourselves too. Plenty to go around. When the mackerel come in, you'd be able to fish them out with a bucket from the pier. Even someone like you would be able to do it, Reverend Mother,' he told her, his face animated and his very blue eyes glowing. She was touched and moved by his enthusiasm. And then a shadow came over his face.

'I'd give anything to be back there.' His lips closed over the protruding teeth. 'Don't like that place. It's boring.' There was an unchild-like look of determination on his face, and, perhaps, the look of one who feels he may have said too much.

'So you don't fancy spending your life working in a shop?' The situation intrigued the Reverend Mother as she half-listened to his description of how boring all of the adults in the shop were – though he did make an exception for the major, who was, according to Christy, a gas man. The boy from the country had already picked up the Cork slang word 'gas' and the Reverend Mother listened with amusement to the major's efforts to amuse the young apprentices and astonish them with stories of tricks played in army life. But then she went back to thinking about Christy. The journey to Baltimore could take six hours by horse and cart to the city of Cork. What had brought the boy to a shop here in this city that he hated? If the boy wanted that sort of work, then there must surely be plenty of shops in Skibberean.

He shrugged and made a face when she put the question to him. 'It was me mam's idea.' And then reluctantly he continued, 'Me brother was drowned and she didn't want me to go on the boats, too.'

'I can understand that,' said the Reverend Mother. 'Are you the youngest boy?' It didn't, she thought, explain the long distance. The substantial town of Skibberean would have been relatively near. She was sure that Skibberean had plenty of big shops, if a career in a shop was wanted for the boy. And then inspiration struck.

'Was your mother from the city here?' she asked.

He gave her a quick upwards glance. A smart boy, she thought. There was immediate comprehension in his face as if he had followed her thoughts.

'She talked me uncle into it. My Uncle Séamus,' he said more formally.

'Séamus?'

'Mr O'Connor. Gents' Shoes. I live with him and me grannie.' His explanation was succinct and explained everything. A large family, probably, a dangerous way of making a living, a much-loved youngest son. An obliging brother in Cork and then a boy from the glittering seas of West Cork was transplanted to the dank fogs of this marshy city. He didn't like it and she could not blame him. Life on a fishing boat was exciting and challenging. Standing around in a shop all day was poor exchange for battling with the waves. Being servile to counter hands, employers and customers was an even poorer exchange for the excitement of landing a net full of glittering mackerel. As for death, well, it was not something that a twelve-year-old worried too much about. Nor did the Reverend Mother. Christy, she thought, had more chance of picking up the deadly tuberculosis in this fetid city as of being drowned among the Atlantic waves of West Cork.

'You'd like to go back to Baltimore.' Not a real question and he didn't proffer any reply, but his lips closed tightly again over his teeth and there was something very dogged about the face that gazed out into the murky depths of the polluted river. Her mind turned over various ideas. The connection between Séamus O'Connor and the apprentice made Miss Mulcahy's benign and maternal attitude to her young apprentice appear understandable. But in her experience, uncles were not that interested in nephews. What did she hope to gain?

And even if Séamus O'Connor was devoted to young Christy Callinan, a jacket from the Munster Arcade for the man's nephew was an excessively expensive way of currying favour with the uncle. The Reverend Mother looked down at the determined face and turned matters over in her mind.

And then she pounced. 'Why did Miss Mulcahy buy you that jacket?' she asked bluntly.

He was very taken aback. She did not take her eyes off him, but stayed looking appraisingly at the sulky face. A hen scuttled past them, giving a sudden squawk, but he did not move, just stayed looking defiantly up at her. Boys, she thought, reached a growth spurt much later than girls and some boys did not start to shoot up until they were seventeen or eighteen. He had broad shoulders and looked well-fed, well covered with flesh, but undoubtedly small for his age, something that probably endeared him to Miss Mulcahy who could regard him as a child. But there was now something quite unchild-like about his face. He had heard something in her voice, had extrapolated some hidden meaning in her words and it had made him wary. He opened his mouth, displayed the protruding teeth in an endearing and child-like grin.

'She's ever so nice,' he said winningly.

The Reverend Mother raised her eyebrows at him.

It worked with him, worked as well with boys as with girls, she told herself. He knew that she didn't believe him. The blue eyes flickered as he began to talk, quite rapidly, and in a voice that held a note of anxiety as he strove to convince her.

'I do be doing lots of jobs for her,' he said, a child-like cadence in his West Cork sing-song voice. 'I'd do be picking up things from the floor, and polishing the counter and tying the ladies' shoe laces and putting shoes back into boxes and dusting the footstools and . . .' His invention began to run out and the Reverend Mother was unimpressed. She nodded her head impatiently.

'That's right,' she said. 'That would be what an apprentice would have to do, wouldn't it? I was talking to Brian Maloney and he was telling me the jobs he had to do in the Men's Shoes department.'

She left it at that, interested to see what he would say to it. He was disconcerted. She could see that, see the way that his eyes flickered and his lips tightened once again over his teeth. Had he been teased about those teeth, she wondered. If he had, he bore few scars. A young man very sure of himself and very sure of his ability to deal with women. His mother's pet, in all probability.

'And so you were in the stock cupboard sorting out the boxes at the time when Mr Fitzwilliam fell.' There had been, according to Patrick, a discrepancy between the stories told by three of the apprentices, those attached to Kitty Fitzwilliam, her sister Monica, and Maria Mulcahy. All of these three ladies had said that their apprentice had been with them during that time, but Henry Spiller said he was in the basement, Tom Donovan had denied loading the change barrel and said that he had gone to fetch some more brown paper and Christy Callinan said that he had been in the stock cupboard.

'I made a mistake.' Christy widened his blue eyes at her. 'If you make a mistake, you must own up,' he added in virtuous fashion, no doubt believing that was the sort of thing that you parroted to the teaching profession. 'I'm going to tell the peelers that when they come around next. I'll tell them that I made a mistake. I wasn't in the store cupboard at all. I was back at the counter.' He kicked at a hen investigating his shoelace and looked petulantly around the empty convent garden.

'Think I'd better be getting back, now,' he said. 'Miss Mulcahy will be looking for me.'

She ignored that. 'Tell me about Mr Robert Fitzwilliam. Is he kind to you, just like Miss Mulcahy is.'

He made a face at that, but didn't reply, just peeped at her tentatively. She didn't press the question.

'And his brother, Major Fitzwilliam?' she asked.

His face cleared at that. It brightened to a smile. 'The major is great gas,' he said, using the Cork slang word without appearing conscious of its appropriateness in the circumstances. 'He do be telling us about the tricks that the drummer boys play and the fun that they have. Nearly frightened the life out of their sergeant once. He was choking and coughing. He thought he was a goner! Though he'd die! Brightened up a dull Monday, that's what the major said.'

She thought that sounded a stupid anecdote to tell young boys, and interestingly he seemed to read her thoughts. 'I'd never do things like that,' he said virtuously; 'just do what Miss Mulcahy tells me to do, that's why she gives me presents.' He looked around to see whether there was anything else of interest to do in the convent garden and gave an elaborate shiver. 'I'd better be getting back,' he said again. 'She might be worrying about me.'

'Yes, you go back,' said the Reverend Mother. The air was

damp and she felt slightly shivery herself, but she doubted whether a healthy, well-covered young boy, wearing a tweed jacket, could really be cold. A bit of an actor, young Christy Callinan, she decided. Nevertheless, her curiosity had been satisfied and so he could go back to his admirers. 'But first of all pop into the kitchen and tell Sister Bernadette that I have a visitor,' she said, looking towards the gate.

He went off with alacrity, running quite fast down the garden path and through the back door. She did not follow him, but turned towards the front of the school. The brief spell of sunshine was over and the fog was closing down over the city again, dense and heavy. Soon it might rain. She had seen a pair of car headlights come slowly along the street. A battered Humber had pulled up at the front gate and her feet had begun to feel cold. A hot cup of tea and a chat by the fire with the knowledgeable Dr Scher would probably be more fruitful than trying to get information out of this boy. She was, in any case, now quite sure why Christy Callinan had got that expensive present. Had Maria told a lie to the police and now was relying on Christy to back her up? He would not betray any secrets when questioned by the police. And the jacket, something that might have cost a week's salary for Miss Mulcahy, was to ensure his continued silence; there could be little other reason for it.

But if Miss Maria Mulcahy, niece to the virtuous Sister Philomena, had been involved in the murder of Mr Fitzwilliam, there was another question to answer.

Why should she? What was in it for her? Were Séamus O'Connor and she on such intimate terms that the sending up of the gas cylinder could have been planned between them. Or had it been her own idea, the last desperate act of a woman who had seen her youth dwindle away and was now faced with the prospect of a childless and lonely old age unless her proposed husband could be brought to the point of proposing. Or could she have sent up the gas to help Robert to inherit his father's fortune? It could have been so easily done. The Men's Shoe department, though the fitting rooms were blocked off from each other by a discreet screen, was almost a continuation of the Ladies' Shoe department. And Miss

Mulcahy had been left in charge of both. It would have been quite simple, thought the Reverend Mother, as she opened the gate, for her to have got rid of Christy on some errand and to have popped down to the other counter. A steady nerve, a steady hand and she could have been back, standing next to her own till, almost before the change barrel from Men's Shoes went flying up on its wire. And she may well have had something of her own to go up also, something that had not required change.

Probably only a sharp-eyed boy, who thoroughly understood the business, might have speculated about what she had been doing when she had sent him on an unnecessary errand.

But if Miss Maria Mulcahy had bribed the boy, ensured his silence with that expensive jacket, which marriage was she contemplating? The long-awaited marriage with Séamus O'Connor? Or the new, secret affair with the son of the owner? Dangerous one that. Robert had been warned by his father that he would be disinherited if he did not give up that business. What if the murder had been planned between the two of them? Robert knew that his father proposed changing his will. Might have confided in her. She would have listened to him with dismay. If Robert were to be disinherited there would be no chance of him embarking on a marriage to a woman with no money of her own. Would she think that she had to act immediately? Maria Mulcahy knew that if she was going to get married, it had to be soon, or else her hope of bearing a child would wander into the realms of an extremely unlikely dream. The Reverend Mother thought that it was a possible scenario. Robert, Mr Robert, as floor manager, would be here and there, all over the shop, but wherever he went, eyes would be upon him. They would all be aware of his presence, perhaps apprehensive of receiving a reprimand, certainly alert for any instruction or command. No, thought the Reverend Mother as she went to greet her guest, if Robert was involved in the murder of his father, the strong probability was that he had an accomplice.

By the time that she had reached the gate, Dr Scher was already out of his car and was locking away the starting handle into

the boot at the back. She waited while he did that and then
accompanied him back into the convent.

'So, Dr Scher,' she said as soon as the door of her room
was securely closed behind them, 'tell me, what is the news
on the town? Will he sell, or will he keep?'

He didn't pretend to misunderstand her. 'Sell, of course.
What does he want with that place? He's off to Palestine. Nice
hot climate, good place to live if you're from the top drawer
and have a good job.' He put the poker in the fire and riddled
it vigorously, and added an artistic arrangement of carefully
placed coals on to the smouldering remnants of the morning's
stoking. 'You must keep warm, Reverend Mother. You're no
chicken, you know. Something like pneumonia is dangerous
at your age. Cork is a bad place for pneumonia and pleurisy.
People die like flies from them. And I don't like the sound of
that cough of yours.'

'Funny, I was just thinking about the city of Cork,' she said,
turning the conversation. 'I was thinking about Cork and I
was comparing it with Baltimore, a lovely village, just on the
edge of the far south-west coast of Cork. Get good fish, there,
or so I am informed.' She sank down into the chair on one
side of the fire and placed her damp feet on the well-polished
fender and smiled as he raised an eyebrow. 'So, Dr Scher, old
Mr Fitzwilliam dies and suddenly life changes for many people.
One person gets the money to set himself up in style out there
in Palestine, and another may be able to select a marriage
partner of his own choice, and yet another, not so important
perhaps, will be able to go back to Baltimore, that's if he's
clever and doesn't allow himself to be bribed by a lesser
reward. A fourth, perhaps, may be able to fulfil his life wish
and join the British army. And then again, another may get
her heart's desire and be married soon enough to bear a child
before her fertility fades into old age. And a man's family may
be freed from the servitude of making money by standing in
a cold, draughty shop for more than seventy hours in the week.
And another would hope to escape disgrace and disinheritance.
So many motives, are there not? And, of course, I do remember
Patrick's exasperation at the very sparse information that
he had obtained from these boys who were at an age to be

sharp-eyed, sharp-eared and perceptive. But, of course, these are not natural boys. These are boys who have been trained to repress all impulsive speech and to concentrate on pleasing those above them. And so it is very difficult to get information from them. But that does not say that they do not have that information. And that means, I fear, Dr Scher, that some of them may well be in danger.' She thought about the boy Christy Callinan and his expensive jacket for a moment and then moved him to the back of her mind. There were other and more pressing anxieties.

'It's a dangerous situation, Dr Scher, when a man, or a woman is brought up to worship money and is kept waiting and waiting and then is denied of their heart's desire,' she said.

'Like Robert,' said Dr Scher, adding two more pieces of coal. 'There's no doubt that he must have been reduced to a state of fury when he heard the news. I think ever since I can remember, Robert has been serving in that shop. Not a very interesting or rewarding occupation for a boy or a young man. And now he is a middle-aged man and when he heard his father say that everything was to go to the eldest son, to Major James Fitzwilliam, well then he would be a saint if he did not feel furious.'

'And Robert's sisters,' put in the Reverend Mother. She would not, she thought mention Robert's mother. The woman would not want for much. She had the air of a person for whom life held little interest. 'I remember Patrick saying how often Mr Fitzwilliam changed his will in the past. For some people it is an occupation.' Dr Scher, she noticed, frowned a little at that, but made no comment. He was stroking his chin and looking into the fire.

'The talk on the town is that Robert is a tricky piece of goods,' he said after a minute. 'Owed money to a lot of people. Made deals about invoices – marked up goods before selling them and pocketed the difference. Well known for these shady deals. His father's fault in all probability. Brought the boy up not knowing where he was. Promised things and then withdrew the promises. Led him on to believe that he would leave him the business, and then told him that he wouldn't. That must have been a very difficult position for Robert. He never knew what his future was and I don't think that it was a piece of cake to work for a bad-tempered old man.'

'I doubt that he had ever been completely cut out of his father's will before now,' said the Reverend Mother. She spoke as one who speculates, but Lucy had been fairly open about the whole business.

'So they say on the town,' agreed Dr Scher. He gave a grin and she knew that he had spotted her surprised expression. 'Not a man to keep his family affairs to himself, old Mr Fitzwilliam; lots of stories circulating in the bar of the Imperial Hotel last evening,' he added.

'Don't know why you keep calling him old; he was no older than I and not too much older than yourself, if truth be known,' she said crisply, but she said it with a smile. He had relieved her anxiety in case she and Lucy, between them, were betraying Rupert's confidences. She should have guessed that Rupert, of all men, would know what was known and what was not known 'on the town'.

'Tell me about Robert,' she invited.

'Not fond of his mother,' he said briefly.

'Nor of his father, perhaps,' she suggested. Why not the mother, she wondered.

'Could have been a few good reasons for that,' he said. 'He has not been well treated, so I've heard tell,' he added hastily. 'Worked from morning to night in that terrible shop. Always under the old man's thumb. And then to hear that your brother who never lifted a finger to help, was to get everything, just because he was the eldest, well that must have been a bitter pill to swallow.'

'I suppose the same thing happens to royalty,' said the Reverend Mother. 'The present king of England has many sons, but only one of them can become king.'

'Well, I suppose that the sons of George V are in a different position. They've known that since they were tiny children. Religion comes into it, too. The divine right of kings. Religion, Reverend Mother, as both you and I know, plays its part in making sure that everyone knows their place.'

'I think that you are trying to distract me,' said the Reverend Mother, good-humouredly. 'Don't worry. I won't pry.'

'Tell me about Baltimore. Not Baltimore in the United States of America, I presume.' Dr Scher seemed to want to change the subject. He had not smiled, nor had he followed up on her lead. That, she thought was not like him. Surely after all these years of friendship he could trust to her discretion. Nevertheless, she told herself, friendship is never an excuse to pry and so she switched the conversation to Christy Callinan and told of his views about Cork city and its polluted river and of his longing for the clean sea air of Baltimore and the tasty fish, fresh from the Atlantic Ocean.

'But you can't think that he had anything to do with it; a little fellow like that. How old is he, ten or eleven?'

'He's twelve,' said the Reverend Mother sombrely. 'And at that age, he would think of his own needs and desires ahead of the needs and desires of the adults around him. And he might not really think too much of the consequences of his actions. There are children like that. I've come across them.'

'So while Miss Maria Mulcahy answers the call of nature, attending whatever facilities that the Fitzwilliam family have afforded their staff, well, young Christy Callinan pops a gas canister into the barrel and sends it whizzing up. Ridiculous,' said Dr Scher heartily.

'Or else, Miss Maria Mulcahy sends her young apprentice off on an errand and then sends up the gas in her own change barrel, or perhaps in the change barrel from her—'

'Young man's counter,' interjected Dr Scher. He had an amused smile on his face. The Reverend Mother was glad to see the brooding, worried look had gone and that the doctor was now relaxed. Why had he been so tense and worried? That was a question that lingered at the back of her mind, and she thought that she knew the answer to it, but she responded to his changed mood and kept the conversation light.

'Thank you,' she said. '*Young man* will suit my purpose. I was about to say *fiancé*, but then I suppose that is wrong. The young, or not so young man, has not, according to Sister Philomena, yet popped the question. And he's been leaving it a long time, if my memory is correct.'

'So despite the lack of a popped question, you think that she might have trusted him enough to do murder in order to give him a leg-up in his position in the shop. It's just not enough of a motive,' said Dr Scher impatiently. 'Goodness, gracious me, Reverend Mother, you talk as if the taking of a human life is as small a matter as throwing a stone at a man's hat.'

'You think that emotions have to be violent in order for murder to be committed.' The Reverend Mother brooded over that. It was, she thought, a valid point, but it might well lead them back onto dangerous ground. 'Odd, isn't it,' she continued, 'that neither of us is thinking about the major. After all, he is the one who really does benefit, wouldn't you agree?'

Dr Scher scratched some rather prickly hair on the nape of his neck. He bore the look of one who longed to agree, but felt constrained to disagree.

'Well, he wasn't actually in the shop at the time, as far as anyone knows,' he pointed out. 'Though he could perhaps have popped in through the back door before driving around to the front door. But, in any case, he's just not that kind of fellow,' he said after rubbing his chin uneasily for a few moments. 'He's easy-going, gets on well with everyone. Not the man to do a murder. Though I can see him ordering a battalion over the top. But, that would be a different matter, wouldn't it? Murder at one degree removed, wouldn't it be? Once they move up in the army, everything is more civilized. Would suit him. He's that sort of relaxed fellow. Enjoys life. Good salary. Someone told me that the army will make him a judge when he goes out to Palestine. They have a good life, these army officers. The British have got themselves put in charge out there, mandated, they call it, and they don't mind bringing the odd Irish man along with them, provided he is monied and educated. Major Fitzwilliam will have a great time. Better, of course, now that he is a rich man, but do you know, of all the family, I think he would be the most unlikely to do the deed . . .' Dr Scher stopped. Up to now he had spoken freely and openly, but now a change came over his face. His eyes were on the carpet and he held his chin in a triangular grasp between thumb and forefinger. The Reverend Mother looked at him compassionately.

After a long minute's silence while she watched him struggle with his thoughts, she spoke. 'You can trust me,' she said. 'Sometimes it helps to unburden a worried mind.'

There was no answer. The light from the window dimmed and the room darkened. No sound. Just a heavy mist descended, as wetting as any rain, but falling silently, cutting out the remaining daylight, streaming silently down the window pane, rendering it opaque. They both sat in silence for another minute and then the Reverend Mother spoke again.

'Forgive me,' she said. 'Friendship and trust are of importance, but the sacred oath, the Hippocratic oath that you swore when you became a doctor; that comes first.' He had written it down for her and she had memorized it, regretting that she did not know Greek, but revelling in the sonorous phrases of the English translation. They went through her mind now: I swear by Apollo the Healer, by Asclepius, by Hygieia, by Panacea, and by all the gods and goddesses . . . to use treatment to help the sick according to my ability and judgment, but never with a view to injury and wrong-doing . . .

Aloud, she said, speaking softly and not looking at him, '"And whatsoever I shall see or hear in the course of my profession, as well as outside my profession in my intercourse with men, if it be what should not be published abroad, I will never divulge, holding such things to be holy secrets".'

What had Dr Scher heard or seen in the course of his profession which had filled him with such anxiety?

The Reverend Mother's mind went to the shrill voice of that badly-used wife, exhausted by the unrelenting work of standing behind a counter for over seventy hours in the week. A woman to be pitied, certainly. Her lips tightened, however, when she thought of that accusation aimed at Brian Maloney. Brian was alone in the world and had been a pupil of hers. He was vulnerable. Children, in the Reverend Mother's most sacred creed, had to be protected by the adults around them. She, the Reverend Mother, was bound by no Hippocratic oath and she would make sure that the innocent should not suffer in the place of the guilty.

FIFTEEN

Eileen MacSweeney did not know whether to tell her exciting news to her mother first, or to Reverend Mother Aquinas at the convent where she had been educated. The single stroke from the bell at the Holy Trinity Church told her that it was only quarter to five. Her mother would not be home for another half an hour. She would see the Reverend Mother first of all. And so she tucked her hair into her leather helmet, fastened it, opened the throttle of her motorbike and sped down the quays towards St Mary's Isle.

The Reverend Mother, for once, was not writing letters when Eileen was shown in by Sister Bernadette. She was sitting in front of a bare desk, in an almost dark room, her hands tucked into her sleeves, not reading nor writing, but just staring at the wall. She seemed, almost visibly, to bring herself back from some dark thoughts as Sister Bernadette bustled about the room, turned up the gas lamp, exclaimed at the state of the fire while emptying half a scuttle of coal upon the embers, and thrust a poker amongst them to accelerate the flames. Eileen took a seat and looked affectionately at her former teacher. She owed so much to the Reverend Mother who had taught her, stimulated her, praised her, challenged her and encouraged her to use her brains. She would be pleased to hear the news. It would cheer up the poor old thing. She even looked visibly better already, seemed to shake off whatever was worrying her.

'So, Eileen, something good has happened,' she said as soon as Sister Bernadette left the room.

'I think it's going to be quite exciting,' said Eileen, noticing that her voice was slightly breathless. 'There's a professor at the university, a Professor Alfred O'Rahilly, and he's got a notion of starting up a publishing company at the university, Cork University Press. It's going to publish books that he and the other professors write. And . . . .' Eileen stopped. The news was almost too exciting to tell. 'And he used to be a Republican and so when he was looking for a printer he came to see Mr Langford, at the Lee Press, and he recognized me and . . . and well, they were talking for ages and then Mr Langford came out to see me and I am going to be working at the university after Easter, in the *Aula Max*, Reverend Mother! Just imagine me there, in the library and . . . and . . . well, I'm going to be typing out the first books and getting them ready for printing, and be on the spot to explain to all the professors what we can do and what we can't do. And Mr Langford told the professor that I was a clever girl and that I knew the printing business inside out and that these university professors would just have to listen to me and if I said something couldn't be done, well they'd have to think of something different . . .' Eileen ran out of steam and stared at the Reverend Mother. She could see how the gloomy, pre-occupied expression had now been replaced with a look of excitement. They looked at each other and Eileen knew that the same thought had flashed through both heads. There she would be, Eileen MacSweeney, sitting in that library, all of those books around her, with access to professors and to a scholarly life.

'And, the *Cork Examiner* have offered me £2 a week if I keep sending in articles! I can live on that if ever I . . .'

'Eileen,' said the Reverend Mother solemnly. 'When you were sixteen years old you made the decision not to try for a university scholarship, but to leave school and join the Irish Republican Army. I think now that you have a chance to reverse that decision. Your School Certificate marks were of the highest and there is nothing to prevent me registering you now to sit the Honan scholarship next June. I can easily put you on the school register,' said the Reverend Mother, with a wave of the hand, which dismissed inspectors, bureaucrats and education offices from her consideration. 'I can easily manage it; I'm sure.'

'The Honan scholarship,' breathed Eileen. 'I'd work every hour of the day and night!'

'That would be stupid,' retorted the Reverend Mother. 'Work a sensible amount of time and don't forget to fit in some amusements and fresh air. Now go home and tell your mother and let me work out how I am going to slip your name back onto the school ledgers. For the Honan Scholarship, you will need to sit a paper in five subjects, so you will have to think what you will do other than English. Latin, of course. Your Latin was excellent. And History – that was excellent, also. Well, I'll leave you to think about another two subjects.'

She said nothing about the help that she would give, the books that she would obtain, the essays which she would correct, but Eileen was not fooled. The Reverend Mother's eyes were gleaming with excitement and Eileen knew that whatever she needed would be forthcoming.

Eileen was scanning her mind for long-buried Latin verbs when she turned into Barrack Street on her bike. She waved happily at Patrick who was standing outside the police barracks, looking preoccupied and worried. She felt sorry for him. Why hadn't he worked a bit harder at school and tried for a university scholarship? Why get a boring job like being a policeman? Suspicious of everyone. Liked by few. Even now there was a young boy, ducking behind a wall as he passed on the far side of the road. Afraid of being nabbed for something, poor little geezer.

Eileen chugged her way up the hill, sparing the engine of her elderly motorcycle by going at walking pace. She thought of Eamonn who had sold her the bike. She and he had been in that safe house belonging to the Republican movement but both had got sick of the never-ending violence. Eamonn was now back at university studying to become a doctor, financed by well-off parents. She would have to go around to his house tonight and tell him the news, she thought, as she turned into the side lane and then up to the back-garden gate of her mother's house. Her mind was still on Eamonn, even after she had put her bike away and she was smiling slightly as she came around to the street again. And then she stopped. The boy whom she had seen earlier was now there, standing pressed tightly up against the front door. For a moment she was alarmed, but then she thought there was something familiar about the freckled face and the mop of flaming red hair.

'Eileen . . .' said the boy tentatively.

'Jesus!' said Eileen. 'You gave me a fright. What are you doing there?'

'Don't you know me, Eileen?' The boy spoke in a whisper and cast a furtive glance down the steep hill. 'I used to be in the infants when you were one of the big girls, don't you remember?'

'I remember you now,' said Eileen. 'Brian Maloney. That's right, isn't it? Terrible little gutty you were too. Always fighting. I remember the red hair.'

'Can I come in?' Once again he turned his head to look down the hill. He flattened himself a little more against the door.

Eileen hesitated. She was looking forward to talking over the future with her mother. She might even go out and buy a cake from the shop, she had thought. Make a celebration. Having young Brian Maloney would be a nuisance.

'What's the matter, Brian?' she asked. He looked worried, she thought. Freckles standing out against a very pale face. Not as cocky as he used to be.

He gave a hasty look around. 'Wondered if you could get me in with the Boyos, Eileen. I could be a messenger boy or something.'

For a moment, Eileen thought he was asking for a job at the printing works and then she understood his meaning. The Boyos was used to describe IRA men when it was dangerous to speak their name. She frowned heavily at him.

'You'd better come in, Brian,' she said curtly. She produced her key and noted how he once more scanned the hilly street before tumbling into the dark little house. 'Now tell me what is the matter,' she said as soon as the door was closed and both stood face to face in the kitchen. Without waiting for an answer, she began to tear up some newspaper, crumpling the sheets up and arranging them in the fireplace. Always plenty of newspaper in the house as her mother would pick up used copies from the public house and bring them home once the floor was scrubbed and the glasses washed. 'What's the matter?' she asked as she struck a match and then piled some loose pieces of turf onto the fire. A certain amount of smoke in the beginning, but she never minded that, liked the peaty smell in the kitchen. It was only when the fire was blazing vigorously and the damp chill of the room had begun to evaporate that she realized she had not received an answer yet.

But when she turned around, saw how white he was and how there was a hint of moisture in his eyes, the sandy eyelashes dark with tears, she began to feel a bit ashamed of herself.

'What's the matter, Brian,' she said gently. He hadn't been a bad little fellow when he was seven and she was one of the big girls. A bit of a show-off and a bit of a fighter, but no real harm in him. 'Sit down and we'll have a cup of tea and then you can tell me all about it,' she said encouragingly. He'd have a chance to dry his eyes and pull himself together while she filled the kettle from the tap in the back yard and got out the old biscuit tin where they kept their tea.

'They're all after me,' he said when she had hung the kettle on the iron crane over the fire.

Eileen turned around to face him. His voice had sounded quite steady now.

'Who?' she asked.

'Everyone at the shop, at the Queen's Old Castle; they all think that I killed Mr Fitzwilliam.'

He sounded very upset and she remembered him very clearly now. A bit of a play-actor, a mammy's boy. Trying to get attention; that was Brian Maloney when he was at the convent school. Been working as an apprentice at the Queen's Old Castle. She remembered her mother telling her that. Very shocked Mam was that Mrs Maloney had gone back to her own people in Mallow and left Brian to look after himself. Went off with another man, too, and left her son behind. Missing his mam and a bit frightened, now, she thought.

'Did you kill him?' she asked in a nonchalant manner. Best to calm him down a bit.

He was indignant. 'Course, I didn't. What do you take me for? What would I be doing sending one of the gas canisters up to an old man?'

'But you didn't, is that what you're saying?' she enquired. The fire was blazing up now, and she moved the long arm of the crane so that the kettle was hanging directly over the flames. Of course the death of Mr Fitzwilliam was the talk of the town. For a moment she felt a rush of pride when she thought about her article in the *Cork Examiner*. Everyone in the pub, according to her mother, had been talking about it for the last few days. No one particularly worried about the old man, of course. He had been a mean old cadger, by all accounts, but everyone was really interested in who had sent that gas cylinder up to him and poisoned the old git.

'What would I be doing that for?' It had worked. He sounded a bit better, not so upset. More indignant.

'Well, why do they think you might have done it?' she asked, pouring the boiling water onto the tealeaves. While he was here, she might as well find out as much of the truth as he knew. If she worked it out, she might make a present of the solution to Patrick. She suppressed a giggle at the thought of his face. He'd be furious that she was cleverer than he was. Always had a bit of a chip on his shoulder. That was Patrick. Anyway, she'd get another good article for the *Examiner* out of it. 'So who did kill him?'

He shrugged his shoulders. 'How do I know? But that crazy old woman, Mrs Fitzwilliam, is trying to pretend that she saw me send a gas thing up instead of a change barrel. She says that I did it from the empty counter, from Mr O'Connor and my counter, when Mr O'Connor was down in the basement stocktaking. And now Mr Robert and Miss Kitty are saying they saw me nip behind that counter, too. Nobody believes me. They'll hang me!' The boy's face had whitened even more and there was a look of desperation in his eyes.

'They don't hang people of your age. You'd have to be sixteen,' she said briefly. She had seen that in a law book.

'I'd prefer to be hanged than stay in prison for the rest of my life. I'm not scared,' he said with a swagger that reminded her of the time when he had been six years old. Always trying to act the big man.

'You can stay here for the moment while I work out what to do with you,' she said briefly. It was that or the IRA, she told herself and there was no way that she was going to hand over this young fellow to Seán Hurley. She wondered whether to send him out for a cake, but that might risk him being nabbed. An apprentice, she knew, couldn't just walk out of a job. The Fitzwilliams might well have sent around for a policeman when he disappeared. She wasn't going to leave him alone with her mother, either, she decided. He had a frightened look in his eyes and frightened people did violent things. She had seen enough of that when she had been a member of the IRA.

'Turn your pockets out,' she said then. Should have done it the moment he came into the house, she thought.

'I never carry a gun when visiting friends,' he said with such a grown-up air that she almost giggled. Still, the most unlikely people in Cork had guns, so she patted his pockets and felt his coat in a professional manner. The British army, especially the infamous Black and Tans, had been notoriously careless and when drunk had a habit of leaving guns behind them in public houses, or else dropping them in the street. Half of the IRA were equipped with stolen or lost British army guns and ammunition. 'Now sit down by the fire and drink that tea, and behave yourself when my mother comes in,' she said warningly as she heard the footsteps outside and the sound of a key in the door.

Maureen MacSweeney, unlike her daughter, was delighted to see Brian, remembered him well, enquired after his mother and could hardly get out of her coat before sitting down to a nice gossip about the state of affairs at the Queen's Old Castle.

'So, Brian, tell me now, who do you think murdered the old man?' she asked eagerly.

'They think that he did it,' said Eileen drily. She thought at times that she and her mother had changed places. She felt elderly, distrustful and world-wise, whereas her mother was young and naïve and believed every word that even the greatest liar could tell her.

'Get-away-out-of-that!' exclaimed her mother. 'As if! Look at the little innocent face of him! Here, I've a few biscuits that were left behind in the pub. Have one, Brian. You poor little fella.'

Now what am I going to do with him, thought Eileen, as her mother was gasping enjoyably over the story of the gas canister inside the change barrel and what the old man looked like when he fell down from the sky-high balcony in the Queen's Old Castle. *He can stay the night. But what will I do with him afterwards? I know him. He won't stay quietly hidden. He'll be popping in and out like a Jack hare. Someone will spot him and then the guards will be up and they'll arrest him and Mam will get into trouble over the whole business.*

'So who did kill him, then, Brian?' she interrupted the story of Mrs Fitzwilliam's mad screams.

She thought he would say that he didn't know, but he surprised her by hesitating a little, looking from one to the other, just like someone who was wondering whether he could be believed.

'Me and the lads think that we might know,' he said after a minute. 'Henry Spiller got us onto it.'

'Who is Henry Spiller?' Maureen leaned forward, eager for a gossip.

'He's Miss Kitty's apprentice. He's old, nearly as old as you, Eileen, he's sixteen now and he sees what's been going on. She and Mr O'Connor, Mr Séamus O'Connor. He pretends to be doing a line with Miss Mulcahy in the Ladies' Shoes, but he's gone off her since she went to the pictures with Mr Robert. If he had a chance with Miss Kitty, he'd jump at that. Miss Kitty is always calling him over to give her a hand with the bundles of linen. She sends Henry off on a message and then she calls over Mr O'Connor to give her a hand. Henry told us all that he turned back once to ask her where he'd buy the lavender and he saw the two of them in the back room and they were kissing.'

'G'wan out of that!' said Maureen. The expression, in Cork, meant disbelief, but the huge enjoyment on her face turned it into an enthusiastic encouragement. Brian grinned widely. His colour had begun to come back, the freckles were not so noticeable and he had, noticed Eileen, finished up the half packet of biscuits that her mother had produced from her handbag. She'd have to get him out of here first thing in the morning. Someone was bound to have seen him on Barrack Street and the guards would be after him, cross-questioning her mother and confusing her into an admission of guilt. In the meantime, let him sing for his supper and tell the whole story about the strange happenings at the Queen's Old Castle. Her own exciting news would have to wait, she thought, as she got to her feet and took out some bread and butter from one of those tin boxes that Maureen collected so as to keep their food safe from mice and rats.

'Sure, I would have thought that he'd be a sight too low for her.' Maureen was deep in the love affair between the shop man and his employer's middle-aged daughter.

'Henry Spiller heard Miss Monica giving out like mad to Miss Kitty, telling her that she was making a show of herself. And,' said Brian with huge enjoyment, 'listen to this, Missus, you'll never guess what Miss Kitty said . . .'

'What?' said Maureen, absent-mindedly accepting the slice of bread that her daughter had handed to her. She was leaning forward and her eyes were wide with excitement.

'She said, and you'll never believe this, but there's not a word of a lie in what I am telling you.' Brian Maloney took a large bite of bread and sat back in his chair, chewing it meditatively. He was spinning the tale out for as long as he could, building up the excitement.

'G'on, tell us.' Maureen held her own slice untouched while she waited for the end of the story.

'She said, "I'll marry who I like, even if it's over the dead bodies of the whole family!" And when Miss Monica came out, Henry Spiller thought that she looked like she was going to cry.'

'What did she say to him, to your man, Henry Spiller? Did she see him? Did she know that he was listening?'

'Naw,' said Brian with scorn. 'He was under the counter, pretending to pick up some pins. She didn't see him. But wait till I tell you . . .'

I'm going to have put a stop to this, thought Eileen. Her mother was a softie. They'd have him on their hands for the next few years. Hard enough for us to manage with the rent going up again. Brian, absent-mindedly, had reached out and taken the last quarter of the loaf, meant for the morning break- fast, and was now chewing it contentedly. Her mother poured him another cup of tea and waited patiently for the rest of the story. There wouldn't be much in it, she thought. Miss Kitty Fitzwilliam was getting on, desperate to get married and would take anyone. And Maria Mulcahy was the same. She'd make sure to keep Séamus O'Connor sweet, even if she played about it with Robert Fitzwilliam whose father would never allow him to marry a shop girl. Interesting, she thought. All sorts of people had motives for murdering one old man. She would think about it, but in the meantime she had to deal with the runaway apprentice. Eileen got to her feet.

'I'm just off to the shop for some more bread, Mam,' she said. Neither even looked at her. Brian was chewing the last crust of the bread and her mother, with eyes wide from excitement, tossed some more turfs onto the fire. Eileen took her coat down from the hook on the door, but left her leather helmet behind. She'd walk. Almost as quick and much less conspicuous.

'Could I see Inspector Cashman?' she asked the guard behind the desk when she came through the door of the barracks.

'Business?' Just the one word. Didn't bother lifting his head from the ruled journal before him.

'Private,' she said curtly. He annoyed her.

He lifted his head at that. Gave her a long look.

'Name,' he demanded, rather than asked. Just as if old Tommy hadn't known her since she was three years old, chased her away from the railings often enough, knew about her connection with that daring gaol break, too, she'd take a bet on that. Still, if he wanted to play games, well, so could she.

'Miss Eileen MacSweeney,' she said and then waited, looking at him steadily. He was in a quandary, she knew that. After all, she might have valuable information about the IRA and he would be in trouble if he sent her away with a flea in her ear. In the end, after staring at her for a moment, he pressed a bell and a sergeant came out of his room. Tommy jerked a thumb at Eileen. 'Wants to see the inspector,' he said.

Eileen gave Joe a dazzling smile and saw, with satisfaction, that it was having a good effect. 'I'm Eileen, Eileen MacSweeney,' she said confidentially. 'Patrick and I were in school together.' A lie. He had left the convent and gone onto the Brothers by the time that she came to school, but it sounded good.

Joe got a little red in the face. 'Come this way, miss,' he said in hushed and confidential tones and she followed him, resisting the opportunity to give a backward glance at the duty sergeant. Tommy the Proddy, the kids used to shout at him and he would roar with anger and threaten to throw them all in the cells. Stupid, really. The man couldn't help being a Protestant. But that was the way they were brought up. *Proddies* and *Cat-Licks*. When it came to exchanging insults there wasn't much to choose between them.

Patrick was studying his notebook when Joe ushered her in, announcing her, to her pleasure, as 'Miss MacSweeney'. It gave Patrick such a shock that he dropped the notebook and jumped to his feet looking embarrassed and slightly alarmed to see her. Boys are so immature and so slow to grow up, she thought and felt pleased to hear her own voice sounding so confident and friendly.

'Goodness, Patrick, aren't you cosy,' she said. 'And a fire all to yourself. And a bookshelf.' She walked across and examined the books on the shelf. 'Law and everything,' she said admiringly. 'Well, I can see that I have come to the right place. Now, tell me, Patrick, what is the protection for a witness?'

His eyes narrowed a little, but he sat very still and said nothing. Not something that Eileen ever liked. A conversation, replies, meeting questions almost before the questions were formulated; that was something that she always enjoyed, not these long silences. She looked defiantly across the desk at Patrick. He had stood up when she came in, and Joe had pulled forward a chair for her, but now she was still standing and he had sat down again, looking at her with a very poker-straight face. She stayed very still, not sitting down, but looking straight into his eyes.

He was the first to crack.

'You'll have to give me some more information, Eileen,' he said.

Had he won? Or had she? Eileen wasn't sure, but she was

too impatient to wait any longer. At least, she thought, he has called me Eileen. She hated it when he became all distant and addressed her as Miss MacSweeney. She gave him an appraising look.

'Another question for you,' she said. 'The law on apprenticeships. Tell me about that.'

This question startled him; she saw that instantly, following his mind in a flash. He had thought she was talking about the Republicans; that she had some information, was going to inform upon her former colleagues, but now he was puzzled. She tightened her lips to conceal her amusement. Let him work it out.

'Apprentices . . .' he said slowly.

Eileen felt superior to him as she watched him turn the matter over in his mind. Slow, she thought. Just plain slow. Men could be like that. Don't suppose that they will ever have women as police officers, though they would probably solve crimes more quickly than these men.

To her surprise, he said with a note of surety in his voice, 'I suppose you are talking about the Queen's Old Castle murder.' He sat back in his chair and raised an eyebrow at her.

Improving, she thought. Not so slow after all. She leaned her forearms on the back of the chair and smiled at him. But she said nothing and after a moment or two he began to speak.

'A boy, an apprentice, one of the boys who was there on that morning . . .' Speaking more to himself than to her. His mind was turning over the matter; she could see that. His eyes were withdrawn and his mouth a tight line. 'Young Brian Maloney,' he said then, with a note of sharp interest in his voice. 'I thought there was something familiar. That's who it was, of course. Lived up our way, didn't he? The young lad, fatherless, wasn't he? I remember feeling a bit sorry for him when my mother told me that Mr Mahoney had skipped off to England. I was at the North Mon. then and I gave him a penny for sweets one day on my way home from school. They used to live in that cabin out there at the top of the hill. I should have known that red hair. That's who I saw. He was in the Queen's Old Castle on that morning. I noticed him there.

He's an apprentice, isn't he? Was wandering around the shop, had been assigned by Mr Fitzwilliam to help the Reverend Mother to collect some flood-damaged goods for her charities, so I was told.' Patrick sat back, grimly satisfied with himself and Eileen nodded.

'Go on,' she said encouragingly.

'He saw something, is that right?' Patrick leaned forward. 'Or else heard something?' he continued. 'Something said when no one knew that he was present. Or else one of the other apprentices told him something. And now he wants to know would he be protected? Would his job be protected if he spills the beans? That's it, isn't it? I thought I saw that red-headed young shaver bobbing down behind the wall earlier on.' And then Patrick sat back again and looked at her. 'Why don't you sit down, Eileen,' he said mildly. 'Sit down and relax. You're making me nervous.'

Eileen laughed. She placed the chair at bit nearer, sat down and put her elbows onto his desk. 'Between ourselves, Patrick, he was thinking of joining the IRA to get away from the place. I thought he might be safer with you.'

Patrick's gaze sharpened. He leaned back. 'Why was he thinking of that?'

'Because the old woman, as he called her, old Mrs Fitzwilliam, she said she saw him do it. Of course he said that he didn't, but they were all ganging up against him; so he says. Miss Kitty apparently said that she thought she saw him at the shoe counter, and she wondered what he was doing there when he was supposed to be with the Reverend Mother and "what, in the name of the Good Lord could a nun from a convent want with men's shoes?".'

Patrick, Eileen was pleased to see, grinned a little at her imitation of Miss Kitty Fitzwilliam, but then he grew serious. She saw him turning the case over in his mind.

'How much do you know about this business, Eileen?' he asked.

She gave a grimace. 'More than I want to. We've had a blow-by-blow account, myself and my mam, every last detail, especially of how the old man fell from the balcony.'

'God be with him,' said Patrick mechanically, but Eileen

didn't echo the sentiment. Religion was indeed the 'opium of the people', she had decided, ever since Eamonn had given her a book by Karl Marx. It made people put up with conditions that they should be rebelling against. That's what she and Eamonn had decided. She never went to mass, now, though she pretended to her mother who would otherwise worry about her only daughter burning in the fires of hell for all eternity.

'I suppose that one of his family murdered him,' she went on in a nonchalant way. It would be good if he were to discuss the case with her. She was sure that her wits were quicker than his.

'Do you think that young Brian Maloney has any useful information?' He flipped through his notebook and then went to the door. 'Joe, could you just pop in for a minute?' He called and Joe appeared before Patrick had got back behind his desk. He had a notebook in his hand.

'The Queen's Old Castle?' There was a query in Joe's voice. Eileen noticed how he had shut the door before saying that. Everything very hush-hush, even inside the barracks.

'Just check your notes, will you, Joe? An apprentice. Brian Maloney. Was with the Reverend Mother at the time.'

'Yes, sir.' Joe leafed through the notes. Not from Barrack Street, posher than herself and posher than Patrick, very respectful to him, though. 'Nothing of interest, sir, same as all of the rest.'

'He's turned up at Miss MacSweeney's place, wants her to hide him. Says that the family are trying to blame him for it. Mrs Fitzwilliam did say something about seeing him send up a barrel. She did actually accuse him and now, apparently, one of the daughters is saying that she saw him go to the Men's Shoes' counter – where he normally worked, of course, but he had no business there on that morning.'

'And one of the six change barrels came from that counter. And, of course, since all of the barrels were empty when I checked, well . . .' Joe and Patrick looked at each other and Eileen stopped herself from saying anything. She wanted to, but she wanted them to go on talking, to forget that she was there.

'Apparently, Mr Fitzwilliam had the habit of dealing with

six barrels at a time and . . .' Joe stopped again and looked at Patrick. And Patrick looked at her. In a moment, he would be telling her that she could go and he had not yet answered her question.

'And one of the barrels came from the Gents' Shoes, but three of them came from the man's own family,' said Eileen rapidly. 'Brian told us. One from Miss Kitty, one from Miss Monica and one from Mrs Fitzwilliam, herself.' She stopped and looked sideways at Joe. Should she mention the gossip about Miss Kitty in front of him? Why not! 'And Brian says that Miss Kitty is in love with Séamus O'Connor and her apprentice, well, he says that he saw them kissing.' She enjoyed the sharp look of surprise that passed between them. Cork, she thought, was a terribly snobbish place. The idea of the daughter of the owner kissing a counter hand had given them both a shock. 'And,' she continued, 'this fellow heard Miss Kitty tell Miss Monica to mind her own business and that if needs be she would marry Séamus O' Connor over the dead body of her family. She probably meant,' said Eileen with an eye on Patrick, 'over the dead body of her father.' She gave him a few moments to absorb this and to her pleasure saw him make a note in the small book in front of him. 'After all,' she continued, blandly, 'her mother is a poor misfortunate old woman. Everyone knows that. And when it comes down to it, well, what right had her brothers or her sister to interfere. The father is a different matter. Would be one of those old-fashioned men who think that they are better than women. And one of those six change barrels did come from the Haberdashery department, didn't it?' she said with an eye on Joe. And she saw with scorn that he immediately checked down through the page of his notebook. No confidence in themselves, these men. Couldn't rely on their memory.

'Yes, well.' Patrick placed his hands flat on the desk after receiving a nod from Joe. In a moment he would stand up to signal that the interview was over.

'Brian Maloney is worried that he is in danger,' she said rapidly, addressing herself now to Joe. 'He feels that the family will find it convenient to blame him. He wants – he needs police protection.' And then she sat back in her chair, giving,

she hoped, the impression that she was there to stay until a
suitable bargain had been worked out. After all, spies got
police protection. Why not a fourteen-year-old boy? She saw,
with satisfaction, how they exchanged glances as she looked
keenly from one to the other.

'I wonder could we leave you for a moment,' said Patrick,
rising from his seat. 'A cup of tea, perhaps?'

'No thank you,' said Eileen politely. 'You don't mind if I
read your books while I'm waiting?'

'Oh, I don't think that we will be that long,' said Patrick,
looking up at the well-filled shelf.

Definitely improving; that was an attempt at a joke, thought
Eileen, as she went across and chose THE METROPOLITAN
POLICE GUIDE 5th EDITION. She opened it. Published in
1910. You'd think that this shining new government of Ireland
could afford to buy some more up-to-date books for their
police inspectors. And written for the Royal Irish Constabulary.
By the British government, no doubt. Well, well, well!
Perhaps, she thought, if I qualify as a lawyer, I can write
them an up-to-date version, especially for Ireland. She smiled
at herself and at her dreams, but that little thrill of excitement
that had awoken when the Reverend Mother had mentioned
the Honan Scholarship made her feel warm all over and she
closed the book.

She had hardly replaced it when they were back.

'Right,' said Patrick.

Trying to sound decisive, she thought, but she echoed his
word. 'Right?' she said and put a note of query into her voice.

'Joe and I have decided the best thing to do,' said Patrick
steadily. 'The boy should go back tonight. Strictly speaking,
no one should harbour a runaway apprentice, so you did the
right thing to come to us. You go and do some shopping or
something and I'll drop up to your mother's house, looking
for you, meet the lad and persuade him to come back to the
Queen's Old Castle with me. I'll have a word with someone
there, make up some excuse, say that he remembered something and felt that he should tell me. I'll smooth it over and
get him back where he belongs. But I will make it very plain
that the police are interested in his welfare and that it is the

responsibility of the owner of the shop to look after him. Don't you worry about it any longer!'

'He doesn't like the place,' pointed out Eileen.

'Well, that's just hard luck,' said Patrick unsympathetically. 'We've all had to do things we don't like. I'd say the place is probably a paradise compared to the North Mon. on a wet Monday with every single one of the Christian Brothers in a bad mood and looking for someone to make a mistake.'

And with that he took his coat and cap from the back of the door and walked off, leaving Joe to show her out.

SIXTEEN

I t was eight o'clock in the evening when Patrick and a reluctant Brian Maloney reached the Queen's Old Castle. The last stroke of the bell from St Peter's Church in North Main Street sounded just as Patrick pushed open the front door. The shop was still open. Patrick grabbed the boy's elbow and steered him in. Mr Robert was there, but his back was turned, gossiping with a man dressed in a shiny suit. John Callaghan, a rep from Blarney Woollen Mills; that's who it was. Patrick recognized him. Been in school with him. Always in trouble for talking at the North Mon. The job as a salesman probably suited him. A man who could talk for Ireland; so they said. He would keep Robert Fitzwilliam busy for a while and Patrick hastily steered young Brian to the far side of a group of women who were examining a curtain held up by Michael Dinan.

Just as well not to involve Robert in this affair, thought Patrick. Easier to deal with the man rather than the master. Séamus O'Connor had no customers and was busy fitting pairs of shoes back into their boxes. Patrick approached him rapidly, still keeping a grip on Brian's sleeve.

'Brian wants to apologize to you, Mr O'Connor,' he said and barely waited for a choked out 'sorry' from the boy before saying rapidly, 'he remembered something that he felt was urgent, something that he had forgotten to mention to the sergeant when he was being interviewed, so he nipped out to see me.'

'Indeed!' Séamus O'Connor glared at Brian and Patrick felt the boy tremble. Poor little fellow, in for a beating, he wouldn't be surprised. Still, better than being homeless on the streets of Cork, he told himself. Not much compassion from Séamus O'Connor. Must be fifty if he was a day. Never been married, though he was reputed to have a fine sum of money stashed away, according to Patrick's mother. O'Connor had opened his mouth to ask a question, and it might be a difficult one to answer. What could the boy have wanted to tell the police? Patrick rapidly ran through various possibilities in his mind. Still, the police were in charge here and dealing with a murder case, Patrick told himself and he stiffened his backbone.

'I'm sure that a man like you knows better than to ask me to talk about police business,' he said rapidly. 'Nothing must be said or done about the boy's absence. I'm happy that he did the right thing in coming to me so promptly. And if anyone asks you about it, well, you know what to say. *On police business*,' he repeated slowly and emphatically. Séamus O'Connor was now looking a bit flustered and that was all to the good. 'Now, Brian, I'm sure that Mr O'Connor would like you to carry on with that work that he has had to do in your absence,' he said severely to Brian and waited until the boy began packing away the shoes, before raising a finger to beckon Séamus O'Connor to his side.

'Something that I omitted to ask you,' he said. 'Could we have a quiet word?'

'Come down to the stockroom. No one there.' Séamus O'Connor eyed him with a searching look. As they passed the Ladies' Shoes department, Patrick noticed a quick exchange of glances between Miss Maria Mulcahy and her fellow worker. Nothing much, just an impression that he had, but he saw the man's lips tighten with annoyance. He led the way downstairs and made sure that the door was closed behind them before saying in a nervous fashion, 'What's he been saying? Terrible boy for making up stories.'

Patrick ignored that. He got out his notebook. 'Something that I wanted to ask you, Mr O'Connor,' he said. 'Who was it who told you to be in the stockroom, last week, on the day when Mr Fitzwilliam died?'

'It was Mr Robert, inspector. He's the one to give the orders. No surprise, though. I was not going to be that busy. On a Monday morning you'd get mainly women. The men who have jobs wouldn't be shopping. The ones out of work have to queue up at the labour exchange on a Monday morning and then after that they'd be queueing at the docks waiting for an unloading job. No, there'd be no problem in having my counter empty and Miss Mulcahy at the Ladies' Shoes would keep an eye and send a boy down to get me if there was a customer.'

'I see,' said Patrick. Joe, of course, had noted all of that information but it had made a handy lead in and the man now looked more relaxed. Patrick looked up and nodded at the empty shelf. 'You've put the gas cylinders away, I see.'

'The major packed them up and has them in his own room in the house. Under his own eye. Very upset he was.' The man's face was wooden, but Patrick saw his eyes glance quickly from himself and then to the empty shelf. How easy it would have been for Séamus O'Connor to put one of those gas canisters into his pocket, pop up to his own counter, insert it into the change barrel. Leave it. And then return to the counter sometime later, perhaps pretend to make a sale; be seen wrapping up a shoe box and shoot off the little barrel with its deadly contents.

'Of course we all thought that they weren't that dangerous,' said the man, almost as though he had read Patrick's mind. 'The major opened one when I was standing beside him, just opened it and flung it on top of the pile of dried-out, flood-damaged bedsheets. Didn't do us a mite of harm. I smelled the gas, but just like you would have smelled a bit of gas before you lit it. They used them to fumigate trees out in California, the major told us that; took the mould from them, that's what he said. Used to throw them up, first of all, but then they got machines to carry them into the trees. And then they started to use them on uniforms of prisoners, got the lice out of them. No problem in the open air and no problem either in a big room like this.'

'Just in a small room like Mr Fitzwilliam's office.' Patrick nodded. His mind went to Dr Scher's report of the autopsy. Death from heart failure induced by the inhalation of gas. Still murder was probably intended, thought Patrick. 'But I suppose the major, being a careful man, explained that to everyone,' he said aloud. 'About the dangers of releasing the gas into enclosed spaces.' Major Fitzwilliam had said that he had done that, but Patrick always liked to check and double-check every statement.

'I suppose so.' Séamus O'Connor shrugged his shoulders. 'I wasn't that interested, to tell you the truth. It was mostly the young lads that took a fancy to them. All excited they were. Keen on being soldiers, all of them. Had to give young Brian a clip around the ear to bring him back to the real world.'

'And now Major Fitzwilliam is the new owner of the business.' The news of the will was all around the town and Patrick was not surprised when Séamus nodded. He was surprised though to see that the man showed no sign of anxiety. And yet, few people could have believed that Major Fitzwilliam would keep the business on. Selling the shop might mean the staff would be without a job. However, it might just be kept on with the present counter hands and apprentices. Or, perhaps Séamus O'Connor had got himself a new job, or even something better. Patrick's mind went to young Brian Maloney's story about the secret kiss and the liaison between Miss Kitty Fitzwilliam and Séamus O'Connor. Perhaps the two of them were going to pool their resources, set up a little shop on their own. There would be little that either of them had to learn about the shop-keeping business in the city of Cork.

'Well, that's all, Mr O'Connor,' he said aloud. 'Thank you for your co-operation. And perhaps you would tell the other staff what I said about allowing apprentices to have free access to the police, with no questions asked. These young lads have sharp eyes and we all do want this business of Mr Fitzwilliam's death to be cleared up as quickly as possible.' He doubted whether the apprentices would actually be told that they had a right to take time off work in order to visit the police, but his words reinforced what he had said about not punishing Brian Maloney. He would, thought Patrick, be able to tell Eileen with a clear conscience, that he had done his best for the boy. He half-smiled to himself as he went out of the shop. Funny girl, Eileen MacSweeney, he thought. Still, at least she had given up all of that IRA business and seemed to have settled down to a steady job. And that article in the *Cork Examiner*, which everyone seemed to think had been written by her, had brought into the police barracks a flood of information from the customers in the Queen's Old Castle on that morning when Mr Fitzwilliam fell to his death.

SEVENTEEN

'Y ou'll never guess what I did last night.' Lucy hardly waited for Sister Bernadette to close the door behind her, before she came out with this pronouncement.

'You were attending a dinner party,' suggested the Reverend Mother. She sipped Sister Bernadette's homemade cough mixture. The honey and carrageen seaweed seemed to soothe her chest.

'Wrong,' said Lucy triumphantly.

'You were giving a dinner party.'

'Wrong again,' said Lucy.

The Reverend Mother sat back. She was going to be enlightened and the sooner the better. Any more guesses would only hold up the news and from her cousin's face she could guess that she had something of interest to communicate.

'Go on,' she said.

'We*eell*,' said Lucy, drawing out the word, 'you know what I am like about servants – spoil them! That's what Maud O'Reilly said to me the other day when I met her for lunch. "Lucy, you spoil your servants." That's what she said.'

'So! Get to the point, Lucy!' said the Reverend Mother impatiently.

'And so I give the cook the evening off every Tuesday, *every single Tuesday*,' said Lucy with emphasis on the last three words. 'Well, she was used to Sundays when she came to me, but I couldn't have that. Poor dear Rupert! His only full day away from that wretched office of his!'

'So what does poor, dear Rupert do on Tuesday?' enquired the Reverend Mother.

'Takes me out to dinner in the Imperial Hotel, of course,' said Lucy triumphantly. 'And that is the point. There we were, just the two of us, just like a dear old Darby and Joan couple, drinking our coffee and sipping our brandy in the lounge of the Imperial when who should come along?' Lucy paused dramatically. She leaned back in her chair and looked across at her cousin with a quizzical air.

The Reverend Mother thought about it. 'Major James Fitzwilliam,' she said with a fair amount of promptitude.

Lucy sat bold upright. 'You are annoying, Dottie. You have no social manners at all. You should have said: "I haven't a clue!" You've spoilt my story, now.'

'No, I haven't,' said the Reverend Mother unrepentantly. 'Go on, Lucy, tell me what he said.' It had been, she thought, an easy guess. Of all the people whose names now drifted in and out of her head, of all the people who might have been guilty of putting a premature full stop to the life of Mr Fitzwilliam, only his eldest son, Major Fitzwilliam, was likely to be frequenting the expensive precincts of the Imperial Hotel. She sat back and waited for what was to come. Lucy, she knew by the sparkle in her cousin's eye, had a piece of gossip to relate.

'Well,' said Lucy reluctantly and then the love of a good story overcame her sense of grievance. 'Well,' she said again and this time the monosyllable had a completely different sound. She leaned forward and said in hushed tones, 'Wait until I tell you the whole story.'

The Reverend Mother poured herself a cup of tea in order to do justice to the atmosphere, and to remove the bland sweet taste of the carrageen moss and honey from her mouth. Then she sat back. 'There you were, you and Rupert, enjoying your after-dinner cup of coffee . . .' she prompted.

Lucy's eyes sparkled. 'When who should appear, but Major Fitzwilliam,' she said. 'As a matter of fact, I was just returning from powdering my nose and he didn't see me for a minute. He just came through the door and then almost ran across the room and seized Rupert by the hand. "My dear fellow" he kept saying and you could see that he had had a bit too much to drink. "My dear fellow. The very man. I want you to do an enormous favour for me. Won't take more than ten minutes of your time. But I need some support." Well, you know, Dottie, when I heard that, well, I hung back a bit, checked my hair in the mirror by the door to the cloakrooms. Didn't want to intrude,' said Lucy virtuously. 'As a solicitor's wife, well, I'm used to that sort of thing. You'd be amazed to know the number of people who after a few glasses of brandy suddenly remember that they should have made their will, or changed their will and nothing will serve them but to go charging up to Rupert and wanting him to do it there and then. He always gives them an appointment for eight-thirty o'clock on the following morning, and they never turn up,' said Lucy with a chuckle.

'But Major Fitzwilliam . . .'

'But Major Fitzwilliam wanted a bit more. He wanted Rupert to come around to the Queen's Old Castle with him, there and then, and explain his father's will to all of the staff. "We'll get a taxi, old boy, and be there for eight o'clock," he kept on saying. "You explain everything to them, make it all sound much more professional." Of course, I kept out of the way. Took up a magazine and started to look through it. Rupert was saying, "My dear fellow, what is the problem?" You know that soothing voice that he puts on; doesn't do it to you, of course; he's a bit afraid of you, thinks you are formidably intelligent, but he does it to me.'

The Reverend Mother smiled to herself. When was it, she wondered, that family and friends had decided that of the two cousins, similar in age, brought up and educated side by side, that Dottie was to be the intelligent one and Lucy the social butterfly? Probably when it became apparent that Lucy was going to be the pretty one and her cousin the plain one, she decided and then turned her mind back to the problem of Major Fitzwilliam.

'He's sold, or has had an offer for the Queen's Old Castle,' she said.

'That's right!' exclaimed Lucy, too carried away, now, by her story to resent her cousin's interpolation. 'You wouldn't believe it, would you? So soon! Probate barely granted.'

'Not for a shop, then?' queried the Reverend Mother. She thought not. The major wouldn't need the services of his solicitor if the news was going to be good.

'That's right,' said Lucy nodding her head wisely. 'Just as I thought myself as soon as I heard him. Anyway, he said that Rupert could help him to explain to the staff about everything.

Notice and that sort of thing. "You'd be so good at it, old man. Soothe them down. Make them see that I had no choice".'

'I see,' said the Reverend Mother. A lot of worried homes last night, was her first thought and her second was that Christy Callinan would have his heart's desire. He'd be back in Baltimore for the spring fishing.

'You can just imagine how my eyes were popping and then Rupert started doing the perfect gentleman act. "Sorry, old man; I have to take Lucy home. Oh, there she is. Come along, my dear. We must be off." And, of course, I couldn't put up with that sort of thing so I just strolled over. Didn't make any pretext of not having heard. I always think these sort of things are so tiresome, just went straight up to the major . . .'

The Reverend Mother sat back with a smile. She could just imagine the scene. Rupert, under the mask of the perfect gentleman, inwardly fuming; Lucy, both hands outstretched, smiling sweetly, playing the role of the acquiescent wife and inwardly determined to see what all of this was about. 'I suppose that you said that you would be perfectly happy to stop off at the Queen's Old Castle,' she suggested.

'Well, I put it better than that,' said Lucy, never one to baulk at giving herself credit. 'You should have heard me. I did it very well. "The Queen's Old Castle. Goodness, I don't think that I have been there for more years than I can count!" And of course, the major perked up at that and Rupert looked furious, but he couldn't say anything. You should have heard me, Dottie, I did it very well. "I won't be in anyone's way. I'll just sit in the kitchen and read my magazine". And then I just snatched up the hotel's copy of *Vogue*, tucked it under my arm and went out the door. And, of course, as soon as dear Mr Flynn saw us coming, he sent a boy for our coats and another for the chauffeur and there we were, up the South Mall and down the Grand Parade before Rupert could think of anything to say. To give him his due,' said Rupert's dutiful wife, 'he didn't say a word, just listened to the major's account of the great deal that he was going to make, and how he wanted to have everything run as smoothly as possible.'

'And the deal . . .?' put in the Reverend Mother. She had guessed, but thought that she should be tactful.

'You'll never guess,' began Lucy, but then began to laugh. 'Oh, all right then, you have guessed. Yes, not been sold as a shop, but for building – apartments – all the rage now, so I've heard. Two-bedroomed apartments. They should sell like hot cakes. Can you imagine! Right in the centre of town. But of course . . .' Lucy grew serious and she grimaced a little.

'All of the workers out of work, that's it, isn't it?'

'Very upset, poor things. I sat in the kitchen. And I heard it all. They have a little stove there with a kettle and one of the boys, a very thin, nervous-looking one – Burke was his name – he lit the fire for me. And he put the kettle on. And then he went back inside. I gave him sixpence, but he still looked very upset and worried. I suppose they had all begun to guess that something was up when they were asked to stay behind after work. But that's not what I was going to tell you about.'

'Was Mrs Fitzwilliam there?' asked the Reverend Mother.

'I knew you'd guess. It's impossible to tell you anything!' Lucy's eyes were alight with interest. 'But I don't think that even you will guess the next bit of the story. Yes, she started to cry and I could hear her shriek. I could hear her very plainly. "My son is going to throw his old mother out on the street. He wants to kill his old mother." That's what she shouted. And there was a deadly silence from the shop. I could just imagine what everyone was thinking. And then Rupert and Monica brought her into the kitchen and by this time I had the kettle boiling and the teapot warming. You should have seen Rupert's face. Never had known me to be so domesticated! And I didn't ask a single question. Just put a cushion for the old lady onto a chair just by the stove. Monica fished out the tea canister. You wouldn't believe it, Dottie, but they keep it locked up, just in case any of their shop assistants would pinch a few teaspoonfuls from it!

'Rupert went back in, then. I could hear his voice explaining the law to the workers. Poor things! You won't believe it, but they only get a week's notice. I couldn't hear much because Mrs Fitzwilliam kept moaning about being thrown into the street and then we heard someone coming . . .' Lucy paused and said dramatically, 'Monica jumped to her feet

– glad to get away, I'd say. She went out and I heard her say. "Kitty!" . . .' Lucy paused. 'Now here comes the really strange part of the story, because Kitty said, quite loudly, "Is she any better? Keep her there, anyway! Keep your eye on her. We don't want her sticking a knife into James, just as she did to Pa!" Well, what do you think of that, Dottie?' Lucy paused dramatically, her eyes very widely opened and both palms held up as though she were a bishop greeting a crowd of worshippers.

'Is it true?' asked the Reverend Mother.

'It could be; but I wouldn't know,' admitted Lucy reluctantly. 'You see my housekeeper's sister only got the job less than a year ago. Otherwise, well, I'd say that I would have heard something.'

'But none of your acquaintances, did any of them ever drop a hint? Any rumours on the town,' she added. Her mind went to Dr Scher. His protective attitude to Mrs Fitzwilliam might now be explained.

'I don't know where you pick up expressions like that,' scolded Lucy, 'but, no, I've heard nothing about that. She is odd, and people do talk about her a bit, but then we don't really belong to the same set. And you couldn't expect me to be on visiting terms with a woman who works in a shop. Perhaps she did stick a knife in him. It probably wasn't too serious. Just a flesh wound. Of course, I wouldn't dream of gossiping about her, though I did hint, just hint, to Rupert to tell me the whole story. But he got all tight-lipped and had the cheek to turn the conversation and ask me when I intended to return that copy of *Vogue* to the Imperial Hotel. As if! We leave enough money there, I told him. What between dinners and lunches and solicitors' meetings in the bar, well, it's no wonder that they can afford to build a new entrance. But anyway, never mind that. What do you think, Dottie?'

'It's a very sad and terrible story if true,' said the Reverend Mother. Nobody had really considered Agnes Fitzwilliam and yet one of the six change barrels had been from her millinery counter. Could it have held the gas canister? 'The boy,' she said aloud, 'the boy who lit the fire for you, Lucy, the boy named John Joe Burke, was he still with you?'

'What? Who? Oh, no, no, he'd gone back inside once the stove began to heat up; but never mind about him. What do you think about Agnes Fitzwilliam? Could she have murdered that miserly husband of hers?' said Lucy impatiently.

The Reverend Mother thought about the matter for a while. In the end she just said, 'Why?'

'To get out of going to that cold shop every day. It really is a most miserable place.' Lucy shuddered.

'But why not tell him? After all, Agnes must be over seventy now. It would be a good enough excuse, wouldn't it?'

'Too scared of him?' Lucy cast an enquiring look at her cousin. 'I bet you know all about them,' she added. 'You usually do know things. You sit here like a spider weaving your web and people bring you little flies of information.'

The Reverend Mother's lips twitched. She rather liked the simile. She shook her head, though. 'Murder,' she said authoritatively, 'takes resolution or desperation. It would be surprising if Mrs Fitzwilliam could bring herself to murder her husband, but not to tell him that she did not feel up to going to the shop every day. Wouldn't it have been easier to just tell him? Say that she is not well.'

'The trouble is that if you are sane and sensible, that makes sense, but my housekeeper says that her sister tells her that Mrs Fitzwilliam is a bit crazy.'

'Crazy, how?' The Reverend Mother thought about this. Lucy liked a good story, but she had an accurate ear and an acute retention of what was said. This, she thought, is serious.

'Well, I'm just telling you what she said. In fact, she, that's the Fitzwilliam housekeeper, actually said that it wouldn't take much to push that woman over the edge. She never takes a holiday, never ever. Monica and Kitty take holidays, Robert takes holidays but their mother doesn't. Neither did Mr Fitzwilliam, but then everyone knows that he is an old miser. Anyway, enough of that. I haven't finished the story. There we all were, all four of us, Monica, Kitty, Agnes and myself, all huddled around that miserable stove, none of us knowing what to say, when Agnes suddenly stood up.'

The Reverend Mother lifted her head and looked with keen

attention at her cousin. She had, she realized, been waiting
for something like that.

'She just shrieked the words, didn't look at me; hardly knew
that I was there, I guessed, but she looked straight at the two
girls. You should have seen her, Dottie. Her mouth was
working, a bit twisted, and her eyes, well crazy was the only
word for them. And she screamed out, "James killed his father.
Don't you understand? It was James. He sent that boy, that
young Maloney boy over to do it. But it was James who got
him to do it. I saw it all." That's what she said, and apparently
that was what she said in the shop. Well, what do you think?'

'I think,' said the Reverend Mother soberly, 'that Mrs
Fitzwilliam is a woman who needs help.' She turned the matter
over in her mind while Lucy sat looking across at her with
an expression like an alert robin. 'Leave it with me,' she said
eventually and so authoritatively that she saw it had an effect
on her cousin. 'Now, Lucy, tell me, what is the latest news
about Charlotte?'

After Lucy had been driven away by her chauffeur, the
Reverend Mother lingered for a few minutes, staring through
the window and thinking hard. Eventually, she closed the
curtains, shutting out the fog and the rain and then she went
down the corridor and lifted the receiver. '4567, please,' she
said to the woman in the telephone exchange and waited,
drumming her fingers thoughtfully on the telephone shelf and
turning over words in her mind.

'I'm sorry, Reverend Mother, there's no answer from that
number,' said the telephonist after a few minutes. 'Dr Scher's
housekeeper has her afternoon off on a Wednesday and he's
usually in the Mercy Hospital on Wednesday afternoon.'

'So he is; well, thank you, Miss Turner.' The Reverend
Mother put down the receiver. Despite her anxiety she could
not stop a smile puckering her lips. Cork was a great place to
live if you wanted to know the last detail of everyone's daily
life. And of all the occupations in the city, the life of a telephonist afforded the most food for gossip. She seemed to
remember that when telephone numbers were allocated
originally, there had been quite a bit of emphasis put on secrecy

and on the anonymity afforded by giving each customer an anonymous number. Well, that might have worked in places like London, or even Dublin, but certainly not in Cork.

The smile, however, faded from her lips as she went back towards her room. Lucy's story had worried her. She stopped by the window in the dark corridor and fished out her pocket watch from its place deep down in her pocket. A quarter to five. Even a conscientious hardworking doctor needed an evening meal. She went into her room, took her warm cloak from its hanger behind the door, put the fireguard in front of the fire, swept her correspondence into a drawer of her desk, switched off the gas lamp, locked her door and went towards the kitchen.

'Sister Bernadette, I'm going for a short walk. I shall probably drop in to see Dr Scher. Please don't bother about supper for me,' she said, speaking rapidly to avoid disturbing the hardworking lay sister from her comfortable position by the fire.

'It's his housekeeper's day off,' said Sister Bernadette, her face as worried as though the Reverend Mother was going on hunger strike. 'Still,' she said more cheerfully, 'she'd be back by five o'clock. I'm sure that she'll rustle up something.'

The Reverend Mother smiled vaguely, repressing a feeling of irritation. A novice, recently, had baulked at taking her final vows, returning to the bosom of her family after confusedly explaining, 'It's just this feeling that everyone knows everything about you, day and night.' The Reverend Mother didn't try to argue her out of her decision, but had applauded her courage and her clear thinking. Even after more than fifty years, she thought as she walked along the quays, the same feeling irked her. And yet she had never regretted her decision. These were small things, she decided. The important things were the times when she had managed to make a difference to the lives of the poor and the unimportant children and parents of the city of Cork. Her mind turned over the picture of Brian Maloney, one of her children. He had passed through her hands, had been a cheerful boy, bright and enterprising, popular with his classmates, good at football. Her mind busied itself with him. She could not, she decided, stand back and allow him to be the traditional whipping boy. Yes, she was sorry for Agnes Fitzwilliam, but Brian had his life before him. Children had to matter more than adults. Such had always been one of her main guiding principles. She would not allow herself to be talked out of the decision she had come to by platitudes such as 'truth will prevail'. The Reverend Mother had little faith in Cork juries. The clan system in Ireland had never been totally extinguished. It had just gone underground. There was always someone related, someone with influence; someone who could do or who had done a favour. 'Sure, I'd never get a job in a bank, Reverend Mother. I've no one to spake for me,' had said a bright girl with a mathematical brain, and a great head for figures.

But first of all, because of their long association, *friendship*, amended the Reverend Mother, and because of the trust that existed between the two of them, she would have to talk to Dr Scher and tell him of her decision.

The doctor had just hung up his hat and had one arm out of the sleeve of his overcoat when he opened the door in answer to her knock.

'Well, well, well, look who's here,' he said, half to her and half to his housekeeper who had appeared from the back hallway. 'And what brings you here at this hour, Reverend Mother?'

'I've come to see your silver collection,' said the Reverend Mother promptly.

'Indeed,' he said. He raised his eyebrows, but allowed the excuse to pass, although he had often teased her for her lack of appreciation for the beautiful silver produced in her native city, telling her that those born into the cream of society were blinded to the value of their surroundings.

It satisfied the housekeeper, though. She murmured a welcome, plumped up the cushions on the easy chairs before the fire, promised supper in a few minutes, took the Reverend Mother's cloak and then withdrew. Dr Scher made no attempt to open the cabinet where he kept his silver treasures, but escorted her to a chair, carried over a small mahogany tea table, placing it between the two chairs, took a linen cloth from its drawer and spread it across the shining wood.

'See how domesticated I am,' he said, but she saw from his eyes that he was anxious. A man of great susceptibility and a keen sharp intellect. He, she felt sure, guessed the reason for this surprise visit.

'Warm your toes,' he commanded. 'I'll fetch the tray.' Another indication. His housewife was a true Cork woman and very chatty. She would be likely to spend five minutes enquiring about the health of the various members of the community, remarking on the latest news in the city and commenting on the weather. If Dr Scher himself went out to the kitchen and collected the tray, he would give the Reverend Mother the opportunity of coming straight to the point.

Now she was sure that he had guessed the reason for this visit, unheralded, and unusually late in the day, also. He was giving her a few minutes alone in which to collect her thoughts and allowing her to skip the usual small talk and discussion about the weather. She followed his lead and said nothing when he returned, allowing him to pour the tea and to help herself from a plate of hot fishcakes.

By the time that she had munched her way through the outer edge of the crunchy slab, the Reverend Mother had made up her mind to be completely direct.

'Dr Scher,' she said, putting the fishcake back on her plate. 'I am thinking of talking to Patrick tomorrow morning about Brian Maloney, the boy who was with me in the Queen's Old Castle on the day of Mr Fitzwilliam's death. I am very worried about the fact that Mrs Fitzwilliam has now twice accused him, in front of other people, of being guilty of her husband's murder. This, of course, means that Patrick, as a conscientious policeman will have to question Mrs Fitzwilliam and will, perhaps, have to warn her that such accusations cannot be tolerated. Either she has evidence, and in that case, it should be given to the inspector in charge of the investigation; or else she must be told firmly that she should refrain from voicing such suspicions in public places. Of course,' concluded the Reverend Mother, 'it may be that she is not responsible for what she says, but if that is true, steps should be taken to make sure that she retires to a nursing home, or stays confined to her bedroom until her nerves have recovered. The boy's safety cannot be put at risk.'

And then she sat back in her chair and drank the rest of her tea. Those fishcakes would not pass muster if sampled by young Christy Callinan. His mother, she felt sure, would do better with the fish straight from the Atlantic.

Dr Scher was thinking hard. He did not press food or drink upon her, but stared meditatively into the fire. She had, she knew, put him into a quandary, but Brian Maloney would risk a life of imprisonment if this murder was pinned to him. And it would be an easy solution. Despite Lucy's disdainful words, the Fitzwilliams were related to many powerful and wealthy families in Cork. To pin the murder onto a disgruntled apprentice was a very easy solution and it would not, she feared, take most Cork juries too long to reach a verdict. She eyed the pensive face and wondered whether she should depart and leave him with his dilemma. But no. Something obstinate in her forbade the acceptance of such an easy solution. She had to have an answer. The open accusation at the meeting between Major James Fitzwilliam and his employees would by now be circulating all of the streets, shops, bars and hotels of the city.

After a few moments he spoke. 'A solution occurs to me and I hope that it may be acceptable to all.'

'All, including Brian Maloney, a fourteen-year-old boy who is alone in this city,' she said.

'Indeed,' he said and bowed his head.

The Reverend Mother sat back and relaxed a little. This was the old Dr Scher. The word had been said with a depth of feeling and of understanding. This man who spent much of his time tending without payment, or even recognition, to the sick and dying among the poverty-stricken denizens of this unhealthy city was not a man to ignore the plight of a young boy on his own and at the mercy of his employers. She kept her eyes on the anthracite stove and waited for him to speak.

'I thought,' he said, 'that I might have a word with the major. I'm all in favour of people being open and honest about illness, whether it's physical or mental. In fact,' he said, warming to his subject, 'we might have less tuberculosis in this city if people didn't try to hide it, didn't think of it as a shameful thing. And I feel the same about mental illness. So I shall suggest to the major that he talk to his staff about the fact that his mother has been under a great strain and that . . .' Dr Scher paused for a moment, his chubby face creased with thought and then his eyes lit up. 'I've got it,' he said. 'What do you think of this, Reverend Mother? The major makes a speech to the staff assuring them all of bonuses on leaving, of good references, etc, and finishes up with something like this: "My mother has been under great strain and I hope that young Brian Maloney will be able to forgive the things that she has said and will realize that Mrs Fitzwilliam, like us all, has a high regard for his integrity." I'll go and see the major first thing tomorrow morning. Will that content you?'

'Write it out for him and be with him when he says it,' said the Reverend Mother. She was somewhat sceptical about the possibility of getting Major Fitzwilliam to say something like that in public, but if it was put to him, she thought that he could be relied upon to keep an eye open for young Brian. Judging by what the boy had said, the major had been kind to him, talked about the army to him. Dr Scher's presence should surely ensure that Brian was not made the scapegoat for this. She gave the doctor a nod of approval.

'You can eat your fishcakes now with a free conscience,' she said.

'You've taken my appetite away. I don't think that I want them,' said the doctor looking gloomily at the breadcrumb-covered slabs.

'You're probably all the better without them,' said the Reverend Mother briskly. She selected a couple of pages from the middle of yesterday's *Cork Examiner* and wrapped up the contents of the plate. 'These will go well with the baked potatoes for the children tomorrow,' she said. 'We're running low on potatoes. I must get the gardener to sow double the amount next March,' she said. There was no need, she thought, to speak any more about the Queen's Old Castle murder, nor of the accusations made by the wife of the dead man. And so she chatted about her scheme to provide a hot and nutritious midday meal for the poorest children in her school and told him of how even the children who usually had a slice of bread and jam were now turning up with nothing, as the scrambled eggs and hot potatoes, straight from the convent oven, had proved to be so tasty. By the time that she rose to return to her convent, Dr Scher had recovered his usual good humour and had not only found her a shopping bag to accommodate a large part of his supper, but insisted on driving her back to St Mary's Isle.

She would say no more to him about Mrs Fitzwilliam, she resolved as she went through the door. She was satisfied that she had taken all possible steps to ensure the safety of fourteen-year-old Brian Maloney from accusations made by the widow of the dead man.

But, she wondered, as she absent-mindedly greeted Sister Bernadette and handed over the goodies that would garnish the potatoes for the hungry children tomorrow, was Brian Maloney now safe? He was, she thought, a very convenient scapegoat.

EIGHTEEN

B rian Maloney thought that everyone must be able to smell the gas. He hesitated for a moment at the door of the dormitory where he and nineteen other apprentices spent their nights. And then, after a smart kick in the shins from seventeen-year-old Henry Spiller, he followed the others. No one spoke. Séamus O'Connor was the counter hand in charge of the boys and he stood, candle in hand, bored and eager to get away and join the others in the pub on North Main Street. They'd all suffer for it if he put the man in a worse mood. Brian moved further in. The smell, he thought, grew worse as he went down the room towards his own bed. He hated that room, in wet weather its damp ancient stone walls drooled strings of green slobber, festooned, in places, with clumps of strange bright orange fungi. He hated the glass just above his head, the incessant thunder of rain on wet nights, the dense eeriness of the fog that pressed down just above his face and occasionally the pale cold glaring light of the moon that penetrated even shut eyelids. Just two tiny barred windows set high up on one wall and no one had ever seen them open. The long narrow room smelled of mildew and of damp; of strange moulds and of the sweat of the twenty boys.

Foggy tonight! Place was wetter than ever. The raw damp had made the walls stream. No glimmer of light from overhead. Just blackness pressing down. Cloudy, wet, foggy evening. Just the one flame illuminating a man's sour face and yellow teeth as Séamus O'Connor got ready to count down the moments until the room would be left to odour-filled darkness.

Tonight, there was definitely something different about the familiar smells. A stink of rotten eggs. Gas! His heart jumped into his throat, choking, retching. For a moment he thought of his mother, gone off with her fancy man and leaving him alone. He blinked the tears from his eyes. He had to manage on his own.

'Get on, Maloney, get on with you; undress; get into bed. I'm warning you, all of you. Sixty seconds! And then I blow out the candle. One . . . two . . . three . . .'

Brian took off his shoes and then his suit as fast as he could. If it wasn't hanging up within seconds there would be trouble. It didn't matter about inner clothes, but the outer had to look smart and clean. Three fresh shirts a week. Suits cleaned every three months. That was the rule. He sat on the edge of his bed still wearing his shoes and socks. He felt something hard beneath the thin flock mattress. He pulled on the old pair of trousers and tattered jersey that he wore to clean the glass. He would sleep in those. Nothing odd in that. Many of the boys did it. The place was freezing at night. But he felt strangely shaky. The smell was stronger by the minute; not just the usual dust, dry and itchy to the nose, nor the usual moulds, rotten and pungent, but the deadly sweet smell of gas. And it was coming from his bed. Too near to him! He nerved himself to scream. Scream! Quickly! Quick before the door was closed! But just when he needed all of the power of his lungs, his throat closed over.

'. . . fifty-eight . . . fifty-nine . . . sixty!' And then darkness.

'Christ! I smell gas,' shouted Henry Spiller. 'God, Maloney, it's coming from your bed. Help! Gas!'

But it was too late. The door had slammed shut. The key had rattled in the door. Footsteps echoing down the flimsy staircase. They were locked in until six a.m. on the following morning. Brian felt around the edge of his bed, lifted the flock mattress. Knew what would be underneath, on top of the iron springs. Screamed! Small, rounded, barrel-shaped. Hand moving over, counting, mechanically counting. 'Gas canisters! Under my mattress. Six of them! Christ Almighty!'

'Don't touch them, Maloney!' Too late! He had sat on them! The lids had fallen off. Tom Donovan, almost hysterical. Henry Spiller screaming 'Help!' John Joe retching. Christy Callinan crying, 'Mammy! Mammy!' Wished they'd shut up. He had an idea. Something to do. Now it had come back into his mind.

He needed to unscrew the metal ball on the top of his bed! Had done it often enough out of sheer boredom when the thunder of the rain on the glass roof had kept him awake. But now was different. Now his hands trembled and his mind was foggy. Couldn't turn it. Didn't open! Sick and dazed! Wrong way! Stupid!

Now it was coming, travelling smoothly on the metal grooves! Not too much time to waste. Getting giddy. Tried to ignore it, to keep calm, to take the time needed. If only they'd stop screaming and shouting, bursting his eardrums. No point in it anyway. The whole of the Queen's Old Castle had been empty except for Séamus O'Connor when they were sent up to bed. He'd be long gone by now.

The ball on the iron bedframe was off. 'Take cover!' It was all that his lungs could manage to spit out. He was gasping for breath and struggling against nausea and the pressing need to vomit. He raised his hand. Heavy as a ton, that iron ball. His muscles almost refusing to move. He should have told them all to stand back, to go towards the door, but he knew that there was no way that his befuddled brain could get the words out. The gas from the six canisters had affected him very quickly. He tried to remember where the wall was, and then recollected that it must be an arm's length in front of him. If it had to brain someone, it had better be Henry Spiller. The thought was in his head when he gulped hard and knew that he was going to vomit.

It was no good. His hand, weighed down by the heavy iron ball dropped down to his side. He wobbled and then reached out and held onto the iron frame of his bed. His legs trembled and his head was sick and dizzy. He tried to straighten himself, tried to stop the dizziness overwhelming him and swallowed back the vomit. *Not now!* The words shrieked through his ears. He gathered up his remaining shreds of energy, raised his arm and flung the iron ball as high as he possibly could.

The crash when the glass smashed into smithereens miraculously restored him. Raw damp foggy air flushed the sick sweetness of the gas from his mouth and nose. He felt blood trickle and then flow down his face. He reached up, touched his head and found it wet and sticky. Sliced by a shard of glass. The pain from the cut overwhelmed the nausea. He sat on the side of the bed and bowed his head in his hands.

'Christ Maloney! You've gone and done it. They'll kill you.'

'They'll string you up!'

'I'm cut!' Christy Callinan sounded about seven years old.

'God, my bed is covered in glass!'

'Don't think that we're going to cover up for you. You're the one that done it and you're the one to take the blame!'

'You'd better cut your throat with one of them pieces of glass. They'll hang you for that.'

No, they wouldn't. Won't get a chance. He said to himself. He had his shoes and his socks on. Could move about. The glass crunched beneath his feet. He touched his head once more. Getting stickier now. He didn't care. Still a bit of a smell of gas, but it was going, evaporating, mopped up by the raw, wet air. He grabbed his bedclothes, dirty old blankets, sheet and pillow and the mattress, too. He could feel his way. Should know this room as well as the back of his own hand. Bundled the bedclothes under one arm, hand fastened onto the top of the mattress, dragged it onto the floor. Three steps forward, turn left, between the beds now. Could hear them all shouting and complaining. Didn't care. Better to be wet and cold than to be choked to death by the gas in that stinking room with no windows.

He stumbled once, but got to his feet again. The voices guided him. The two oldest boys, Henry Spiller and Tom Donovan, had beds nearest to the door and Henry Spiller never stopped talking, never stopped complaining though he was the furthest away from the broken glass. Still, he was glad to hear him for once. He guided himself that way. A black night with not a star or a slit of a moon to help. No smell of gas left, though. No gas left! He repeated these words again and again. They seemed to help. No wet down this end either. Should have told the kids, Christy and Jimmy, to follow him, but he was too weak and sick to make the effort.

'What are you going to tell them, Maloney? Christ! O'Connor will flog you raw in the morning.'

Good! Keep talking, Henry, lad! Brian stumbled on, dragging his load with him. It was important to get to the door. Another few steps. He tried the handle, but knew that he wouldn't be able to do anything. That door was locked every night with an enormous key the size of his foot. Without replying or saying a word to anyone, he dropped the mattress, and the pillow just in front of the door.

By now he was quite reckless and knew that there was no future for him in the Queen's Old Castle. By feel, he stripped off the pillow slip, made a pad with half of it and then tore the rest into shreds so as to bandage his head and stop the flow of blood over his face. And then he dropped down upon the mattress and covered himself with the threadbare old blankets, pulling them right over his ears so that he didn't have to listen to Henry Spiller any more. A sharp pain from his lacerated scalp, but he smothered it with plans for the future.

A faint grey light had filled the attic room by the time that Brian Maloney woke up. The woman who came in to scrub the floors stumped up the stairs every morning, banging her bucket on each step, rattling the mop handle against the hand-rail and the newel rod, shouting, 'Up all of ye!' at the top of her voice. The quicker she could get them out, the quicker she could get the stairs, the passageway to the office and the office itself, mopped out. Brian was ready for her as soon as the key turned in the lock.

In a flash, he was past her. Running down the stairs. No trace of sickness, now. His head hurt, but the bleeding had stopped. He snatched off the blood-stiffened pad of the pillow slip and dropped it on the stairway. It bled again a little, but only a little. Before the first boy, carrying his pot of night soil down to the yard, had put a foot on the stairs, Brian had turned the key in the front door and was out on the pavement of the Grand Parade. Nobody much was around, just a few people going to six o'clock early mass and communion in the Augustinian church nearby. They gave him a few curious looks and he guessed that he had dried blood on his face. He stopped at the fountain in the middle of the Grand Parade, dipped the end of his sleeve in and then changed his mind. Let it alone, he thought and crossed back over to South Main Street and headed towards the convent on St Mary's Isle.

NINETEEN

The Reverend Mother spent longer in the convent chapel after the six o'clock early morning service than was her wont. The celebration of the feast day of the Irish Saint Brigid had reminded the convent chaplain that he had not yet been provided with a set of green robes to do full honour to his native country. The Reverend Mother, suffering from a pain in her chest, but aware of the dangers to her reputation of appearing parsimonious to the Church, had listened very carefully to his grumbles, had agreed wholeheartedly with his speculations on how good they would look, but was sorrowfully lacking in ideas as to how money should be raised for this purpose. She listened to various suggestions with a dubious face and slightly raised eyebrows, and then when he ran out of ideas said, with a sudden flash of inspiration, 'I know what I'll do, Father. I'll write to the bishop. I'll do that straight away.' And with an air of decision, she left him and strode quickly down the path towards the back door, smiling to herself as she foretold the bishop's pained response about the lack of diocesan funds for such a cause.

It was just as she had lifted a hand towards the latch that someone spoke from behind a bush.

'Reverend Mother,' a hoarse, cracked adolescent voice, but one that she knew well.

'Brian,' she said, 'what on earth . . .' And then she stopped. Brian Maloney had edged his way past the laurel leaves and presented a face shockingly smeared with dried blood.

She assessed him quickly. There was a patch of blood-hardened hair on his scalp, cuts, lightly scabbed over, on his hands, and one, long, narrow slit running down one cheek. All superficial, she guessed.

'Come into my room,' she said. She held the door open until he was through and safely in the passageway and then she led the way. His story could wait. By now Sister Bernadette

would have placed her breakfast and a pot of tea on a tray
and the fire would have been burning since before the early
morning service. A cup of tea, some food, some warmth and
then he could tell his story. The rest of the community had
filed into the refectory to eat their porridge and boiled eggs
so they met no one on their way. The Reverend Mother
unlocked her door, ushered him to a seat by the fire, poured
him a cup of tea and set a plate of bread and butter beside him.
'Wait here,' she said, but took the precaution of locking the
door before she went up the corridor and secured some warm
water and an old face flannel.

By the time that she came back, he had eaten and drunk
all that she had provided for him. Nothing much wrong with
him, she thought as silently she mopped his face with the
flannel. His hair she left untouched. Scalp wounds bled
profusely; she knew that from all of her years of coping with
playground falls. She wouldn't risk disturbing the healing
scab that had spread over the dried blood. She was rather
touched by the trusting way in which he turned his face up
to her and submitted to her thorough cleansing of the blood
from his face and about how patiently he waited until she
told him to tell her what had happened.

She listened carefully until he came to the end of his story.
A brave boy, she thought, and she admired the quick thinking
that had spurred him to undo the iron knob from his bed and
hurl it through the glass roof of the Queen's Old Castle.
According to his story, his resourcefulness had saved his own
life and perhaps the lives of those in the beds on either side
to him. He had told that story well, she thought. Had made
her see that dormitory with its damp, unplastered walls, and
the ten beds on either side of the long room beneath the
glass roof, made her hear the exclamations of the boys, had
made her almost experience the horror of that moment when
he had plumped down on that flock mattress and smelled the
dangerous odour.

'I think, Brian,' she said after a few moments' thought, 'I
think that I should send for Inspector Cashman. This sounds
as though it were an attempt to kill you.' She sat back and

looked for his reaction. Not too upset by the whole affair, she thought, considering that he was only fourteen years old. These children grew up very quickly. They became accustomed to unpleasant, difficult and dangerous situations from a very early stage in their existence. It wasn't so much bravery as a certain stoicism, an acceptance of what life threw at them and a clear understanding of how much, or how little, they could influence events around them. The poor, she thought, were more cynical about the powers of the police than the society to which she and her cousin Lucy belonged were. He bore a resigned look upon his newly washed face now, she thought. Much more resigned than relieved. There was no impression to be got from him that he, in any way, felt that this would solve his problem.

'I suppose that you'd have to,' he said, rather more to himself than to her.

She had risen to her feet in order to go to the telephone, but then something in his voice stopped her. She cast a glance at the clock over the door. A bit early, anyway, she thought, and she sat back onto her chair again. His phrase interested her.

'Is there anything else that I could do?' she asked respectfully, thinking that after his heroism and his quick thinking the night before that he deserved to be consulted.

He thought about that for a while. 'I knowed, before now, that they were out to get me,' he said eventually. 'The old woman. Miss Kitty. Tom Donovan. Mr O'Connor. They were all saying that I was the one that dunnit. Saying they saw me send up a change barrel with a gas cylinder in it. I went to see Eileen, you know, Eileen MacSweeney, she used to be one of the big girls when I was a little mickey man here in the convent. I thought that Eileen might get me in with the Shinners, get me a bit of protection, like.'

The phrase amused her, but she was careful to keep a smile from her face. He deserved serious attention. There was little doubt in her mind that the presence of six gas canisters in his bed did appear to be strongly connected with the murder of Mr Joseph Fitzwilliam.

'And what did Eileen say?' she enquired with interest.

'She put the peelers on to me,' he said in disgusted tones.

'I see,' she said. Just as she had intended to do herself. It obviously hadn't worked then, and it might not work now. She looked across at him. 'And what did Inspector Cashman do?' she asked.

'He took me back. Talked to Mr O'Connor. Told him that he wasn't to blame me for going to the police, that it was police business. Did his best, I suppose.'

'But what did Mr O'Connor do?'

He thought about that. 'Told Miss Kitty,' he said. 'Told her that I had been to the barracks. Said I had been complaining. Henry Spiller, her apprentice, told me. Said I was in bad trouble. The two of them had their heads together, talking about me.'

That had been an unexpected reply. She had expected that the owner of the business might have been involved.

'And Miss Kitty had been one of the ones that had accused you . . .' The Reverend Mother thought about the complexities of this business. 'And what happened next?' she asked.

'Nothing,' he said. 'Didn't say nothing.' And then added, 'That scared me.'

Once again she silently applauded his astuteness. He would, she thought, have preferred punishment.

'I told myself to be very careful.' He said that as much to himself as to her. A reminder, she thought it was.

She nodded approval at his words. And, indeed, she told herself, it certainly behoved him to tread carefully. That seemed a rather unholy alliance between the daughter of the owner and an ambitious counter hand.

'And then the major made this speech. Said his old mam was a bit gaga-like, but . . .'

The Reverend Mother bit her lip. 'But, it didn't work.' She finished his sentence for him and then sat and thought what was best to do.

'Well, the old lady hasn't been in the shop since then. Miss Kitty had to take her place, gave John Joe Burke a bad time. Could hear her shrieking at him. Didn't say a word to me, though.'

'So nobody said anything to you, since the major spoke to them, is that right, Brian?'

'That's right. Though I'd prefer they'd be slagging me off than poisoning me. That's a terrible way to kill anyone. Just like rats in the tunnel, the whole twenty of us there in the dormitory.'

The Reverend Mother shared his horror. Though from what she had been told of those gas canisters, she reckoned that they would not have been powerful enough to kill the boys in that dormitory with its unplastered, roughly laid, stone walls and its high glass roof. Nevertheless, Brian, himself, had probably been in acute danger, especially if, like lots of children, he had stuck his head under the bedclothes. Keeps your nose and lips from freezing, a five-year-old girl had explained, displaying to the Reverend Mother the picture that she had sketched of herself and her four sisters, outlined as five neat lumps under one blanket.

'Brian,' she said. 'Who could have put these gas canisters in your bed?'

He looked at her with the slight amazement that children show when their teacher admits to not knowing the answer. 'It was Mr O'Connor, wasn't it? He's the one that keeps the key to the dormitory.'

'So it's kept locked during the day, is that right?'

'Except on Sunday,' he said.

'And where does Mr O'Connor keep the key?'

'Dunno,' he said.

A routine response, she thought, and waited.

'In his pocket, I suppose,' he said. There had been an interval of silence while he thought about the question. 'In his coat pocket,' he went on, speaking quite slowly now and with a very serious, thoughtful look on his face. 'He'd be wearing his coat when he locks us up at night. And he'd be wearing his coat when he unlocks. He's the one that opens the shop in the morning. He keeps the keys. He'd give the key to old Maggie and she'd give it back to him, or to Mr Robert, sometimes, but usually he has it.'

'And where does he hang his coat?'

'In the cupboard, behind the counter. All the counters have these cupboards, that's what they're called but they're more like little rooms. He hangs his coat up there and spare boxes of shoes and boots are in there. Not much room for anything.'

The Reverend Mother reflected on this. The shop had seemed hectically busy on the morning when she had visited, but she supposed on normal, non-sale days there might well be slack times when the counter hands visited each other, indulged in a few minutes of chat.

'Miss Kitty is always coming over to borrow one of our rulers, or our tape measures,' put in Brian, as though he had guessed her thoughts.

'Do you think that she might have been the one to put the gas cylinders in your bed?' She put the question bluntly to him, but he was not taken aback. He considered it carefully.

'Nah,' he said decisively. 'They'd be in it together, the pair of them. If they made up their mind to croak me off, then he's the one to have done it. Nobody would wonder if they saw him go into the dormitory during the day time, but they would wonder if they saw her.'

A good point, thought the Reverend Mother. 'And who else could have gone up those stairs and had no one wonder what they were doing?'

'Mr Robert,' he said immediately. 'He's up and down the stairs all day, now. He's taken the old man's place in the office. He has the job of sending the barrels whizzing back down.' There was a distinct note of envy in his voice, and the Reverend Mother suppressed a smile. This matter, she told herself, was a difficult and a dangerous one and it was a matter that she had to solve quickly. She couldn't keep a fourteen-year-old boy immured in a convent of nuns, but neither could she condemn him to being sent back to that shop. That glass roof that he had broken would cost a large sum of money to repair. It was possible that Brian's unfortunate mother or her family would be asked to pay for it. She had heard of such things before now. In any case, the thought of those deadly gas canisters worried her. Six of them had suddenly appeared. Were there others lurking around in the shop, or in the possession of someone connected to the shop? Something terrible could result from any unconsidered action of hers.

She made up her mind.

'Brian,' she said, 'I have no way around this. I have to call the inspector and ask him to come here and to listen to your story.'

To her surprise, he nodded. 'I was thinking that you would have to do that,' he said.

She applauded his pragmatic and sensible attitude. 'And have you any idea of what I could do with you?'

He looked at her hopefully. 'You could maybe dress me up as a nun?' His voice held a tentative note.

She looked at the spotty, adolescent face with the slight moustache on the upper lip and the sprouting hairs on the chin.

'No, I couldn't,' she said firmly.

He showed little surprise or disappointment. Just turned the matter over in his mind. She had thought he would suggest that he be sent back to his mother, but that did not seem to be a solution that had occurred to him, or if it had, he had dismissed it as impossible. Sister Bernadette, who knew all the gossip, had hinted strongly that there had been another man involved in Mrs Maloney's removal from the city.

'I suppose that the inspector could put me in a cell,' he said eventually. 'Not for ever, but just while he was sorting things out. I wouldn't mind. Give me a bit of a rest, like. And then I couldn't be blamed if anything else happened? If someone murders the old woman or someone, then no one could say it was me. And if I had a ball, I could play hand ball against the walls.'

The Reverend Mother looked at him speechlessly. This offer had taken her aback. Brian, however, was looking more cheerful, almost as though he felt that he had solved all of his problems.

'How big do you think that a cell would be, Reverend Mother?' he enquired. 'What sort of space between the walls?'

The Reverend Mother seized on the question. 'I don't know, Brian,' she said seriously. 'But I'm sure that it is something that Inspector Cashman could tell you.' She could see that he was turning over the possibilities of a private handball court within the precincts of the police barracks. It wasn't, she thought suddenly, an utterly impossible idea. At least it would bring safety, would allow Patrick a certain amount of time to work out the problems. But then her heart sank. Poverty and desperation brought its own intense problems to this distressful city. Seldom had a night gone by without the noise of gunfire. Drunken fights on the quays were hardly reported these days. The gaols were overflowing and only the other day she had read about the scandal of convicted criminals having to be housed in police barracks as there was no place available for them in the gaol. Patrick would not be able to allocate a cell for the safekeeping of this boy.

'Or else,' said Brian, watching her face carefully, 'you could send for the major, Reverend Mother. He might get me smuggled out of the country and send me over to the British army. That's what I would really like to do.'

'What would your mother say to that, Brian?'

He shrugged. 'Wouldn't care. She's gone off.'

'Have you got her address, Brian?'

'No.' The monosyllable was curtly enunciated and the boy's face closed in a forbidding manner.

'Never mind,' said the Reverend Mother. 'I'll do what you suggest and send for the major, but I think I must send for Inspector Cashman, also. There is this matter of the broken roof. We'll have to sort that out, make sure that it is on record that you did that, not out of wilful vandalism, but because you were in danger of your life. You, yourself, must tell the whole story to Inspector Cashman.'

She thought that he might protest at that, but he shrugged his shoulders.

'If you like. Don't mind. But the major 'ud be the one that would look after me. You'll get him to come along, won't you, Reverend Mother?'

'Yes, I will, Brian.' The boy was probably right. She should notify the major. Legally Brian was bound to the owner of the Queen's Old Castle Stores and it was only right that the owner should be informed of his presence here at the convent. 'Now, while we are waiting for all those people to get out of their beds and have their breakfasts,' she said cheerfully, 'I think you might give Sister Bernadette a hand in the kitchen. She needs help with scrubbing the potatoes and putting them in the oven for the little children's lunch. You don't mind helping, do you, Brian?'

He seemed enormously relieved at that and assured her that he would like to help. And chop wood or draw water or anything that needed a man's strength. He was quite effusive in his offers to do any jobs she wanted done. To the Reverend Mother's pleasure, he remembered Sister Bernadette and had a story to tell about her giving him a piece of cake once when he had been knocked over in the playground. It had been, she thought as she walked him down the corridor, a flash of inspiration. He was unlikely to be a great reader and the parlours were chilly and lonely places for a boy who was used to plenty of company. She left him to Sister Bernadette and went off to telephone Major James Fitzwilliam.

TWENTY

The major was the one who answered the shop phone when she had called and he already knew the whole story. 'I'll be with you in under five minutes, Reverend Mother,' he said.

The Reverend Mother felt that she needed to see him before Brian burst out with his side of the story and so once she had put down the phone, she lingered in the hallway, near to the front door, passing the time by examining carefully, for the first time in years, the rather faded pictures that hung there. Her cousin Lucy had told her of a convent in Waterford where a picture that hung in the parlour for almost a hundred years had been found to be painted by some Italian artist and to be worth a considerable sum of money. The Reverend Mother did not think that she was an expert, but, nevertheless, she doubted whether any of these uninspired paintings of St Therese of Lisieux, entitled 'God's Sweet Little Flower', or the lurid scenes of the crucifixion would draw any splendid offers from some connoisseurs. She had begun to speculate upon the possibility that in some dark corner of an upstairs corridor there might be lurking an early work by Daniel Maclise, famous for being a friend of Charles Dickens, but a native of Cork city, when a military-sounding step clipped its way along the path to the front door. She slipped a cough lozenge into her mouth and opened the door before the bell could be rung, anxious not to interrupt Sister Bernadette or, indeed, to have Brian Maloney appear prematurely upon the scene.

'Come in, Major,' she said politely and ushered him through the hallway and into her room. Presumably he had been served with breakfast in his father's house not too long ago, so she saw no need to press cups of tea and slices of cake upon him. The sooner they had their talk, the better, and she bade him hang up his coat and hat in clipped and

authoritative tones. She moved her chair near to the fire. She
was chilled to the bone since her session with the chaplain
in that cold chapel. Still, this business about Brian had to be
settled.

'I'm very worried and concerned about this affair at Queen's
Old Castle last night, Major,' she began.

He made no pretence of misunderstanding her. A man of
keen wits and a lot of self-possession.

'Do I understand that young Maloney came here this
morning,' he enquired coolly.

'He is a past pupil of the school here,' retorted the Reverend
Mother, doing her best to suppress her cough, but having to
yield to it. She wished now that she had ordered tea for the
wretched man. Something hot to drink would have helped
to soothe the tickle in her chest. 'He was deserted by his
mother once she had placed his future and his well-being in
the hands of the proprietor of the Queen's Old Castle,' she
said once she had recovered. Surreptitiously she slipped
another clove lozenge from her pocket and popped it into
her mouth. Sabres out, she thought and looked steadily at
him. Brian had spoken of him with touching faith, but she
could not help thinking how convenient it would be for the
Fitzwilliam family if Brian could be the scapegoat.

'My father,' he returned.

'And now you, yourself, of course.'

He sat back in his chair and regarded her with a certain
degree of amusement. 'You hold me responsible for sorting
out any differences between the young apprentices of a shop
in which I have no interest and which I hope to have sold by
this time next week,' he observed.

'I hold you, and all men, responsible to prevent wilful murder
of a boy entrusted to the care of your family's business,' she
said swiftly and felt a stab of pain in her chest.

He sat up rather straight at that. 'Murder is an odd word,'
he remarked.

'And a most unpleasant affair,' she said. 'And if the death
of your father is counted as murder, then the attempted
death of young Brian Maloney must be reckoned to be
attempted murder. Don't you agree, Major Fitzwilliam?'

He sat back. 'Let's hear what his story to you was, Reverend Mother.'

His tone was perfectly polite, but she resented his manner. She was not accustomed to being spoken to like that. For over fifty years she had worked in Cork, had been a Reverend Mother for almost forty of those years, and she had become a person of influence and of importance in her native city and had during these years never hesitated to exploit her position whenever she needed to do so. She looked across at him steadily. A thought had come to her mind.

'Could you tell me why you brought these gas canisters home with you, Major? A whole suitcase of them, I am informed.' He looked taken aback at that and she followed up swiftly. 'Rather unusual in someone of your position to misappropriate army property,' she said. And then she sat back and surveyed the position as if it were a chessboard.

'As to that, there was a whole roomful of these things at my barracks, of little or no value,' he said stiffly. 'Does that answer your question?'

'Not really,' she said. A poor explanation, she thought, but she refrained from drawing an analogy with the theft of one gun from amongst many. She was sure that any foot soldier who had done such a thing would have been court-martialled.

'We seem to be wandering from the question of young Maloney,' he said. 'But since you seem interested, these gas canisters are not often used these days. Surplus to requirements, you could say. DDT is a more effective substance. And as to why I brought some of the gas canisters home with me, well, I did so at the request of my father. I had been talking to him on my last leave about how they remove odours and he was interested in that because of the problem with damp in the Queen's Old Castle. The place should have been pulled down a hundred years ago,' he added.

'And that's what is going to happen to it now?' The Reverend Mother excused herself this piece of curiosity. Lucy, she knew, would never forgive her if she passed up on the opportunity to acquire any additional details.

'That's right,' said the major curtly. 'Once all of the stock is sold off. Three four-storey new buildings can be fitted into that space.'

He was only just restraining himself from asking what business of hers it was, she thought, and hastened to absolve herself from idle curiosity. 'Presumably, then, all of that dangerous glass will be removed from the roof before work begins on demolishing the building. Brian will be pleased; he has a great admiration for you and would not want to have done you any harm,' she explained.

To her surprise, he looked touched. Rather embarrassed. Smoothing his hand over the glossy wing of his swept-back hair. 'I suppose he panicked,' he said awkwardly.

'Understandingly,' she replied and was satisfied to hear a tart note in her voice. Really, those clove lozenges were excellent. She must remember to compliment Sister Bernadette upon them. 'After all,' she continued, 'not much more than a week ago, Brian witnessed the death of your father from just one of those gas canisters.'

'Wouldn't have done him any harm as long as he didn't breathe in the gas,' he said with an annoying air of indifference.

'And your father? It did him harm.'

'My father was an old man with a bad heart.'

'Was that known?' she asked.

'He told me, but no, I don't think that anyone else knew. He would have been afraid of upsetting my mother.'

The Reverend Mother hoped that her face did not betray her scepticism, but she found it hard to believe in that motive. Dr Scher, she would be almost sure, had not been aware of anything wrong with the man's heart. There was perhaps a chance of the man going to a specialist in Dublin, but in that case, surely it would have shown up during the autopsy. Still, she told herself, the major would be quite right in hinting that this was none of her business. Her concern now had to be for Brian and she turned over in her mind a way of ensuring his safety.

'I presume that some of the gas canisters were stolen,' she said. 'Who do you think placed six of them in Brian's bed? Just under his mattress, so he told me.'

'That's right. I went up and had a look when my brother

phoned me about the broken glass. He had been in early that morning so he had the whole story. Yes, there were six of them, all with their lids off, lying on the bedsprings. I'd say that they were left almost unscrewed and then when he sat on the edge of the bed the lids popped off.'

The Reverend Mother nodded. 'That would fit with what he told me, but why should anyone have wanted to kill him?' She would, she thought, bring him to acknowledge that Brian should not go back to the Queen's Old Castle. Perhaps the major might pull a few strings to get the boy into another shop immediately, rather than remain until the stock was sold.

The major pursed his lips. 'Another boy playing a trick,' he suggested. 'Not that much gas in those things, Reverend Mother. Only dangerous if there is no air in the place. That's a big room. Went up there this morning. Didn't think that anyone, except perhaps the boy himself, would have been in any great danger.'

The Reverend Mother left a silence. A particularly stupid suggestion, she thought. From Brian's description, every boy in the dormitory had been terrified. He had painted a vivid picture of the screaming and the choking noises until he had broken the glass ceiling with the iron knob from the bedstead.

'They are locked in every night, Major,' she said after a moment. 'Locked in from nine o'clock in the evening until six o'clock in the morning. Every boy would know that. Would know that there was no escape. It must have been quite terrifying for them.'

He shifted uncomfortably. 'Be glad to get that place off my hands,' he muttered and then looked around as there was a gentle tap upon the door. He sat back on his chair and looked pointedly at his watch while the Reverend Mother called out, 'Come in.'

'Excuse me, Reverend Mother,' Sister Bernadette said apologetically, 'but Miss Fitzwilliam is here, wants to see you urgently. That's what she said.'

'Miss Fitzwilliam?' queried the Reverend Mother. She glanced at the major and saw that he looked astonished.

'Miss Fitzwilliam, which Miss Fitzwilliam, sister?' His

manner was polite, but very authoritative. A man who was used to giving orders.

'Miss Kitty, Major,' faltered Sister Bernadette. 'It's Miss Kitty Fitzwilliam. Says that she knows that you are here.' She stopped, her colour high and she appeared confused and embarrassed.

The Reverend Mother felt annoyed. Sister Bernadette was gentle and hospitable. This woman had upset her and the Reverend Mother rose to the occasion.

'Oh, dear, Sister Bernadette,' she said, 'I'm sorry that you have been disturbed, and on your busiest day of the week. I am so sorry this has happened.' She left a pause and then changed her tone of voice for an authoritative one. 'Major,' she said firmly, 'please go with Sister Bernadette and bring your sister to see me. I presume she came to see me.'

Sister Bernadette looked startled and even more embarrassed at the prospect of the major in all the splendour of his uniform, being sent on this errand, but the Reverend Mother felt rather pleased with herself. She stayed sitting down until they had left the room, but then left her seat and went through into the corridor to wait in stony silence to receive her uninvited guest. And, of course, to avoid any whispered conversations between the two as they walked through the empty space.

Kitty, she thought, had a belligerent look about her. She glimpsed the Reverend Mother, standing in a pool of light outside her door, but she did not call out a greeting and instead talked to her brother, loudly and aggressively, about the huge amount of money that the broken glass roof would cost. She did not even greet the Reverend Mother when they arrived at the door to her room, but went on talking about glassmakers to the major.

'Nonsense,' said the Reverend Mother firmly. 'A couple of sheets of hardboard will tide you over until the shop is emptied. Now do come in, Miss Fitzwilliam. Come in and sit down on that chair by the window. What we need to discuss now is the problem of poor Brian Maloney. After all, for a fourteen-year-old boy it has been a terrifying experience. To find out that someone is trying to kill you would be horrendous for any adult, but for a child of that age . . . .!' She left her sentence unfinished and eyed them both.

The major was looking uncomfortable and ill-at-ease, but Kitty threw her hands in the air and exploded into a hearty burst of laughter. The Reverend Mother suddenly recollected the words spoken by her cousin Lucy. *I believe that one of the twins, Kitty, I think, used to go in for amateur dramatics at one stage.*

'That boy!' exclaimed Kitty when she had milked the last drop of merriment from her laugh. 'That boy, Reverend Mother, he is the greatest liar that you could ever meet. You wouldn't believe it if I were to tell you some stories!'

The Reverend Mother turned an interested and attentive face in her direction which disconcerted her for a moment. The words flowed on, but now she directed them at her brother.

'Robert will tell you, James, the trouble we have had with Brian Maloney. Mr O'Connor took such pains with him because his mother disappeared once she had paid down the apprentice fee and Mr O'Connor was sorry for the boy. But there was no doing anything with Brian Maloney. A liar and a thief, Reverend Mother! That's Brian Maloney for you!' She had whirled around to face the Reverend Mother. The silent reception of her words seemed to disconcert her again. She looked from one face to the other, stopped to draw breath and then said emphatically, 'I wouldn't believe a word that he said.'

'What would you expect him to say?' The question, thought the Reverend Mother was an innocuous one. And she uttered it blandly. It interested the major, but it irritated his sister.

'Lies!' She almost spat the words. 'He'd tell lies. That's what I would expect.'

'But he did have six gas canisters placed in his bed.' The Reverend Mother glanced at the major for corroboration, but he remained silent.

'Put them there himself,' snapped Kitty. 'Looking for attention, making trouble.'

'Who would he have been making trouble for?' The major asked the question before the Reverend Mother could frame it. She was conscious that there was a shake in the woman's voice. What was she so worried about that the boy might have said? During the silence that followed her mind went to Brian's words. Only one person had possible access to the dormitory during the day and that was Mr Séamus O'Connor. The boys were only allowed to go there during the day on a Sunday, otherwise the room was kept locked, and the key in his possession, until nine o'clock bedtime when the twenty apprentices were herded in and locked up until six o'clock in the morning. Brian's story about a possible love affair between Séamus O'Connor and his employer's daughter came to her mind and she decided that there was probably some truth in it. She looked across at the major and saw irritation, but not suspicion on his face. He did not appear to want an answer to his question, or at least he didn't feel inclined to push for one, because he followed up his words without waiting for an answer.

'I don't know what all of this is to do with you, Kitty,' he said in authoritative tones. 'Now I think it would be best if you got back to the shop and leave this business for me to handle. Come along, Kitty. The Reverend Mother will excuse you, I'm sure.' And then he took his sister by her arm, ushered her through the door and in a moment his firm footsteps sounded in the passageway outside.

Kitty had gone with him, had gone without a word of protest. There had been an odd sound to the major's voice, almost a warning note. Did he know something about his sister, something that ensured her obedience? He was an intelligent man, a qualified barrister; had acted as an army judge on occasion. It would, she thought, be hard to pull wool over his eyes. On the other hand, he would want no scandal, no suspicions that a daughter might have been involved in the murder of her father. The Reverend Mother put a few more pieces of coal onto her fire and sat back on her chair and awaited, with folded hands, the return of Major Fitzwilliam to her room. And while she waited, she turned over the whole matter in her mind, bringing up the various points such as profit, accessibility, knowledge and probability. In the end, she sighed. It had to be like that, she thought and the consequences of the revelation would have to be faced. Murder could not be ignored. She sat very still and stared, without seeing anything, through the window and into the fog-wreathed bushes in the garden.

He was longer than she had expected. She heard his voice. Greeting Sister Bernadette, assuring her that she could rely on him to close the front door carefully, joking with her, commenting on the weather and that cold north-easterly wind, congratulating her on the beautifully polished hall table, pretending that he was scared to dull it by placing his hat on its surface. A dialogue. The major's jokes, Sister Bernadette's giggles, her soft country accent. But not a word from Kitty as he took her out to the front door. Not even after Sister Bernadette had returned to her kitchen.

But there would have been words. Kitty, thought the Reverend Mother, must now be in her forties. This late romance would have come at a time in her life when she had almost given up hope of escaping the dreary treadmill of her existence. And Major James Fitzwilliam would not want any inter-ference in his own plans. Sell the shop, settle his mother, pay off his brother, get one sister, at least, married and off his hands. She tried to imagine what the last words exchanged between the brother and sister on her doorstep might be and came up with one phrase. *Leave it to me*, she imagined him to say and then there was a crisp bang of the front door, quick footsteps coming back down the corridor, her door opening without a knock, or even a hesitation.

'Now, Reverend Mother, perhaps I could see the boy.' The words were uttered before the door was closed with a smart click. This was a man who had a piece of business to accom-plish and was determined to get it over and done with as quickly and smartly as he could. The Reverend Mother consid-ered the matter.

'Why is your sister involved in this affair?' She asked the question with an air of mild surprise and told herself that he couldn't object to her curiosity. After all, the manager of the shop was Robert and he had not made an appearance.

The question flummoxed him for a few seconds. And then he made a quick recovery.

'She takes a strong interest in the welfare of the apprentices,' he said blandly and then when she said nothing but looked at

him with what she hoped was an expression of mild surprise,
he hastily amended his reply. 'Yes, welfare, behaviour, all of
that sort of thing,' he said with a careless wave of his hand,
and then reverted to his question. 'And the boy; where have
you hidden him?'

In answer, the Reverend Mother got to her feet. 'Follow
me,' she said and went straight through the door and down the
corridor. As she approached the kitchen she could hear Sister
Bernadette chatting to a young lay sister. Her normal practice
was to knock and to wait for an invitation to enter, but she
knew that Sister Bernadette would not mind and so she opened
the door very quickly and walked through, allowing him to
follow her. Her eyes were on Brian as he looked quickly from
her to her companion.

The expression on the boy's face was one of pure relief.
No hesitation whatsoever. He had been on his knees in
front of the opened oven door of the enormous black range
where Sister Bernadette and her assistants cooked meals for
the community, but as soon as the major appeared, he was on
his feet, his eyes shining.

'Finish your job, lad,' said the major and the Reverend
Mother silently applauded the words. There was something
much friendlier about the word 'lad' than the rather cold and
contemptuous use of a surname only when addressing a boy
not far past childhood. 'Well-scrubbed potatoes,' he added
approvingly. 'What do you think, sister?' He addressed himself
to Sister Bernadette and she beamed approvingly at him.

'Brian was always a good lad,' she said fondly. 'I remember
him when he was no higher than that stool there. Never known
him to tell a lie,' she added with a slight measure of defiance
in her voice.

'So he's told you the whole story, has he?' The major lowered
himself onto the stool and absent-mindedly ate a piece of raw
pastry from the edge of the rolling pin.

Sister Imelda silently brought forward a chair for the
Reverend Mother and she sank onto it and watched the boy
and the man.

'Terrible, wasn't it?' Sister Bernadette chopped deep lines
into the rim of an enormous pie and then pierced a few holes

around the centre of it. Brian hastily lined up the baked potatoes onto the bottom shelf and then got neatly out of her way.
He went straight to the sink and cleaned out the left-over dirt
from the sides. He then picked up the empty potato basket
and went off to the yard with it, carefully closing the door
after him. The major, thought the Reverend Mother, gave him
a glance of approval as though he were a new recruit to a
regiment, but said no more until the boy returned to the kitchen.

'How's he getting on?' he asked, then, directing the question at Sister Bernadette as she bent down to put the tray in
the oven. Brian stiffened and looked at the nun, also.

'He's a good lad,' said Sister Bernadette straightening
herself. 'A good worker. Could do with him every day, couldn't
we?' She addressed the words jokingly to her helper, young
Sister Imelda, but the major took her up instantly.

'You'd have plenty of work for him, then, around the kitchen,
would you?' he said sounding like someone who has just been
struck with a good idea.

Sister Bernadette looked dubiously at the Reverend Mother.
Brian looked surprised and then interested. He stood there,
looking from one to the other and the Reverend Mother was
struck by the expression of hero worship on the boy's face.

'Yes, Brian is a good boy,' she said and waited for the next
move in the game.

'He'd like to be a soldier, isn't that right, Brian?' The
major's eyes were on Brian. Was there a hint of something
akin to a challenge in his voice? The Reverend Mother found
it hard to be sure of what she heard, but was sure that there
was an undercurrent.

'Yes, sir.' There was no mistaking the boy's enthusiasm.

'What I was thinking of, Reverend Mother, was if Brian
could stay here for a few days, he would be . . .' The major
hesitated and then finished by saying, 'He would be happy,
here.' The Reverend Mother wondered whether he had been
about to use the word 'safe'. 'And then,' he continued, 'if
Brian wished for it, my batman is going over to Liverpool in
few days' time, on the night ferry and . . .' He hesitated again
and then finished by saying, 'You're still keen on joining the
army, Brian? Is that right?'

'Oh, yes!' Brian breathed the words, his eyes shining.

'Surely, he's too young,' said the Reverend Mother. But she was conscious that her voice held a questioning note and that she did not, out of hand, reject the notion.

'Not to be a drummer boy,' said the major. 'I'll cover the expenses,' he added.

For a rich man it would not be an over-large sum, but it was, nevertheless, a generous offer. Moreover, it seemed as though it would involve the major in a fair amount of trouble. Why was he doing it? Was it sheer goodness of heart?

'What do you feel about that, Brian?' she asked.

'You won't be a nuisance to the sergeant, will you?' put in the major. 'Not too much chatter.'

'I won't say a word,' breathed Brian. His face was pink with excitement and his eyes shining with sincerity.

'What about your mother, Brian?' asked the Reverend Mother. That thought about the boy's mother had been so much in her mind that she was surprised when he turned a bewildered face towards her. The major, also, looked taken aback.

'She won't care! It's nothing to do with her! I'm grown up, now. She don't want nothing to do with me.' There was a note of almost panic in the boy's voice. Frightened lest the dream of joining the army would be shattered at the last moment. His eyes were fixed imploringly on the major.

'Do you write to your mother, Brian?' The major sounded, thought the Reverend Mother, as though he knew the answer to that question.

'Nah, I told you, sir. She don't write to me and I don't write to her.'

There was a ring of truth in that. Sister Bernadette raised her eyes and looked fleetingly at the Reverend Mother before lowering them again to the flour-covered table. Sister Imelda washed the pastry cutters as silently as she could. Sister Bernadette folded dishcloths and stuffed them into a drawer, but her eyes were alert. The Reverend Mother thought about what Sister Bernadette had told her of Brian's mother, but decided not to involve her in the conversation.

'Has your mother gone back to where your grandparents live, Brian?' she asked and he shook his head violently.

'I don't know where she is. She could be in Timbuktu for all that I know. She told me that I was getting a new dad, but I never saw him. Don't want to either. I'm too old for any new dad. I look after myself. I'm an adult. You can rely on me, sir.'

Brian addressed the last words to the major. He had, thought the Reverend Mother, sized up the situation and was willing to throw in his lot with an unknown future in the British army as a substitute for the unsatisfactory and uncongenial position as apprentice in a shop which was now about to be closed down. And, perhaps he was right. She got to her feet.

'Perhaps I could have a word with you, Major. You stay here, Brian. Sister Bernadette will find you something to do.'

Once they were back inside her room, she made up her mind. 'Mallow isn't a big place, Major. Would you be willing to send a messenger there to track down his mother?'

He frowned in an irritated fashion. 'You're asking too much of me, Reverend Mother,' he said, raising his voice to a pitch which she felt more suitable to the parade ground than to the cloistered quiet of a convent. 'You may not realize it, Reverend Mother, but I'm an extremely busy man. You wouldn't believe all that I have to do. I'm arranging for my brother's situation as a manager in Blarney Woollen Mills. Much of the stock is being transferred there and most of the apprentices, also. And then I have to see to the future of my sisters, and of my mother. I can't possibly run around the county of Cork looking for the mother of this lad. In any case, the chances are that she takes no interest in him and that I would be wasting my time. You heard his words, yourself. No, he has a chance to go to England with my batman, or else he will transfer to Blarney Woollen Mills with the other apprentices. I'll go and have a word with my batman now. He lives not far from here on George's Quay and I'll make sure that he is happy to take the boy with him. Tell the lad to go back to the shop and he'll find out what's happening. I think they are rigging up somewhere for the boys to sleep in the basement so he should be all right for a few days. I'll be in touch, Reverend Mother.'

And then with a decisive nod to her, he took up his hat from the table and let himself out of the front door. He closed it behind him with a very definite click and for a moment she thought that the next click was an echo. And then she realized that it had come from the door of the kitchen. So Brian had been listening in. Well, it was not surprising. After all it was his future. The Reverend Mother went meditatively back to her own room. She would try the effect of a letter, she thought. Marking it: 'Mrs Maloney, Mallow' was not a very accurate address. If the woman was in the town, it might possibly reach her, but Mallow had a large farming hinterland. And Brian's mother might no longer be known by the name of Mrs Maloney.

Nevertheless, she took some care over the letter and explained the situation as clearly as she could to the woman. When she had finished, she sealed the envelope and stamped it and then rang her bell.

'Oh, Sister Bernadette,' she said when the lay sister came in, 'I wonder could Sister Imelda take this to the post for me. And could you send Brian to me, please.'

'Yes, Reverend Mother, well, no, Reverend Mother . . .' Sister Bernadette hesitated a little. 'Brian has gone out, said that he had to go to confession.' Sister Bernadette half-smiled. 'Said that he had a really, really big sin to confess so he had to go straight away. He was gone before I could stop him, Reverend Mother. Went out the door just after the major.'

The Reverend Mother nodded resignedly. Not surprising, really. After all the boy was thirteen or fourteen and had been without a parent for many months. He would consider himself capable of looking after his own future. A sharp boy. There was no doubt about that. But the Reverend Mother recalled a saying by Sister Philomena. 'Too sharp for his own good,' she would declare. 'Mark my words, that boy will cut himself before he's much older.'

Was Brian Maloney too sharp for his own good? And was the mention of a 'big sin' a piece of childish naivety, or was it something else?

The Reverend Mother handed over the letter. A waste of time and a waste of a stamp, she thought. Brian had made up his own mind.

Had he struck a bargain, perhaps? Major Fitzwilliam wanted everything tidied up neatly and above all, she guessed, he wanted no talk about his mother. Even now, he was probably making arrangements for her to be taken care of. Brian would have to promise to say nothing about the woman and the accusations. The matter had been taken out of her hands.

She sank wearily into the chair by the fire. For some reason, she felt dreadfully cold. Despite the glowing coals, her teeth began to chatter. Every breath that she drew seemed to stab her ribs with agony.

'Sister Bernadette,' she said. 'I'm afraid that I may be ill. I wonder, could you call Dr Scher and ask him to pop in with some cough medicine for me.'

TWENTY-ONE

The Reverend Mother leaned back into the easy chair beside her bed in the Mercy Hospital. The effort of getting up and of dressing herself, of adjusting wimple and veil, had exhausted her, but a glance in the mirror showed a familiar figure, tidy and in control, rather pale, but then she was always pale. She braced herself as a knock came to the door; but she called out 'Come in', her voice weak but steady.

'Oh, it's only you,' she said and relaxed.

'You are a ridiculous woman,' grumbled Dr Scher. 'You are just pulling out of a severe dose of pneumonia. You should be relaxing, taking life easy. Why on earth, if you have anything to say to the man, don't you let me give a message to Patrick and allow him to deal with the matter?' He eyed her with a certain measure of curiosity and she looked back steadily at him.

'Now, Dr Scher, you were the one who said that I might have a visitor. Otherwise, I would not dream of going against your professional advice.'

'Well, I meant your cousin, or even one of the sisters. Someone that you could receive lying in bed and who would just chat to you. I heard that you had little Eileen yesterday. Someone like that Sister Mary Immaculate who keeps asking to see you. Wants to tell you how well she is looking after the convent in your absence. Now, she would have been a nice restful visitor, I'm sure, and you wouldn't have felt that you had to get out of bed and get dressed for her.'

The Reverend Mother hauled out her watch and examined it carefully. 'It's very kind of you to pay me a visit, Dr Scher,' she said, 'but I'm afraid that I must ask you to go now. My visitor is due shortly, and I do wish to talk to him alone. And, I assure you, this conversation is nothing with which Patrick can help me.' She watched him go with a measure of regret.

She would have liked to confide in him, but this matter had to be handled by her alone.

When Dr Scher had gone, she carefully poured out a glassful of water, noting how her hand shook and hoped that her voice would remain steady. She glanced once more at her watch. Another three minutes to go. Her visitor would, she thought, be punctual and she kept her watch in her hand until the long hand pointed up to the twelve at the top of the dial. Four o'clock. And at that very moment the sound of firm footsteps on the corridor outside. Walking without hesitation, scanning the room numbers as he went. A man who was very sure of himself. Not a minute wasted. The moment the footsteps stopped, the knuckles tapped out a triple knock on the door.

The Reverend Mother allowed a few seconds to elapse while she tucked her hands within her long loose sleeves and then gathering to her all of her strength she called out in a firm voice, 'Come in, Major.'

He looked just the same, trim in his uniform, well groomed, eyes resolute and steadily meeting hers. 'I'm glad to see you looking so well, Reverend Mother.' The voice was steady. He scanned the room, noted the numerous bunches of flowers, but made no excuse or apology. This, they both recognized, was a business meeting, a venue for measuring strength. A bouquet would have been inappropriate.

There would be no attempt to soften her. He held all of the cards, thought the Reverend Mother.

'Tell me about Brian Maloney,' she said. Her voice, she hoped, did not sound as weak as she felt. She saw him nod and was obscurely pleased that he was not going to waste her time.

'Brian Maloney is, by now, on his way to England with my batman and by tomorrow he should be enrolled into the Drummer Boy Corps and I hope will be well and happy, settling down and performing his duties to the satisfaction of his sergeant. You don't need to worry about him, Reverend Mother.'

'But I do worry about him,' she said firmly. 'I worry about what he has done and what he will do in the future.'

He frowned at her. 'I'm not sure that I understand you, Reverend Mother,' he said.

'Brian Maloney killed your father,' she said and watched to see whether he would pretend to be astonished.

He didn't. His lips tightened and his chin thrust forward. But he said nothing.

'And I know why,' she said.

Again he said nothing. Merely looked at her with a steady gaze. Her respect for him grew.

'Dr Scher said an interesting thing about you once, Major,' she said. 'He remarked that you, in his opinion, were not the man to do a murder.' She scanned through her mind, finding herself, to her annoyance, weak and lacking in energy. 'These,' she said with an effort, 'were, I think, his words: "He's just not that kind of fellow. He's easy-going, gets on well with everyone. Not the man to do a murder. Though I can see him ordering a battalion over the top. But, that would be a different matter, wouldn't it? Murder at one degree removed, wouldn't it be?".' The Reverend Mother stopped, studying his face and also glad to have an opportunity of taking in a few long breaths. 'Murder at one degree, removed,' she repeated and watched his face.

It was immobile, blank, showing no emotion. And then she began to be convinced of his guilt. She had been slightly unsure. Had wondered at times whether the whole affair had not just been a tragic accident, but now she knew. *Brighten up a dull Monday!* The words sounded in her ear with Christy's West Cork accent but, of course, it had been the major who had said them. And had said them just after relating to the boys an anecdote about army boys playing a trick on the sergeant by throwing a gas cylinder through the window of his small office.

'Brian, of course, worshipped and probably still worships you and he thought it would be fun, would amuse you, to play a trick on an unpleasant old man sitting in a small office in a dull shop on a dull Monday morning. I hope and pray that was all the boy had intended. And, I think that I do believe that was all. He would know nothing about the complexity of wills and inheritance and I don't think that a cautious man like yourself would go any further than just to plant the seed. I think, however, that being a bright boy, he understood later on what he had done, knew that it had benefitted you. He was anxious to assure you that he would say nothing. "I won't say a word." Brian said that to you in Sister Bernadette's kitchen when you warned him not to chatter too much to the sergeant.'

'You are, of course, forgetting the reason why Brian came to your convent, you are forgetting that someone tried to murder Brian. Or are you accusing me of that, also, Reverend Mother?'

'No, I'm not,' she said readily. 'I think that Brian did that himself. I think that he was frightened by your mother's accusations, by other remarks that he overheard. He wanted to put himself out of suspicion so he devised that method. He knew, of course, that these gas cylinders were not too lethal, nevertheless, I think that he had planned to break the glass ceiling so as to make sure. And I do think that he planned to throw himself under my protection. Certainly, it was a clever idea. And would remove suspicion from him.'

He was wondering, she thought, how much she knew, wondering what had been said to her, scanning his mind for any possibility of a betrayal of intention on his part.

It did not take long, this process of inner interrogation. He was satisfied that he had not betrayed himself. His face resumed its normal pleasant, competent lines. He even looked slightly amused.

'Someone must have been playing a joke on you, Reverend Mother,' he said. 'And as for young Brian Maloney being guilty of the murder of my father, I'm sure that is not true.'

'And I'm sure that was not what I said,' she snapped back. Suddenly she began to feel strength ebbing back into her. She sat up, keeping her spine very straight and barely resting her wrists on the arms of the chair. 'The word I used was *killed* not *murdered*. I said Brian Maloney killed your father. I don't think there was an intention of murder on his part. He is of the age where a joke is irresistible. I think; no, I know, that you told stories to these young apprentices about pranks played in the barracks using one of those gas containers. A small room, the cylinder thrown through the window, a sergeant bursting out of it, gasping for breath . . .' she continued, watching his face. 'Hilariously amusing picture to adolescent boys. One of the young boys told me how funny you were. A *gas* man is what he called you. The word was appropriate though he, of course, meant it in the local slang word for "funny" or "amusing". Possibly you even went so far as to put into the boy's mind how the cylinder could be introduced to the room your father occupied. I'm almost certain that you did. It would have taken just a throwaway sentence, a remark about the use of these change carriers, a suggestion that something like those change carriers were used to send the gas cylinders whizzing up into trees in California. You, I'm sure, planted the idea. A very, very careful and well-planned murder. It had, of course, an element of uncertainty, but if it didn't work one day, then it might work the next day. And you made absolutely sure that you were not present when the fatal gas container was sent up, something that makes me think that you knew the gas cylinder was going to be sent up on that very Monday morning. You had, perhaps, hinted that the opening day of the sale would be appropriate. "Brighten up a dull Monday". That was your expression, according to young Christy. Your mother, of course, had seen Brian dodge over to the Men's Shoes counter when he had gone off on an errand for me. Easily done in a crowded shop. The matter would have only taken seconds. The Millinery counter is opposite to the Men's Shoes. Your mother had seen him, but no one believed her as she had a reputation for erratic behaviour and suffered from the delusion that her husband wanted to kill her. Others, also, mentioned Brian's name, influenced perhaps by her insistence, or else glad to throw suspicion on someone who was not a member of the family, but, of course, the boy had no motive, no motive whatsoever. Unlike you and your family.'

He leaned back in his chair. 'Have you anything more to say?' He left a short silence as if waiting for her words and then said quite casually, 'You are not looking at all well, Reverend Mother. Your cousin, Mrs Rupert Murphy, told me that you had been very ill. I suppose that a bad fit of coughing might just bring on a heart attack.' He stood up, drew on a pair of thick leather gloves and deliberately knocked his chair on to the rug by the bed and advanced towards her.

The Reverend Mother did not hesitate. Instantly she squeezed the bell concealed within her wide sleeve, repeating the action two or three times. Hurried footsteps sounded from the corridor outside.

The major barely managed to pick up his chair before the door opened. He showed no surprise and no alarm, just greeted the incomer with a pleasant smile.

'I'm afraid I've tired your patient, doctor,' he said, his voice polite and apologetic. 'I'll take my leave of you now, Reverend Mother. I don't suppose that I will see you again as my sister and I take the ship for Palestine in a few days' time, but I leave you all best wishes for a speedy recovery.'

With a nod, the major took his hat, went to the door but then stopped abruptly as it opened.

There were two other figures standing there. He knew them both and instantly seemed to realize the significance of their presence: the uniformed policeman with his hand firmly grasping the shoulder of a white-faced boy. The major gave one hunted glance around, but in that moment of hesitation his way was blocked by two women.

'We've brought him back, Reverend Mother,' called out Maureen MacSweeney. 'Back where he belongs.' She gave an appraising glance at the major and then at her daughter. Eileen closed the door with a slam and stood with her back to it. No one spoke for a few seconds until Maureen MacSweeney once again interrupted the silence.

'We went along with the inspector on to the ship seeing as his mam is too far away. Us being neighbours and knowing him since he was a baby. Poor little *pisawn*. All on his own. I'm going to take him back with me in a minute, Reverend Mother, and he can stay with us for the moment. We'll look after him.'

'As Mrs MacSweeney says, she and her daughter were kind enough to accompany me on-board ship as the boy's mother was unavailable. I had reason to believe, though, that Brian

had been removed without her knowledge or her consent.'
Patrick closed his mouth firmly, looked doggedly at the major
and Eileen nodded approval.

It had been a good idea, thought the Reverend Mother.
Mrs MacSweeney was bound to steamroll any opposition by
the sheer flow of her words. No mere batman would have
stood up to a uniformed policeman and a woman of her
calibre. And Eileen, of course, was quick-thinking and determined. She congratulated herself on having sent the girl with
a message to Patrick. All had gone well. They had boarded
the ship before it sailed for England. Now was a chance to
arrest the guilty man.

The major seemed to come to the same conclusion. He
reached for the handle of the door. Eileen raised her eyebrows
at him, but did not move and Patrick went to stand beside her.
He spoke quickly. 'Just a moment, major. I'd like you to listen
to what the boy has to say. Go on, Brian.'

Brian looked from one face to another. He was pale and his
eyes were circled with black shadows. He looked appealingly
at the Reverend Mother but she ignored it. There could be no
forgiveness, no reassurance while the events of that Monday
morning in the Queen's Old Castle still remained obscure. She
tucked her hands back into her sleeves, lowered her eyes and
waited for the boy to speak.

'Go on, Brian,' repeated Patrick. There was a very firm note
in his voice and Brian responded to it.

'He showed us a photograph, from a forest, showed us the
things they put the gas cylinders in, to send them up through
the trees, just like the change carriers in the shop.' Brian
stumbled over the words. Looking from face to face, looking
at all except the major. That face he avoided, but responded
instantly to an encouraging nod from the policeman.

'He said to us: "What does that remind you of?" And he
was making us laugh telling us about the boys codding the
sergeant, throwing a canister in the window, nearly killing
him. And then when the bell went for our dinner, he told
me to stay behind.' Brian stopped there and now looked
miserably across at the major who was examining the inside
of his hat.

'Go on,' said Patrick and the boy looked back at him with a start.

'Well, he told me to stay behind,' he continued, his voice almost inaudible. 'He said that the regiment was looking for bright boys and that I was old enough to join the drummer boys and that I would do well there . . .'

'Go on,' said Patrick for the third time. 'You've already told me. Speak out now and let everyone hear what you have to say.'

'Poor little *cratur*,' said Maureen MacSweeney. 'Go on, *alannah*, all friends here.'

This time Brian's words came out in a rush. 'He said that on Monday morning I would be downstairs with Mr O'Connor but he was sure that I'd be able to find a reason to pop up to the empty counter. And then he took down a gas container and just said: "Put that somewhere safe, like a good lad".'

'And then?' queried Patrick.

'And then he just strolled off, whistling,' said Brian and he looked sideways at the major and shifted uncomfortably, moving from leg to leg, sticking his hands in his pockets and then taking them out again.

'But you guessed what he meant. You knew what he wanted you to do. He said something else, didn't he?' Patrick's voice was firm. He kept his back to the door and fingered his truncheon.

There was a long silence. Brian now stood very still. His eyes moved, however. They travelled from the stern-faced policeman standing beside him across to where the major stood, very quietly, holding his hat in his hand, his face pleasant and relaxed. After a long minute of silence, Brian seemed to come to a decision.

'No,' he said firmly. 'He didn't tell me to do nothing. It was me own idea. I just thought it was a bit of *craic,* a bit of *codding*-like. I didn't know that it would give the old man a heart attack.' There was an expectant look in his eyes and he stared across at the major, his mouth slightly open and every fibre of his body seemed to be hoping for a word from his idol.

It did not come, though.

'Well, that's that, inspector,' said the major briskly. 'Now, if you'll excuse me, I'd better be going. Have a lot to do.' Eileen and her mother looked hopefully at Patrick, but he moved away from the door, and after a moment, Eileen moved also and allowed the major to go through. No one said a word until the sound of his footsteps in the corridor died away.

And then Patrick spoke. 'Well, I think you'd better come down to the station with me, Brian, and make a statement,' he said. He cast an apologetic glance across at the Reverend Mother but did not speak to her.

She looked across at Brian and nodded encouragement. 'Go with the inspector, Brian and make sure that you tell him everything. In the end it always pays to tell the truth. Tell the truth and shame the devil; do you remember how Sister Philomena used to say that when you were in the infants? Don't worry about anything now. We'll find your mother and you will be taken care of.'

'And we'll go along with you and give you a nice feed when you're through with the inspector,' said Maureen reassuringly.

The Reverend Mother sat silent for some time after they had gone and when she spoke, it was more to herself than to Dr Scher. 'Patrick could not arrest the major,' she said. 'There is no evidence that could stand up in any court. Even if Brian had been willing to say more, it would still be very doubtful. Our only chance was for the major to admit the crime.' And then she looked at Dr Scher with an irritated expression. 'You were too quick,' she complained. 'I knew he'd never admit to it, but if you had caught him in the act of trying to smother me, then he'd have had some explaining to do. Why didn't you wait in the waiting room, instead of lurking in the corridor?'

'It's just professional pride,' said Dr Scher. 'I hate losing a patient. You gave me the fright of my life. I knew that you were up to something. If I had known that Patrick was on his way up the stairs, I'd have felt relieved. But I didn't and I thought that smooth-talking major might do for you. I was waiting in the corridor, listening at the door, in fact. I suppose when Eileen popped in to see you, you sent her over to Patrick with a letter. Well, all's well, that ends well.'

'All is not well,' said the Reverend Mother, compressing her lips. 'A boy has been corrupted, an elderly man has been murdered and the guilty person has escaped, unscathed and in possession of a fortune. I've mismanaged this. I knew he was guilty and now he has escaped. And if you had waited in the waiting room as I had told you to do, we might have got a confession out of him when you came in and caught him strangling me. You could have told him that I was on the point of death, or something, made him admit his guilt.'

'Now, Reverend Mother, I wonder could you explain to a dull old man how you fastened on the major as the guilty one.' Dr Scher had the air of one who wished to change the conversation. He took her wrist and checked her pulse before continuing. 'Patrick was just saying the other day that he never knew of a case where so many people appeared to be guilty. They were all going around trying to fabricate alibis for themselves. Why were they doing that if they were innocent of the crime?'

The Reverend Mother leaned back in her chair and thought about that for a moment. 'Fear, Dr Scher, is like a noxious gas and there was an atmosphere of dread and of anxiety spread over the whole of that shop. I'm not sorry that it is being pulled down. The late Mr Joseph Fitzwilliam kept his wife and three of his four children in a state of nervousness and unease. As he did with his employees and his apprentices. All were used to being blamed for something of which they were innocent. They expected irrationality when it came to apportioning culpability and therefore they became accustomed to producing alibis or blaming someone else. Once poor Mrs Fitzwilliam accused Brian, they all fastened on him as a scapegoat. They did not know what she knew. She was the only one who had seen him, I feel sure, but he made a handy scapegoat. And then, of course, Brian muddied the waters by staging his own murder and trying to make it appear that he was a victim, a witness, perhaps, rather than the perpetrator. It was a strange case, but not a particularly difficult case. One had only to determine who really benefitted from the murder and then to work out how it could have been done. The use of an underling, of course, as you yourself suggested, came naturally to an army officer who would be used to giving commands to kill.'

'Well, there's nothing to be done now,' said Dr Scher. 'Anyway, I don't suppose it would do any good to hang the man. Wouldn't bring back the father, would it?'

'There is one thing to be done,' said the Reverend Mother. 'And I hope that Patrick will have the authority to do it. That boy was taken away without the consent of his mother, about to be launched into a life where killing is the norm. He has now been brought back, but I am seriously worried about him and think that he will need care; that his mother, that all of us will need to think about him. Something which he did, at the age of thirteen, some evil action, almost resulted in a total change in his life, very nearly, in fact, gave him his heart's desire. That is a very dangerous start to adult life and the boy will need to be monitored to make sure that he does not think that the death of another is a solution to problems.' She leaned back in her chair, feeling exhausted and very depressed. Murder, she thought, was like a cancer. Its tentacles spread out and infected those who had been touched by it. A sense of failure had seeped through her own veins. What was she, an elderly unwell nun, doing meddling with crime instead of sitting by the fire and telling her rosary beads? She looked across at Dr Scher, who was delving into his attaché case, no doubt for some remedy. And somehow, as she looked at him, her spirits lightened.

He, she thought, battled on a daily basis against disease. He fought against cancers and tuberculosis and the terrible effects of starvation. He was often defeated, but never gave up. She sat up a little straighter and resolved not to be downcast by one failure.

Aloud she said, 'And it does matter that the man has escaped justice. Thomas Aquinas, as usual, sums it up for us. *Bonum commune praeminet bonum singulari unius personae.* The good of the community must predominate over the good of the individual person. For the sake of the community, murder must never be tolerated.'

She took in a long breath. It stabbed at her lungs but she ignored the pain and sat up very straight. 'And one miscarriage of justice,' she said firmly, 'cannot ever be allowed to make the lawgivers lose heart.'

Lightning Source UK Ltd.
Milton Keynes UK
UKHW010824110920
369735UK00002B/25

9 781847 519566

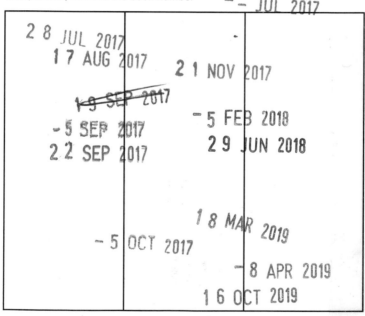